KISS THE FROG

A PRINCES OF DANISLOVA NOVEL

ALICE GAINES

Cover image by Novelstock

Cover Design by Bookin' It Designs

Formatted by IRONHORSE Formatting

ISBN-13: 978-1-940854-04-5

For Therese Rittenbach
Thanks for all your help on these books

ALSO BY ALICE GAINES

The Glass Slipper
Beauty Awakened

CHAPTER ONE

The lot of them were up to no good, and if Felice Larson could read her friends right, they were about to drop the trouble into her lap. What the zoology department laughingly called the graduate student lounge couldn't hold more than five or six people in addition to the ratty couch and the Steelcase table with the ancient microwave on top. With Ben's height and broad shoulders, which he at present was using to block the doorway, her buds from Professor Marc Fanley's lab created quite a crush as they circled in on her. As they came forward, she backed up. And backed and backed until her legs hit the couch and she plopped down. "Okay, what's up?"

Crystal took the opportunity to sit next to Felice, almost on top of her, actually. "We've come to a decision."

"Why do I get the feeling it involves me?" Felice said. "And why are the butterflies in my stomach telling me I won't like it?"

"Oh, you'll like it." Sandra sat on Felice's other side, bookending her. Both women appeared ready to pounce if Felice so much as tried to stand up.

Alex nodded toward Ben. "Better close that door."

Ben did and rested against it. For heaven's sake, this was starting to look like a parody of a gangster movie. Next thing, they'd be threatening her with cement overshoes and speaking out of the sides of their mouths, even the women.

"Are you going to tell me what all this is about, or do I have to figure out what you've decided on my own?" she said.

Crystal dug her index finger into her hair and twisted a blonde curl tightly around it—a nervous habit of hers that manifested itself every time she didn't have an answer to a question and had to stall for time. Felice glanced to Alex but got no more than a view of his faded jeans and university sweatshirt. His brown eyes gave nothing away. Ben wasn't any more help. He simply crossed his arms over his chest and stared at the opposite wall.

Finally, Sandra took charge. She grabbed Felice's hands and leaned forward. "You owe us. You said so yourself, remember?"

"Owe?" Felice searched her memory. She'd used that expression lately. Though she couldn't recall what debt she'd incurred, she had a pretty solid feeling she'd paid it off.

"The research trip," Sandra said. Though she was the smallest of all of them, her red hair made her stand out. She joked that no one should cross her because of her temper, but after getting to know her, you didn't dare laugh.

"I can see I'm not getting through to you," Sandra said. "Kangaroo rats."

A shudder went through Felice at the mention of the word "rats." Ever since reading the novel *1984*, she'd had a terror of the miserable creatures.

"The trip we were all supposed to make to the desert," Crystal tossed in. "The one we let you skip out on. The one when it rained for three solid days and we all came home covered in mud."

"It's not my fault you got stuck with the one week the desert got rain," Felice said.

"We all ended up with colds," Alex said.

"And I sat on a cactus," Ben added.

Of course. Her mind hadn't quite managed to block out the fact that she'd bailed on the rest of them and had stayed in her warm, dry apartment while they'd chased over half of the Sonoran desert counting the population of kangaroo rats. Awful, nasty creatures.

"She's got it now," Alex said.

"We're connecting," Ben said from his station at the door. A man of few words, but every one was important.

"I'm writing half the paper," Felice protested.

"And you're first author," Alex said. "Not enough."

"All right, all right. What do you want from me?"

"Well-ll." Crystal let the blond curl loose for a moment, and then went back to twirling it. "You know Dev."

"Of course I know Dev." The new grad student was kind of an odd bird. A few years older than the rest of them, Dev came from a tiny European country, Latstonia or Bardstokia or something like that. He always mumbled the name when people asked. But then, he swallowed most of his words, making it difficult to know for sure if he was speaking English some of the time.

"He's really nice," Crystal said.

"How can you tell?" Maybe Crystal knew him better than Felice did. He glanced away whenever she looked at him. Poor guy. It had to suck to be that shy.

"I've talked to him," Crystal said.

"We all have," Alex added. "We spent six days in the rain with him, remember? If you'd come along on that trip, you'd know him, too."

"I shared a tent with him. He's a good guy," Alex said.

"Well, I don't know him," Felice said. "He hasn't said more than ten words to me, and he's swallowed six of those."

"He only clams up around you," Sandra said. "Which makes you perfect."

"None of you are making any sense," Felice said. "Perfect for what?"

Crystal's finger gave her hair a work-out, twisting and twisting. "You tell her, Alex."

"Not me." Alex glanced at Ben, whose face turned a bright pink.

"Oh, for crissake," Sandra said. "You're perfect to sleep with Dev, that's what."

"Sleep? Dev?" If Felice thought for a minute, she could probably put those two words into a sentence that would make sense – as long as they didn't have "with" between them. Sleep with Dev. "As in have sex with him?"

"Why not?" Sandra said. "He's a good looking guy."

Maybe he was behind the glasses with the huge rims. If he combed his hair out of his face. And burned the corduroy pants. Lord, did he shop at Dorks R Us?

"Look, Dev's been here for months, and he hasn't interacted with a woman except for the ones in Marc's lab," Alex said.

"Heck, he might never have been with a woman," Ben said. "In fact, I'm pretty sure he's a virgin."

"How in heaven's name could you know a thing like that about him?" Felice demanded. This whole conversation had gone from weird to bizarre to insane within less than five minutes. What man Dev's age would be a virgin?

"We didn't have much to do but talk at night in that tent," Ben said. "I asked about women, and he shut right up."

"I've tried to draw him out on the subject, too," Ben said. "He won't talk."

"Think about it. You could be his first." Ben nodded as if that settled the matter.

If Ben thought that made the whole thing better, he'd missed by a mile. "You want me to take a guy's virginity?"

"Believe me, that's one thing a man never misses." Ben stood there, an immovable tower of certainty, and no one else in the room seemed eager to contradict him. True, the first time meant different things for men than women, but still…Dev ought to share that special moment with someone he cared about.

"It just doesn't seem right," Felice said finally.

"We're his friends," Alex said. "We should do this for him."

"Fine. If you all think that's such a great idea, Crystal or Sandra can sleep with him," Felice said.

"I'm taken," Sandra said.

"So's Crystal," Ben added. The two of them had obviously paired off. They'd been giving off signs for weeks. That only left Felice, or the sane and logical choice, which was to let Dev find a woman on his own.

"Besides, he doesn't look at us the way he does at you," Sandra said.

Felice glared at Sandra. "And how is that?"

Sandra opened her eyes wide and imitated a kind of puppy-dog face. "Like he wants to follow you home."

Good God Almighty. Felice rose and paced to the other side of the room. Her hip bumped the table, rattling the microwave. "You all must be out of your minds."

"He's thousands of miles from home. He only knows us," Crystal said.

"He really needs to get laid," Alex said. Always helpful, Alex.

Crystal's expression brightened. "You could make him feel welcome."

"It's your patriotic duty," Sandra concluded.

"Now, I know you're kidding."

Sandra gave Felice her best menacing stare. "Try me."

"You mean this. You really mean this." Felice glanced at each of her friends in turn, from Ben's stern features, to Alex's open expression, Crystal's smile, and the look on Sandra's face that said she knew she had Felice trapped.

"A little action might do you some good, too," Sandra said.

Felice couldn't stop the gasp from escaping, and she charged across the room to Sandra. "I told you that in confidence."

"Everyone knows you've been…" Alex cleared his throat. "…lonely since whatsizname left on his post-doc."

James. It had been three months, two weeks, and a day, not that she was counting. Even the e-mails were getting short and seldom as James slipped off into the ether of her past.

"Give Dev a shot," Crystal chirped. "He might be good."

"A virgin? Good? The first time?"

"Well…you could teach him," Crystal said. "Show him all the things that turn you on."

"I am not giving Dev VonRamsberg a crash course in the Kama Sutra."

Sandra rolled her eyes. "Do it any way you want. Just do it."

"Right." Felice planted her hands on her hips. "What am I supposed to do? Walk up to him and ask, 'If you don't have anything scheduled between seminars, want a pity fuck?'"

"Of course not. You'd scare him to death," Alex said.

"Well, then?"

Alex reached into his pocket and produced a key tied to a loop of string. "He gave me this when I took care of his pet iguana when he was out of town. Sneak in in the middle of the night and ambush him."

"That's just great." Felice threw her hands into the air. "You want me to assault him."

"It's not assault if he likes it," Alex said.

"How do you know what he likes?" Damn, they had her shouting now.

"He's a guy." Ben counted off the points on his fingers. "He's horny. He wants you."

She turned to the two women for some logic. "You couldn't ask me to do something so stupid."

"We not only ask it, we expect it," Sandra answered.

"You owe us," Crystal said.

Well, shit, they meant it. She paced the room again, what little of it there was. She did owe them. She'd meant it as an expression, but they had her. Technically, she didn't have to have collected the data to write the paper and be first author. But what would Marc think if he found out she hadn't gone on that trip? He prided himself on putting out PhDs who'd had hands-on training. How could she explain to him that what he thought of as cute, little rodents were to her disease-ridden, blood-thirsty vermin just dying for the opportunity to put their fangs into her face? She stopped pacing for a moment. “If I do this, I don’t owe you anything more, right?”

“That’s it,” Sandra said. “Paid in full.”

“I only have to do it once?”

“Unless, of course, you want more.” Crystal smirked at her. Actually smirked. She could smirk easily enough. She didn’t have to skulk her way into a near-stranger’s apartment, get naked, and do the nasty with him.

But then, she’d only have to do it once, and Dev was a sweet person, except for his fascination with side winding rattlesnakes. If he’d never made love before, he might finish quickly, and she could go home to her own bed. Women had put up with worse in their sex lives. In fact, she herself had. She could face a few minutes in the sack with Dev a hell of a lot easier than she could face Marc’s disappointment in her.

“Okay,” she said. “Give me the damned key.”

*

What did you wear to a sexual ambush? Maybe the same sort of thing you wore to a seduction, which meant that Felice didn’t have anything right except for the negligees she’d worn for James. She wasn‘t putting one of those on for another man. She normally slept in sweatpants and t-shirts. Very appealing for a tackling dummy but not so great for a *femme fatale*.

In the end, she threw an oversized sweater over her jeans and blouse and drove to the apartment complex where the guys all lived. The key Alex had given her worked on the outside gate as well as the building’s front door, so she let herself in and searched for number one-seventeen. That lock also turned easily, and she found herself inside Dev’s living room.

As the door closed softly behind her, she glanced around. Aside from the large glass tank on the opposite side of the room—the iguana’s enclosure?—it was a fairly standard space for a graduate student. Light that slipped inside between the blinds showed a couch several years newer and nicer than the one in the grad student lounge and a flat screen television. An arm chair and coffee table sat on top of a throw rug. That amounted to the total of the furnishings.

An archway led off to a small kitchen at one end of the room. The doorway at the other end promised to lead to the bedroom. She tiptoed in that direction. If he didn't detect her presence, she could always change her mind and tiptoe right back out again. Since the afternoon, she'd had plenty of time to conjure up images of what she'd be getting herself into here. And plenty of time to buy some condoms.

She might embarrass Dev. He might jump up and demand that she leave him alone. That would be awkward as all hell. She'd have to apologize and spend the rest of the semester trying to make things right between them. The others would have to apologize, too. She wouldn't take the fall for them when they'd thought up this ridiculous scheme to begin with.

On the other hand, he might take what she offered, more or less fall on her and shove his way inside. She could handle that. It wouldn't give her a lot of pleasure, but it'd get things over quickly. That would only leave the problem of him wanting a repeat performance.

She'd rehearsed that whole scenario in her mind. *Dev, I really like you. You're a good person and a great guy, but it was just a one night stand. You'll find a woman who truly cares about you.. A woman who deserves you. I love you, but I'm not in love with you.*

Lame, lame, lame, but it was all she had. The others might well end up owing her something by the time this all ended. She approached the bedroom and stood on the threshold for a moment. No point putting this off any longer. Operation Seduce Dev T minus zero.

The bedroom proved as unremarkable as the living room. Illumination also snuck in through the blinds here. The room held no more than a dresser, an end table, and a huge bed. For a guy's place, it was all pretty tidy, as was the bathroom, at least from what she could see from a night light in there. The display of an alarm clock showed Dev himself lying face down against the sheet, the covers exposing a broad expanse of naked back. He slept in the nude? Interesting.

With no rational excuse to delay, she quickly kicked out of her shoes and removed her clothing. The air cooled her skin, setting up goose bumps along her arms. She shivered, although the air wasn't really all *that* cold. Across the room, Dev's soft breathing brought home the message. She'd soon cuddle up to his body. No matter how shy, he was still a man with a man's anatomy and a man's needs.

After pulling the strip of condoms from the pocket of her jeans, she approached the bed.

How had she never noticed Dev's size before? Sure, he slumped, but she couldn't have missed the fact that he was easily as tall as Ben. Though not as beefy as Ben, Dev nevertheless had shoulders as broad. The back she'd studied from across the room now appeared like an expanse of flesh, solid muscle with a furrow down the middle.

One of his hands lay splayed near his head, the long fingers spread against the sheet. From this close, he didn't resemble any kind of nerdling. dork, or geek she'd ever seen before. His hair had fallen back from his face, exposing a strong jaw, high cheekbones, and a pair of lips sculpted for sin. Only his long eyelashes suggested innocence.

She shivered again, although this time she didn't try blaming it on the temperature in the room. He suddenly seemed so male and big and, well, desirable. A physical knowledge blossomed inside her body…the sort of communication that didn't require words. Her pussy clenched, grasping for something that it hadn't had for months.

Wicked thoughts formed in her mind. What would those fingers feel like against her breasts, her nipples? Would he have a large cock? Would it stay hard for a good, long time before he came? Would she have the courage to show him how to make her climax?

Still clutching the strip of condoms, she lifted the covers and climbed into bed with him.

*

Christian Devlin Philippe Pascal VonRamsberg, the Crown Prince and Heir Apparent to the Throne of Danislova slept lightly. The trait had persisted in his family from centuries ago when missing the subtlest clues from one's surroundings could mean death by any number of gruesome means. The threat no longer persisted, but vigilance still served him well. He'd realized the moment someone came into his room. The soft footfalls and the pitch to her breathing told him the intruder was a woman. Until she neared the bed, he hadn't fixed her identity, but the moment he caught her scent, he recognized his visitor. Felice.

Fascinating. A woman only crept into a man's bedroom for mischief, and with any luck, she'd come here with the best sort of naughtiness in mind. He'd held himself back from approaching this particular woman for months, and now she'd come to him.

Lying perfectly still, he allowed her to crawl into his bed and press her body against his. Her naked body. More and more fascinating. The perfume that belonged only to her surrounded him. Roses, with a hint of spice and musk. Whether it came from her soap or her cologne, the scent always drew him to her. And it always produced the same reaction. An embarrassing one for a classroom or the lab. It fit much better in his bed.

He'd already been half-hard from a dream that had evaporated the moment she woke him. Now, his cock swelled to full length and readiness. She could have only one reason to be here, obviously. He'd have to find out later why she'd taken it into her head to seduce him. He had more pressing matters to deal with now, namely, taking full advantage of what she offered. He'd do that, certainly. He'd give her a lot more than she'd bargained for.

Though he kept his eyes closed, he'd memorized her appearance well enough to picture how she looked lying next to him. Her straight, blonde hair would hang over her shoulders to the swell of the breasts that blue sweater of hers showed off to such good effect. In the dim light, the green of her eyes wouldn't show, but he could imagine them glowing with the heat of arousal. And her pale skin would have flushed along her cheeks and throat. She always looked and smelled like a confection, one he'd finally get to enjoy, if only for tonight.

He smiled inwardly as she began some tentative explorations. Her breast nestled against his ribs, the nipple stiffening, as her hand wandered his back. Fingertips traced a path down the center to his waist and back up to the base of his skull. Her lips pressed against his shoulder and then traveled along the top to his neck. She had to stretch to reach his ear. Once there, she nibbled on his earlobe. Her breath went into his ear, and he let out an involuntary moan. Too late to pull it back. She must realize he was awake. He'd take over now.

Giving into temptation he'd resisted for so long, he lifted his arm and pulled her beneath him. Her gasp of surprise sounded exactly how he'd imagined. How many times had he awakened in the middle of the night to a fantasy of doing exactly this—of fitting their bodies together, her softness against him everywhere? He claimed her mouth in a kiss, finally tasting the lips that had distracted him so much during seminars. She had a way of pursing them when lost in thought that made him ache to ease them apart with his tongue.

He'd imagined how sweet she'd taste, but he couldn't have anticipated how quickly she'd respond. She ran her hands under his arms and around his shoulders to raise herself to him while she explored his mouth. When she let out a sigh, he took the opportunity to slide his tongue along the seam of her lips. Their breath mingled as the scent of roses filled his nostrils and fogged his brain. Already, he'd slipped from reality into a world of rising arousal, and the way her fingertips dug into his shoulders told him she'd followed.

Delicious. Even better than he'd dreamed. She'd come to him on her own, and now, her body seemed to vibrate with the same need that built inside him. As heat rose between them and around them, he released her mouth and placed his lips against her ear.

"Felice," he whispered, just to hear the sound of her name in his bedroom. As she'd done to him, he blew softly into her ear. In response, she arched against him, obviously as excited by the caress as he'd been.

"Dev?" His name came out on a gasp.

"Mm." As he nibbled his way down her neck, he shifted so that he could cover one breast with his palm.

"Is that really you?"

"You were expecting someone else?"

"No…it's just…oh, that feels so good."

"That's the general idea, I believe." He rolled her nipple under his palm, and when she gave him another happy sigh, he slid lower along her body so that he could take the hardened tip into his mouth.

Making love with Felice was a hugely bad idea. He couldn't become involved with anyone in the United

States, not with his obligations at home. Still, she had invaded his bedroom. Refusing her now would amount to out-and-out rejection. He couldn't do that to her, and honestly, his body wasn't going to allow him to do it to himself, either. His hottest fantasy had come to life and was currently beginning to squirm beneath him. It would take the willpower of a saint to stop at this point, and he was no saint.

That resolved, he moved to the other breast and gave it the same loving, all the while skimming his hands over her ribs and down her side to her hips. She was soft everywhere, curved in the way he most enjoyed. How many times had he caught quick glimpses of her? The way faded denim caressed her ass, enticing him to cup her buttocks. He did it now, running his palms underneath and massaging the flesh. The action parted her legs, and he fitted himself between them. She did nothing to resist but only made more room for him.

Oh yes. This could get really interesting. He went exploring, pulling himself downward and running his tongue along the center of her body. He stopped briefly at her navel and planted kisses all over her belly. She had to recognize his destination. His deepest desire involved her pussy against his face, and by all appearances, he'd have it. He could eat her to his heart's content, until she climaxed hard enough to make her scream. By God, after all these months of wanting and imagining and dreaming, he could finally hear the sounds of her orgasm.

Lower still, he burrowed his nose into the hairs that covered her sex. Her scent had changed to the perfume of an aroused woman…complex and heady. When he brushed her lips with his fingers, the tips came away wet. Such a gift, an honor. She wanted him.

Pride swelled in his chest. He wouldn't disappoint her.

"Dev?" she whispered. "Are you going to..."

He took a breath of her incredible perfume. "I certainly hope so."

"Oh." The sound was half-gasp, half-cry. "I just wondered."

He chuckled and then bent to his work...his utmost pleasure. Slowly, he dragged his tongue over her lips from the back to the front, probing for the hard nub. Ah, there. She stiffened, and this time her cry wasn't half anything. After a moment, her hips relaxed against the sheet, her legs falling farther apart.

He continued, this time separating her lips with his fingers. Now more exposed, her clitoris fairly begged for his caress, so he flicked the tip of his tongue against it. Softly, barely touching the little bundle of nerves. Her hands found his head, the fingers burrowing into his hair while her breath grew rapid and harsh.

A highly aroused woman. The pride of any real man. And the more excited she became, the more his own sex craved entrance into hers. This may have started as an exercise in tantalizing her, but he'd need the inevitable coupling as much as she did by the time it finally happened.

"Don't stop," she said.

"Not until you've finished." Of course, finishing her would nearly finish him. He'd watched and wanted this woman for months, although it felt as if he'd lusted after her for his whole life.

He continued, this time stroking her more firmly, still toying with her. She needed to climax, and he needed to hear her cries ringing in his ears. But for right now, he could enjoy listening to her breath coming in ragged gasps, rising in pitch. Signaling the approaching orgasm. Quickly, he slipped a finger inside her and probed while he continued pressing against her most sensitive flesh. Her muscles tightened around him as her releasing cry built. She'd reached the pinnacle, so he sucked her clitoris into his mouth to make it as good as he could.

The storm broke. The walls of her pussy gripped his finger rhythmically for long seconds. A powerful climax. And yes, she screamed. Exactly what he'd wanted for her first time with him. He stayed with her until she finished and then pulled himself up beside her.

When he tugged her into his arms, she sighed and pressed her face against his chest. "Oh. My. God."

He stroked her back. "Good?"

"Amazing. I can't believe..." She pushed herself back and stared into his face. Even in the dim light, he couldn't miss her expression. Astonishment and confusion. "You've done that before."

"Yes, I rather think so."

She slapped a palm against his chest. "You're not a virgin."

"Who told you I was?"

"Well, everyone. I mean they assumed....that is…"

Hm. Everyone. That would mean the rest of the students in the lab. He ought to be angry, but he'd have to get over being highly aroused first.

"Assuming," he said. "That's dangerous, no?"

She stared at him for several more seconds. "You are Dev VonRamsberg, aren't you?"

She would wonder. Only natural, given the persona he'd adopted. But then, he'd no doubt ruined that effect several minutes ago when he'd feasted on her pussy. That wasn't the action of a man so shy he could barely look directly into her face. When he'd thought up Nerd-Dev, he hadn't considered what would happen if one of his colleagues filled him with lust. He sure as hell hadn't expected that exact coworker to sneak into his apartment and into his bed.

"I'm Dev."

She pushed his hair back from his face, took his chin between her thumb and forefinger, and titled his head from one side to the other. "I guess you are."

"You wouldn't break into just anyone's apartment, would you?" To tell the truth, he could wonder about that question. The idea of Felice making a similar visit with another man didn't sit well at all. Still, he had a pretty good idea who had put her up to this.

"Of course, not," she answered.

"Alex gave you the key, didn't he?"

She didn't answer but shrugged and smiled.

"Never mind. I know he did, and I rather think I know why." That little heart-to-heart he'd had with Ben about how he didn't know any women here. Mostly, he'd tried dodging the question. Yes, he'd avoided romantic entanglements in the United States. He'd eventually have to marry the woman who would best serve his country. He couldn't become entangled with an unsuitable partner, no matter how much he might prefer her...like the woman lying in his arms this very minute.

Despite his best intentions, he'd become involved with her when he'd given her that orgasm, and he was about to become even more entangled. His cock wouldn't give him any choice in that matter.

"So, shall we go along with Alex's plan?" he asked.

"It'd make him happy."

"What about you?"

She shifted and slid her hand between them. When her fingers circled his cock, his vision went hazy around the edges.

"It'd make me happy, too," she said.

Chapter Two

Felice had gone against every bit of common sense to commit breaking and entering and probably sexual harassment. Only she'd ended up happily in bed with a man who very obviously didn't feel harassed. Then, to top that off, he'd given her an orgasm of the caliber that she normally only read about in books. Wages of sin. Nice work if you could get it, and it appeared she'd just gotten it.

And then, to frost the cake and put the cherry on the top, Dev hadn't finished with her, not if the beautiful erection in her hand meant anything. His cock was a thing of beauty, thick and long and giving no indication of going off prematurely. When she stoked it, a lazy smile curled his lips, and his eyelids went to half-mast.

He didn't appear to want to rush things, though. Still smiling, he snaked a hand between her thighs and touched her clit again. After an orgasm like that, she should have been too sensitive to want stroking. But he used so light a touch…no more than a feathering…that in moments, the languor of arousal slipped over her again. As her mind crossed the boundary to the land of pure sensation, one thought managed to creep in. He knew how to deal gently with a woman who'd just come. He knew how to excite her when she felt as if she'd had enough.

The knowledge might have got her wondering who exactly the man was except for the fact that it felt so damned natural to lie here with their hands on each other. She continued stroking him from the base of his cock along the shaft and finally tugging gently against the ridge around the head. His breath grew shallow and erratic, and his eyes closed in bliss.

"I'd better…" He groaned."…get...something."

"Don't you dare move." *Don't stop touching me.*

"We need—"

"I have it." Somewhere. She hadn't thought about the condoms since he'd first kissed her, but they couldn't have gone far. When she shifted, they crinkled beneath her.

He opened his eyes."Is that what I think it is?"

She sat up enough that he could peel the strip off her back.

"Clever girl," he said."You brought three."

She'd only done that because that was how the condoms were packaged. She certainly hadn't thought they'd need all of them. The glint in his eyes told her they would. How could anyone have mistaken this man for a virgin?

After tearing one of the packets open, he slid the condom on and took his place between her legs. This time, he didn't lower himself along her body but propped himself over her. As she stared into his dark eyes, he eased his hips forward, and the tip of his cock pressed for entrance between the lips of her pussy.

Lord, but she'd never wanted a man the way she wanted this one. While he planted tiny kisses all over her face, he entered her slowly, one tantalizing inch at a time. So sleek and hard and big, he stretched the walls of her sex as he penetrated her. Unable to wait another millisecond, she wrapped her legs around his and lifted her hips to take him all.

For a moment, his eyes widened and he held himself over her. Then he lowered his head to the side of her face and began to move.

Surely, this had to be heaven, to have such a skillful, well-endowed lover. He'd made her wet before, and now, she'd become so slick, he moved easily in and out. The sounds of their lovemaking filled the room—her sighs and little cries, his rapid breaths, the slap of their bodies together as she moved with him. One thing was certain—she was going to come again. When she did, she'd have his hardness filling her. Her muscles would grip it, her anchor to reality as her world spun out of control.

Already the orgasm built inside her, coiling, becoming hot and demanding. Words wouldn't form, so she could only communicate with her cries and the force of her movements up to meet him. Somehow he understood, or maybe he only felt the same urgency, because he picked up the pace, thrusting all the way into her and nearly pulling out only to impale her with his next movement.

One syllable finally came to her. His name. She pushed it past her lips."Dev."

"Come for me, Felice."

"Dev!"

The orgasm gripped her like a fist, squeezing the air from her lungs. Then she exploded into it as the current rushed through her. She could only breathe enough to scream as the muscles of her sex went wild around his cock. To complete the miracle, he came with her. His moans built to a growl and then a roar as he plowed savagely into her a few more times and stiffened in her arms. The seconds felt like minutes before it finally ended and the two of them fell into a limp heap against the sheets. Neither of them moved except to suck air into their lungs, but where they were still joined her pussy fluttered in the aftermath of their coupling. She'd never had anything like that and likely wouldn't again.

*

The day after Felice had stolen her way into the lab's pet nerd's bed and had her brains screwed out, she sat in Marc's seminar, trying to make sense of his words. He gave great lectures. So wonderful, in fact, that even the undergraduates loved him. She always got an intellectual charge from listening to him, and from the attentive expressions on the faces of the other students, he hadn't disappointed today. But the pleasantly used feeling in her sex and the continuing post-coital haze around her brain wouldn't let her concentrate on anything.

At least, Dev hadn't shown up. He should have, of course, but she really wouldn't be able to think with him around. Especially given the cowardly way she'd left him, about…she checked her watch…about eight hours before.

The whole thing had her weirded out. Or at least, it had her mind weirded out. Her body wasn't the least confused about anything. It was still glowing with the residual heat that only a world-class fucking could give it, not that she'd had a whole lot of those. The night before, he'd awakened her and given her a second helping of his own special brand of lovemaking.

That guy was not a virgin. He wasn't a nerd. He was something else entirely, and that had created the odd spinning sensation in her brain. At least, she'd managed to get up and out before he woke up so they wouldn't have to talk about what had just happened between them. She probably ought to want to know what lay at the bottom of the mystery, but something told her she should enjoy the sex and leave the rest of it well alone.

Dev did appear, though. The door to the seminar room opened, and he stood on the other side. He'd gone back to his usual Dev, hair in his face and bad posture. At least, he'd ditched the corduroy in favor of jeans.

Marc gestured for him to enter, but he hung back. He mumbled something that sounded vaguely like her name.

Ben turned toward her."He wants you."

"We'll talk after the seminar." She stared ahead at Marc, who now wore a quizzical expression.

She probably couldn't avoid Dev forever, but if she stayed away from him long enough, he might forget the whole incident, and she wouldn't have to explain her behavior. He must think she was a total slut, skulking around men's apartments with condoms in her fist. Oh, why had she let the others talk her into that stunt? Sure, she'd had the best sex of her life…probably a lot of other people's lives, too. But who knew what Dev thought of her?

An elbow nudged her. Ben again. He wore the most self-satisfied smirk, as if he'd watched every moment of what had happened between her and Dev. He jerked his head in the general direction of the doorway. Dev hadn't moved.

"Either come in or not," Marc said.

For heaven's sake, this foolishness was holding up the entire seminar. She rose. "I'll be right back."

She might have heard a snicker behind her as she left. Ben. She was going to have to talk to him about privacy and how he should act around their advisor.

Once she got into the hallway, Dev closed the door, set his palm at the small of her back, and guided her into an empty classroom. Then he shut that door, too, and stood there with his hands in his pockets, his head down.

“Oh for heaven’s sake.” She reached up and brushed the hair from his eyes. “You can cut out the act.”

“Very well.” He straightened and removed his glasses and stuffed them into the pocket protector in his shirt.

The transformation took Felice’s breath away. The easy air of confidence he’d shown the night before came back as the incredibly handsome man who’d made love to her returned. She had noticed his huge, brown eyes before, even behind the glasses, but she’d never seen him clearly by the light of day. His hair fell neatly into an elegant cut, complementing his strong jaw and high cheekbones. He could obviously change himself from dork to heart throb in a matter of seconds.

“Amazing,” she said. “How do you do that?”

“Practice.”

“*Why* do you do it?”

“I have my reasons.” Beneath his dark complexion, he actually blushed. “I’ll explain it to you someday.”

What could she say to that? What could she do except stand there like a dummy while her brain absorbed the scent she’d slept in the night before…when they’d slept. Then, he’d had a stubble of beard, and now his jaw was smooth from shaving. Then, he’d been a creature of the shadows, and now she could see him clearly. Still, he was the same man who’d taken her apart with his hands and his mouth and his cock, and all her body wanted to do was crawl back into his arms and ask for more.

He reached into his jeans pocket and produced the last of her condoms. “I thought we were going to use all of them.”

“Sorry. I had to get home. Feed the cat. You know how that goes.” Anyone who knew anything about cats knew damned well hers could have waited.

“I had hoped we could talk before you left,” he said.

"Not much to talk about." Except that the others had put her up to giving him a pity fuck. She wasn't about to tell him that. "I do want you to know that I don't usually do things like that."

"I thought as much. Why did you do it with me?"

"Alex put me up to it, remember?" she said.

"You didn't have to go along."

"I had my reasons. I'll tell you more when you explain the nerd impression."

"*Touché.*" He fidgeted for a bit, as if he couldn't find a good place to put his hands, even though one of them still held the condom, and he certainly could have done something with that. For a moment, he looked as if he might reach for her. Hell, she was using all her self control to keep from touching him. Then the moment passed, and his expression grew serious, his beautiful eyes going downward at the corners. "We shouldn't have…that is, I shouldn't have allowed that to happen."

"Why not?" Oh, great. She'd asked for an explanation. This was obviously a rejection, and she'd just requested the reason for it, complete with details. Why couldn't she have simply laughed and assured him their night together was no big deal? A lark. Something that had popped into her head when she couldn't find anything on television.

To make matters worse, he didn't answer for several seconds, drawing out the suspense while her stomach did a nosedive inside her.

"It's complicated," he said. "I have…obligations."

"Obligations as in a woman?" She could have smacked herself. Now she'd added outrage and hurt into the mix.

He dug his fingers into his hair, but that did nothing to ruin the casual grace of the cut. "Not exactly."

"It has to be exactly. There's either a woman or there isn't." What if he did have someone special? What if he brought her around the lab?

"I'm not free," he said. "We'll have to leave it at that."

"Sure. Fine." She tried to shrug, but even if she'd managed, the gesture wasn't all that convincing. Dev didn't appear convinced, in any case. He continued to stare at her out of his bottomless dark eyes. Curse them, and curse him.

"You don't have to feel bad," she said. "You didn't come on to me."

"I wish I could."

"What?" Okay now, that didn't make any sense at all.

"I've admired you since I first saw you."

He said it with the same Old World charm he always had, except when he mumbled. He was fluent in English, with a trace of a European accent mixed with a British inflection. Utterly beguiling except for the fact that he had a significant other and had just admitted to lusting after Felice.

"That's not exactly fair to the other woman, is it?" she said.

"I didn't say there was another woman," he said, his voice rising in frustration. "Besides, you crept into my bed, not the other way around."

That stung, and she took a step away from him. "Believe me, I'm aware of that."

"I'm sorry. I don't mean to be ungrateful."

"Grateful?" she repeated. "I didn't do it as a favor."

Of course, she had done exactly that. It had started out as a favor to him and payment of an obligation to the others. Somewhere before her first orgasm, it had turned into something else, indeed. Something he was ending, and she'd better get used to the fact.

"Making love with you was a precious gift," he said. "Something I'll never forget."

He seemed to mean that as he closed the distance between them and took her hand. When she half-heartedly tried to pull it back, he held on.

"You don't have to say that," she said. "The whole thing really was my fault."

"No fault, please." He put the condom in her hand, closed her fist around it, and kissed her knuckles. "Just pleasure. Always remember me."

As if she could forget. The best sex of her life and now romance that could steal her breath.

He kissed her on the forehead and then turned to go. He paused at the doorway. "I'd appreciate it if you didn't…how do you put this?…blow my cover with the others."

At this point, she could hardly care about that. So she shook her head and watched him leave. As his footsteps sounded down the hall, she glanced at her hand. When she uncurled her fingers, she found the condom. A perfect memento for a relationship that never happened.

*

A reptile didn't make much of a companion, but at least Luther didn't demand attention. As Dev dropped the food into the tank, the iguana cocked his head first one way and then the other before chomping the vegetables between his strong jaws. Luther would grow into quite a monster eventually. When Dev returned home, he'd have a reptile room built in his wing of the castle where Luther could move about freely. Luther could have his own house if he wanted and anything else, just as Dev could have anything. He could have any woman he wanted, too, as long as he kept things casual. Things wouldn't have remained casual with Felice. He'd done right to stop before they became involved.

"You got me into some trouble," he said to the iguana as he closed the tank and secured the latches. "If I hadn't given my key to Alex so he could take care of you while I was at home, Felice wouldn't have gotten in."

She'd admitted that Alex had given her the key. Today, Ben had had a knowing look on his face when Dev had called her out of Marc's seminar. The two of them could have talked. Might she have told him he wasn't what he seemed?

Would everyone in the lab figure out who he was? Marc knew, of course, as did the dean. They wouldn't reveal his identity. But now, the others could know he wasn't the shy creature he'd pretended to be. Would his whole persona of unremarkable foreign graduate student begin to unravel? He'd built his whole plan to get the education he craved without the paparazzi hounding him on the fragile hope that he could hide in plain sight for several years. Would it all crumble after no more than a few months?

He checked Luther one more time before settling onto the couch and turning on the television. An American football game came on, or what they called football. It was a truly inscrutable game that seemed to involve huge men in pads and helmets running full speed at each other. When he watched with the others, he'd almost figured out how to cheer in the right places. Alone, the spectacle did nothing to keep his mind off Felice.

He'd never had a woman like that. A lover who gave herself so completely and so honestly. She took and gave sexual pleasure as if she'd invented it for the two of them alone.

Over the years, he'd given plenty of women plenty of orgasms. He'd made sure he knew his way around a woman's body…the right places to touch and how to read his partner's responses. Few, if any, of his lovers had ever faked a climax. But they had a way of gushing over his prowess. He was Prince Christian, after all—Europe's most eligible royal bachelor after the fellow in England. He could make a woman a princess by marrying her. You couldn't blame a woman for hoping, even though he had no intention of breaking off the betrothal his family had made for him in childhood.

The others had made love to Prince Christian. Felice had come to Dev.

Damn, but he got hard just remembering her. The way she'd heated the sheets as if she had a furnace in her. How she'd ridden him the second time they'd coupled. She'd sat astride him, taking every inch of him inside her. She'd cupped her own breasts and toyed with the nipples. Then, he'd found her clitoris with his thumb, and she'd let her head fall back as she shouted. Her sex had grasped at his, milking him for his own orgasm. He needed to do that all again and more. Much, much more.

All of which meant, he'd never let her go if he allowed himself to truly care for her. Best to break off things now before he hurt her and himself.

Shouts came from the television, followed by the crowd's roar. One of the teams had scored. Whether three points or six or one, who could tell with this game?

He could call Felice easily enough. Everyone in the lab had everyone's number. He could ask her over to reassure her that she hadn't done anything wrong by coming to him. He could take the confusion and embarrassment out of her eyes. Yes, and he could get her naked, part her legs and eat her pussy right on this couch while mountains of male flesh hurled themselves at each other on the television. Because, that's what he'd do. The only talking they'd do would be "here, yes, yesssss!"

His phone rang, and he snatched it up from the coffee table. Not Felice, of course. Overseas. He flipped it open and answered.

"Christian," his advisor and his father's oldest friend, Grigori said.

"Is everything all right?" Dev did some mental arithmetic. It would be morning in Danislova. Not a middle of the night call, but Grigori was never one for idle chatter. If he had something to say, Dev needed to pay attention.

"When are you coming home next?" Grigori asked.

"The end of the semester, as we discussed."

Silence settled on the other end. Grigori hadn't liked his answer.

"I already took those days last month," Dev said. "I do have obligations here, too."

"I know that."

"Then, what's wrong? Out with it." That tone worked on absolutely everyone in Danislova, except for his father and Grigori. A bit more silence at the other end was followed by a sigh.

"Your father," Grigori said. "He says he's well. I don't believe him."

Dev probably wouldn't believe him, either. His new friend, dread, settled in his chest like a fist. Though Friedrich, Prince Royal of Danislova, appeared on the surface to be hale and hearty in his sixties, his heart had given them all worries on more than one occasion. He'd kept the news out of the press and away from his country's people, who loved him.

"What are the signs?" Dev asked.

"He tires easily. He sleeps a lot during the day and little at night."

"That's not unusual for a man his age."

"It's not normal for your father. He's always been so…" Grigori's voice trailed off. He didn't need to finish that sentence. Friedrich had been the face of Danislova since his own father had died young in a boating accident. Whole generations had never known another Prince Royal. Solid as a rock, even when rebellions and wars in neighboring lands threatened to spill over the mountains into their tiny country. Friedrich had never shown his subjects anything but calm and strength. The idea that he might be vulnerable to normal human failings was not acceptable as part of his public face.

"Has he been following his doctor's orders?" Dev asked.

"As far as I can tell," Grigori said. "But you should come home. Show the people you're ready to reign. They need continuity."

"I've been brought up my whole life to rule. I'm ready." Dev couldn't keep the hint of anger from his voice. His obligations to Danislova had controlled him since birth. Why couldn't he have a few years for himself and his dreams of a higher education?

"You and I both know you're ready, but what of your subjects? They only see you in those dreadful magazines," Grigori said.

"At least, you should be glad I'm avoiding them here." Anywhere he went in Europe and with anyone, no matter how innocent, ended up in some rag or other.

"That's a start, I'll admit," Grigori said. "Come home so the people can fall in love with you and know you feel the same way about them."

Dev might have laughed at that if it weren't so horribly, undeniably true. Of all emotions, the one his role wouldn't allow him was love. Perhaps he and Astrid, his betrothed, would come to care for each other over the years. But the image of an American with green eyes, blonde hair and an unholy terror of anything with the word rat attached to it came to mind whenever he thought of the word "love." And "orgasm," and "desire."

That taste of the forbidden made him crave it all the more.

"Are you listening?" Grigori's voice pulled him back to the present.

"Of course."

"Will you come home?" Grigori asked.

"I can't. I'm occupied here."

That earned him silence, although Grigori's displeasure came through clearly. Let him be upset. He had a wife he adored, something he'd deny Dev. He could damned well give him a few years to live freely in the United States.

"I'll call father and see how he is," Dev said.

"He'll tell you he's fine."

"I'll be able to judge if he's not telling the truth," Dev said. "It's the best I can do."

"Good then. Do that. We'll see you soon."

"Soon," Dev lied and ended the call.

He stared at the television screen for a moment, barely registering the movements of the men in brightly colored uniforms. Across the room, Luther sat, apparently doing very much the same thing. Reptiles were amazing creatures—simple and yet utterly foreign. Mysterious.

"You don't have a mate, either, do you?" Dev asked.

Luther didn't move a muscle.

"I'll get you one. At least, one of us will be happy."

After using the remote to turn off the television, he rang his father's private number. On the second ring, Friedrich answered with his usual gruff, "Speak."

"It's Dev."

"Of course, it is," Friedrich said. "Who else would it be? What do you want?"

"I want to know how you are, old man." His father absolutely hated being called that, or pretended to, which was why exactly Dev did it.

"Who are you calling old, you young upstart? Are you even shaving yet?"

"I'm thirty-five years old."

"I know that. I was there when you were born."

"So you keep telling me." On the telephone, Dev didn't have to hide his grin. His father was no doubt smiling, too, all the while trying to scowl.

"Enough play. What do you want?"

"I want to know how you are." So far, Friedrich sounded like his usual self, affection escaping through the cracks in his stern exterior. Some day he would fail, but with luck, the Almighty would put that off for years.

"Has Grigori been filling you with nonsense about me?" his father demanded.

"He's worried about you."

"Grigori's an old woman. He'll be measuring me for a casket next."

Dev gripped the phone a bit more tightly. "Are you sure you're fine? Do you want me to come home?"

"I always want you to come home."

That wasn't exactly true. While his father did enjoy having him nearby, he'd nevertheless encouraged him to take this time for himself to be a normal human being.

"It's good you should set an example for our people with your education," Friedrich said. "But we do have a university here."

"I'm studying American snakes, father."

"We have snakes in Danislova."

"Not sidewinders," Dev said.

His father heaved a huge and very exaggerated sigh. "My son studies snakes that wind sideways."

"That's it in a nutshell."

"Well, I suppose you'd better stay in America, then," Friedrich said.

There. His father had given his permission. It meant so much coming from a man who'd had to give up his own life to rule their country at a young age.

"You really don't need me to come home?" Dev asked.

"Bah. What would I do with a young upstart under foot?"

"I love you, father."

"I love you, son." With everything important said, his father cut the connection. Dev held the phone in his hand for a moment, as if it still contained his father's voice.

CHAPTER THREE

Felice had expected the third degree at some point, and honestly, she needed someone to talk to after first her adventures in Dev's bed and then his brush-off. So, she let Sandra and Crystal into her apartment and led them into the kitchenette.

While Felice set the coffee maker to gurgling, Crystal dumped Felice's cat, Sneakers, off the stool at the end of the dining counter and sat on it herself. "You did the deed, right? You went to Dev's at night while he was asleep?"

"Of course, she did. Ben saw them together yesterday, and something had happened between them." Sandra put her purse on the counter and took the stool next to Crystal's.

"You two have to do me a favor and keep the guys from bothering me about this." Things had been awkward enough during the seminar. She didn't need the men questioning her in the lab where Marc might overhear.

"We can do that, as long as you tell us exactly what happened," Sandra said.

"Every detail," Crystal added.

"It's kind of hard to explain." She could say that again. She'd been trying unsuccessfully to explain the past two days to herself, and she'd been there to witness everything.

Crystal started in on her hair and then stopped herself and rested her palms on the counter, instead. "Was it really awful?"

"Awful?" While Felice searched for a word to describe making love to Dev, and the courage to use it, she got the sugar down from the cabinet and then went to the refrigerator to get out the milk.

"That bad?" Sandra whistled softly. "I'm sorry. We'll make it up to you. I promise."

Felice stopped in her tracks, the sugar still in one hand and the milk in the other. "You don't understand."

"Still, it was a really nice thing you did for Dev." Crystal pasted a pity smile on her face. "Don't you think?"

"Nice." She put the milk and sugar on the counter between her two friends. "Nice doesn't begin to describe it."

"Hey, wait a minute." Sandra narrowed her eyes and studied Felice for a long second. "Are you trying to tell us it was good?"

"It was…" She blew out a frustrated breath. "…indescribable. Amazing. Cataclysmic."

Crystal's eyes went round. "Orgasmic."

"Definitely orgasmic. Multiple times."

Her two friends stared at each other in silence and then back at Felice.

"Dev?" Crystal said.

"Our Dev?" Sandra said.

"First of all, he's built. Know what I mean? Where it counts."

"Endowed?" Crystal said the word as if it were holy.

Sandra fanned her face. "Who could have known he had a battering ram inside the corduroys?"

"Not only that, but he knows how to use it," Felice said. "Same with his fingers and his mouth."

"Mouth," Crystal said with the same reverent tone. She was starting to sound like an echo. "I think I'm going to slide off this stool."

"But the guys were so sure he was a virgin. Where did he learn all that?" Sandra said.

"He's no virgin." Felice let that admission hang in the air while she filled three mugs with coffee. While the others served themselves milk and sugar, Felice sipped her drink black.

"I'm having a hard time picturing sweet, stumbling, mumbling Dev as a master in the sack," Sandra said.

"That's the problem. He's not really the Dev we've all come to know and love." Okay, she was breaking her promise not to blow his cover, but she needed help keeping Ben and Alex off her case.

"What do you mean?" Sandra asked.

"Hell, I might as well tell you everything." Felice set her elbows on the counter and leaned toward her friends. "The shy, dorky thing is an act. He can turn it off and on at will. And when it's off, wow, Katy bar the door."

"I always wondered if he was good looking behind the glasses and the hair," Crystal said.

"Not just handsome, but charming and romantic, too." Like the gesture with the condom. She'd brought it home and put it in an old jewelry box, wrapped that with ribbon, and stashed it in her keepsake drawer. Maybe years from now she'd find it and wonder what had made her keep such a dumb thing, but more likely, the discovery would bring back their night together as well as his declaration that things couldn't go any further. "And there's no future for us."

There, she'd said it. The ridiculous idea that they could have had a future had ridden her since she'd wandered home from his apartment in a daze of sexual satisfaction. Now that she had it out in the air where she and her friends could dissect it, they could discuss it to death and put it behind her.

"So." Sandra's eyes got a calculating look in them. "You've discussed a future."

"Only in the sense that there is none." The memory of his face when he'd said it came back to Felice. So serious, thoughtful. As if he carried a burden he couldn't tell her about.

Honestly, did she have to get so melodramatic about this? It wasn't Shakespeare or even a reality television show. It was a one-night-stand with a guy too nice to brush her off as if the encounter had meant nothing to him. He'd put together some nice words to convey the message that they wouldn't have a repeat performance. No more.

Both of the others watched her as they sipped their coffee. They'd caught her with her mind wandering to Dev and the way he'd kissed her hand. They'd almost caught her sighing. Instead, she straightened.

"Did he happen to mention why you couldn't have a relationship?" Sandra asked.

"Something about obligations." Felice tried at waving the thought away with a gesture. Maybe it worked.

"Like what?" Crystal asked. "A wife and kiddies back in the old country?"

"I think he would have mentioned to one of us if he was married," Felice said.

"It could be another woman, maybe someone who's waiting for him," Crystal said.

Her mind had gone there first, of course, but if the matter had been that simple, he would have simply told her, no? Oh, hell why was she even bothering about this? Goodbye meant goodbye.

"It really doesn't matter, anyway." Felice turned toward the sink and rinsed out her mug. When she turned around, she found Sandra standing behind her. She couldn't help but jump. "Don't creep up on people."

"If your mind had been here, you would have heard me," Sandra said.

"Now, really…"

"Really," Crystal echoed from where she still sat across the counter.

"I think this matters a lot," Sandra said. "You're covering it up."

"The psychology department is two buildings over," Felice said.

"I think you ought to pursue him," Crystal said. "Long distance relationships fall apart. What if he hooks up with another woman here? How would you feel then?"

The same way she'd feel at seeing any other woman with Dev, knowing that she'd have tasted his kisses and felt the firm muscles of his chest against her breasts while his member… Stop. She really had to control her thoughts so they didn't wander in that direction.

"Crystal's right, you know," Sandra said.

"You guys are sweet, but you're also deluded. Dev and I are colleagues. That's all."

Sandra and Crystal exchanged glances, but neither seemed eager to argue any further.

"So, I need your help with the guys," Felice said. "When I refuse to give them any details, you have to back me up. This time you owe me."

"I guess we do." Sandra reached around and rubbed Felice's back. "We got you into this."

"And you have to help me get myself out of it, right?"

"Right," Sandra said.

Felice turned to Crystal. "Right?"

Crystal said nothing for several seconds and then shrugged. "Okay."

Less than convincing, but Felice would have to take it for now. "And neither of you will say anything about who Dev really is, whoever that might be."

"Of course," Sandra said.

"Sure," Crystal added. "Makes things more interesting that way."

Felice really ought to ask what "things" Crystal was thinking of and what she meant by "interesting." But then, maybe she didn't want to know.

*

For over a week since the night that would not remove itself from his fantasies, Dev had managed to avoid situations where he'd find himself alone with Felice. Seminars presented a bit of a problem because, with the small groups involved, he usually ended up in a room with her where he couldn't help but notice everything that had drawn his attention in the first place. The clear green of her eyes, her long neck and delicate collar bone, the curve of her breasts below her blouse.

He'd made himself shuffle out the moment the sessions had ended, but for those hours, he'd had to admire her wit and intelligence, even while imagining her voice as it had sounded in his bedroom. Tonight would present a new challenge…their study group. Just the five of them in Crystal's apartment. Before he rang the bell, he checked to see that the glasses with the neutral prescription were in place and his hair hung into his face. Then he pushed the buzzer and waited.

When the door opened, Felice stood on the other side. She'd dressed in something soft that clung to her, outlining her curves. The vision sucker-punched him in the gut, and it took a while for him to drag his gaze from her blouse with sleeves gathered with ribbons and a curving neckline. She'd probably picked it and the matching skirt for its innocence. It didn't do anything innocent to him at all. Quite the contrary.

She seemed as dumbstruck to see him as he'd been with her. For a moment, she just gazed into his face before glancing down the hallway. "Aren't the others with you?"

"I thought they'd already be here," he answered. "Crystal?"

"She had to go out to get something." Neither of them said what they were both thinking…that they were alone.

She stepped back from the doorway. "You'd better come in."

He did, almost brushing her as he went by. The scent of roses clung to her, and she left him a pheromone trail of it as she led him through the apartment to the tiny balcony in the back. Two laptops were open on the table, and a pitcher of iced tea sat next to five glasses filled with ice. There wasn't much room for his own computer, so he took the seat behind Crystal's, across from Felice. Studying the equations on the screen for a minute convinced him statistics weren't going to get through to his brain with Felice so close.

Finally, he pushed his chair back. "I don't see why we have to study this kind of math. We don't use it in our work."

"Trial by fire. A significant number of things we do in graduate school are designed to drive us crazy for no reason."

"Is that so?"

"If we survive, they give us a degree so we can find a faculty job and do all the same things to our own students," she said.

"Marc wouldn't do that."

"Marc's a good guy, but they all do it," she said. "He's probably sitting on someone's dissertation committee making the poor schlub's life miserable as we speak."

"Schlub?" he repeated. "Is that the taxonomic term?"

"Might as well be. *Homo sapiens schlubus*, the common doctoral student." She poured two glasses of tea and handed one to him.

"And how do you know all this, given you're a lowly member of the species yourself?" he asked.

"My parents taught me. They warned me I'd have to take statistics and that someone would try to sabotage my dissertation at the last minute."

"And how do they know all that?" he asked.

"Personal experience. She's an archaeologist, and he's an anthropologist. They're in Peru right now, poking about in things and amusing the locals."

"Don't you want to be with them?"

She shrugged. "I want to be where I am."

She meant the university, of course, but he couldn't miss the fact that right now she was sitting alone with him while the late summer sun turned her hair to gold.

"You must be lonely without your family," he said.

She ran a fingertip around the rim of her glass. "I'm used to it. They've always been gone. Sometimes they took me along. Others, I stayed with my grandparents."

"No siblings?"

"Only child. You?" she answered.

"Two brothers." One serving as ambassador for his country to the United Nations and the other studying art in Italy. Both closer to Danislova that he was.

"Are you the middle child? Baby?" she asked.

"Oldest."

"I've often wondered what it would be like to have a brother or a sister," she said.

"Siblings are good," he said. "For example, if you had a brother, he'd have a pound of my flesh for what happened the other night."

She turned her head to glance out over the building's common courtyard. Her pale skin couldn't hide the blush that rose in her cheeks. He shouldn't have said anything. They'd been getting along so well.

"That wasn't exactly your doing," she said softly.

"I'm sorry I brought it up."

She avoided eye contact. "Shouldn't the others be here by now?"

He checked the time on Crystal's laptop. "Twenty minutes late."

"And Crystal should have come back by now." Her eyes narrowed. "It's a set-up."

"Do you mean, they've arranged for us to be alone together?"

"And with a bedroom handy." She got up from the table. Her face had turned a bright pink. "I'm going to check."

"Felice…"

"I'll be right back." She went into the apartment, and he sat while the birds sang around him and the screen saver came on on Crystal's computer. In a moment, Felice returned. When she held out her hand, a string of condoms unfurled. "I'm going to kill them. All of them."

He rose and went to her, not touching her but standing close. "Don't jump to conclusions."

"They were on her nightstand where anyone would see them."

"They could be for her use. Perhaps Ben planned to stay."

"Then, where are they?"

"Please don't upset yourself." He touched her elbow, and the warmth spread from his palm upward, as it always did when they made contact. "It's kind of funny, actually."

"You're too good." She reached up and pushed his hair out of his face. For a moment, the light in her green eyes softened, and then, she looked away. "I've made such an awful mess of everything."

What she meant by "everything" was a bit of a mystery. And he'd hardly call their one night in each other's arms a mess. Although the bone melting desire for more certainly complicated things, he wouldn't call it a mess. Unless she hadn't told him all of it.

"Why don't you give me the entire story?" he said.

She went back to her chair and sunk into it, staring at her hands in her lap. "The others thought up the plan."

"For you to sneak into my room?"

She nodded, still not meeting his gaze. "They thought you were a virgin and that you were lonely."

"Lonely or horny?" he asked.

Her head shot up.

"I've learned some American slang," he said. "Especially the most important words."

"Yeah, they thought you were horny."

Actually, he had been after months here. That didn't explain the power of his response to Felice, though. Nothing so simple could explain that. "So you agreed to sacrifice your body on the altar of my loneliness?"

"No." Her eyes widened in shock. "It wasn't like that."

He crossed his arms over his chest. "Then, tell me what it was like."

"I liked you. I still do. We all do." She nibbled on her bottom lip for a moment. "Only now I like you in a different way."

That last confession zinged into the general area of his heart, knocking a bit of breath out of him. That shouldn't have surprised him. One didn't make love the way she did if there wasn't a bit more than liking involved. Granted, he'd taken control when she'd first slipped under the covers. But that second time in the night, when she'd come into his arms so hot and eager…no, that was more than liking.

"How it happened doesn't matter," he said.

She stared up at him again. "They're not going to drop it. They're going to pester us until we're a couple, and you have your obligations."

He did, although they seemed more and more distant every moment. He didn't correct her, though.

"They'll get bored," he said. "We'll survive as long as you didn't tell them my secret."

"Secret?" For a second she didn't seem to understand, and then, she buried her face in her hand. "Oh, that."

"You didn't tell anyone I'm not what I pretend to be, did you?"

"Crystal and Sandra. I had to. I needed to talk to someone."

Damn it. Damn it all to hell. "You promised you wouldn't."

"Actually, I didn't. I just agreed. Kind of."

"I don't see the difference," he said.

"I'm sorry, Dev. I told you I made a mess of everything. Now you know what I meant."

She looked so sad with her eyes wide and her mouth turned down at the corners. He couldn't help but feel sorry for her, even though she'd sunk his graduate career here, not her own. One of the others would talk…or both. The word would get out that the student from Danislova had a double identity. The press would find him, and he'd have to leave. His normal life might include running from the paparazzi. The others' lives didn't.

"Please say you'll forgive me," she said, almost pleading. "I'll get the others to leave us alone somehow."

"It doesn't matter."

"I'm sorry, Dev," she said in a tiny voice. "Really."

His cell phone rang, so he pulled it out of his pocket. Danislova, and this time it *was* the middle of the night there.

He answered the call, switching to his native German. The voice on the other end was unfamiliar to him, one of the many people who worked in the palace. In his fear, the words blurred, but he caught the important ones. "Your father…stroke…expected to live."

"What do you mean 'expected?'" he demanded. "Is he going to die?"

"Is something wrong?" she asked.

"That's what I was instructed to tell you," the man said.

"Have you called my brothers?"

"I will as soon as we hang up, Your Highness."

"Then do it. And tell Grigori I'm on my way." He broke the connection and sat for a moment while his insides went cold. Somehow, he'd automatically found the chair and dropped himself into it. Now, Felice stood over him, her hand on his shoulder. On instinct, he took it and pressed his lips to the backs of her fingers.

"I know enough German to recognize the word for 'die,'" she said. "What was that about?"

"My father. He's had a stroke. I have to get home."

"Of course. I'll get on the internet and find you a plane ticket."

When she went to move, he clutched her hand. "It's not necessary."

"But you'll…"

"Not necessary," he said again. This time, she didn't try to leave his side, and the fingers of her free hand stroked his hair. They'd shared passion together. Who would have guessed she could give comfort, too?

"If you won't let me make a plane reservation for you, you have to let me help you in other ways," she said. "I can fill Marc in on what's happened. I can send the statistics take-home test to you via e-mail. I can take care of Luther."

Yes, his iguana. Someone would have to feed him and clean the tank. He should have planned for this better. He'd known Friedrich's health could fail at any time. Why in hell had he ever left the old man's side?

"God, you look scared," she said.

"I'll be all right." But would he really?

"I'm not buying it." She took his face in her hands and forced him to look into her face. "Talk to me, Dev."

Her green eyes filled with the soft light of concern. They had forged a connection that night in his bed, stronger than he could have imagined. She cared about him. She wanted to support him, and God help him, he could use her warmth. The hours would stretch out long ahead of him before he could see his father with his own eyes. Her presence…her touch…could ease those hours, if he was selfish enough to accept her kindness.

"Will you…" he said. "I shouldn't ask."

"Anything. Just tell me what."

"Come with me?" He was insane to ask, but maybe she'd accept the crazy invitation.

"To Danislova?"

"The semester won't end for a few weeks. We can do our coursework on the internet. You can write the research paper." As Crown Prince, he'd never begged for anything. He scarcely knew how to do it, but he was begging now.

"I guess I could," she said softly.

"Alex will feed the iguana," he said. "Do you have a passport?"

She nodded. "And Crystal will take care of my cat."

"Good. We'll have the visa prepared when we arrive."

"But, Dev, we *are* going to need plane tickets."

"No, we don't." He rose and gazed into her face. She was confused. Only natural. She'd find out everything about him now, which was just as well. He'd likely never come back here, and he couldn't say goodbye to her. Not yet. He'd have to later, but please, not yet.

*

Dev had only given Felice half an hour to get ready for a flight to Europe, even though they hadn't bought tickets. Maybe he had some kind of magic with the airlines that she didn't know about. In any case, she'd managed to pack a few things, call Crystal to ask her to take care of Sneakers, and written out instructions when the knock came at her door. It wasn't Dev but a tall man dressed in the livery of a limo driver. He took her bag. "The car's ready, miss."

When he headed down the hall, she quickly locked her apartment door and followed. The stranger had her things, for heaven's sake.

When she got outside, she found him loading her bag into the back of a huge SUV with tinted windows. She walked up to him. "Did Mr. VonRamsberg send you?"

He straightened, obviously startled. "Why, yes. He's waiting for you inside."

The man went around the SUV and pulled the door open for her. When she approached, she discovered that Dev was, indeed, sitting on a couch toward the rear. The other seats had been removed to turn the vehicle into a limo with a glass screen separating the passenger compartment from the driver.

When she climbed inside and got a better view of him, she had an even bigger shock. She knew the relaxed and confident Dev. She'd never met the one who wore a business suit as if he was made for it.

Or rather, as if the suit had been made specifically for him and by an expert tailor. It fit perfectly, the charcoal grey wool emphasizing the breadth of his shoulders and the firm planes of his chest. Above that, the startling white collar of a dress shirt contrasted with the dark glow of his skin.

He patted the seat next to him. "You'd better sit down. Dolf will be ready to leave by now."

She sat. "Dolf?"

"My driver."

"I thought I detected an accent," she said.

"He speaks German, as do most of my people."

She suddenly realized that her mouth was hanging open. No wonder, given all the surprises he'd just handed her. Before she caught any flies, she brought her jaws together. "Dev, is that really you?"

"Yes and no," he answered. "You'll find out soon."

By now, the SUV had merged onto the freeway, headed toward the airport only ten or so miles away.

Dev's hand covered hers on the...of course…leather seat between them. "Thank you for coming."

"Thank you for having me. I think."

"This must be confusing," he said.

"Major understatement."

"It's going to get worse, I'm afraid," he said.

"How? Are we going to go down a rabbit hole?"

"Something like that."

Actually, she'd left rabbit hole behind when she'd first slipped into his bed. Now, she was having tea with the Mad Hatter, and the Dormouse was driving them down the Yellow Brick Road. The limo, for example. Many of her friends didn't even own a car. Then, there was the huge transformation in Dev's appearance…again. And what had he said about his people? As if he owned them or ruled over them or something equally fairy tale.

She stared out the window at the exits she'd passed enough to know by heart. They all seemed part of another reality, a past world she was stepping out of into a new existence. The presence of Dev's hand on hers amplified the feeling as did the scent of his cologne. He'd been a friend before. A bit older than her other friends but not so much that he couldn't fit in. Now, he was a man in his prime, and any woman with any sense knew how dangerous those could be.

Dev didn't speak but stared ahead of him at the back of the driver's head. His eyes didn't really focus there, though. He clearly wasn't seeing the things around him. His face had the same lost expression he'd worn when he'd received the call at Crystal's place. In an inadequate attempt to comfort him, she turned her hand under his so that their palms met.

"Has your father had strokes before?"

"We think very small ones," he answered. "He denies it, of course."

"And your mother?"

"She died at a young age. A horrible cancer that took her quickly."

"I'm sorry, Dev." Though she and her parents spent a lot of time apart, they were still a presence in her life. Losing one would create an empty place in her heart.

"I'm sure he has excellent doctors," she said. Based on the obvious wealth of this new Dev—the third she'd encountered—his father wouldn't want for good care.

"He has the best."

"They have a clot-busting drug now. If they gave it to him in time, he should be fine." Or at least recovered if not perfectly fine.

"If he wasn't stubborn enough to deny what was happening to him," Dev said.

"He sounds like quite a man."

"He is. I take after him in many ways, I hope."

"I'm sure you do." She'd have to be working with gut feeling on that one. She'd never actually known anything about him except for where he came from. He'd shown quite an ability to change like a chameleon, but all of his incarnations seemed sincere and caring. Yes, if his father deserved his respect, Dev deserved hers. Otherwise, she couldn't have trusted him enough to go with him to Danislova.

When they exited the freeway, the limo didn't head toward the passenger terminals but instead drove to the part of the airport where private and corporate jets landed and took off. Dolf pulled up next to a particularly large plane with what looked like a family crest on the side. He cut the motor and came around to open the door for them.

Dev climbed out first and offered his hand to help her down. When her feet hit the tarmac, she stared up at the huge aircraft. "What is this, Air Force One?"

"Not nearly so large," he said.

"Is it your family's plane?"

"Officially, it belongs to the government."

"Then, you work for the government?"

As Dolf brought their luggage around, another man in uniform came down the staircase from the jet.

He bowed smartly toward Dev. "We're ready to leave as soon as you board, Your Highness."

"Highness?" She gazed up at Dev, not even caring if her jaw had dropped.

"Highness." He lifted her fingers to his lips. "You see, my dear, I'm a prince."

CHAPTER FOUR

The couch on the jet opened flat into a bed, but Dev didn't disturb Felice's sleep to make the adjustment. Instead, when he could no long endure watching her and not touching her, he lay down next to her, pressing her front against his chest and her back against the cushions. They barely fit into the narrow space, but their bodies merged like two pieces of a jigsaw puzzle.

The last call from Grigori had held good news, and the fear had drained out of him. Or most of it. This trip hadn't been strictly necessary, but now that the danger was over, he could have Felice beside him for a while. He could show her his native land, the country he'd dedicated his life to. For the next minutes, he could enjoy the comfort of her body, safe in the knowledge that they wouldn't find tragedy when they landed.

After a moment of snuggling, she stirred but didn't rouse completely. As he'd removed his jacket, her hand rested against his shirt.

"How much farther do we have to go?" she mumbled.

"A few hours still." Hours he'd spend in an agony of wanting her. He'd already become erect sitting on the chair and picturing all the things he could do to give her pleasure. Now his cock pressed through the layers of their clothing into her belly. So near to what it needed, it had begun to throb.

"Prince Dev, huh?" she said. "I still can't believe it."

"Actually, Devlin is my middle name, or one of them. I'm Prince Christian."

He waited for the reaction. She'd now connect him to the scoundrel in the tabloids, the bastard who went all over Europe breaking women's hearts. He might have disappointed a few of the women he'd dated. What well-meaning person hadn't done that unintentionally? But he'd always been honest with his lovers before entering the relationship. He couldn't marry for love. His future wasn't his own.

Which meant he shouldn't be lying here now, basking in the warmth of the embrace. He shouldn't be calculating how best to get his hand inside her clothing nor where the clasps of her bra might be.

"I think I've heard of a Prince Christian," she said. "Are you the guy in the gossip rags?"

"I'm afraid I am."

She stretched, rubbing her body against his in all the most delicious and unfortunate places. "I don't read those."

"I'm glad."

"I mean, what can you believe in a paper that has the picture of an alien dog baby on the cover?"

"Then you don't think I'm a pampered, self-indulgent womanizer?"

"Virgin Dev? I don't think so."

"I'm even gladder of that." He held her against him, her head tucked under his chin. Being this close to a woman had stirred his lust many times. It had never created such protective urges in him before. As if as long as he kept her here, he could keep her safe from any of the world's unpleasantness when, in fact, he would soon be the cause of more than a little when they had to part.

"The paparazzi are likely to try to swarm us when we land," he said.

"Let 'em. I'm not afraid of having my picture taken."

"They'll link you with the notorious Prince Christian."

"Good. I'll be the mystery woman." She tipped her head back and kissed him just below his jaw.

Against every shred of sense of decency he had left, he tugged his tie loose and undid the top two buttons of his shirt to give her more room to explore. She took advantage, her fingers parting his collar so she could nip him at the base of his throat. Oh, this was a bad idea. A very, very bad idea.

"They can drive themselves crazy trying to figure out who I am," she said.

She'd drive *him* crazy in another minute. "What if your parents see your picture?"

"They don't read those rags, either."

She continued her assault on his neck, covering it with kisses and tiny bites, even smoothing those spots over with her tongue. He'd always known how sensitive a woman's throat could be, but he'd never imagined his own could draw such a response. In a moment, she had him so hot he could forget he wasn't supposed to make love to her. So he stopped her mouth the most effective way possible, by bending to cover it with his own.

The kiss caused more problems than it solved as she opened her lips under his, demanding that he fall completely under her spell. How could he not? Her breath was honey sweet, narcotic. As his last scruple threatened to unwind, he tugged her blouse from her skirt and slid his hand up her back.

Her bra was a tiny, silky thing, and the clasps unfastened easily. She let out a little moan when her breasts fell free, and he moved his hands over her ribs to catch one against his palm. Already stiff, the nipple tightened into a hard nub as he flicked his thumb over it. Restless with rising arousal, she kept moving against him as he continued to knead her soft flesh.

"May I touch you?" Lord, he hardly recognized his own voice.

"Yes," she whispered.

"I'll give you an orgasm. You can go back to sleep, and I'll…" What? The plane's bathroom had a small shower. He could douse himself with cold water, or he could make the water hotter and do something he hadn't done since his teenage years…use his hand for some relief.

"What about you?" she said.

"No condoms on the plane."

"Check in my purse. There's a box."

Luckily, the handbag in question lay on the floor beside the couch so he didn't have to get up to find it. He reached inside and found something that felt like a jewelry box. When he pulled it out, she propped herself up on one elbow to watch him.

"A present for me?"

She gave him a lazy grin. "Look and find out."

He undid the bow and opened the box. "You store condoms like this?"

"It's a special one. The one we didn't use."

"Clever, clever girl." He had to twist to find the switch on the intercom next to the couch.

"Your Highness?" the pilot's voice came on.

"Do not interrupt me for the next half hour, no matter what."

Half hour? she mouthed silently.

"Understood, Your Highness." Dev let the switch fall closed.

"I plan to take my time," he said. "And then, I'm going to want to hold you."

"It sounds wonderful." She raised her hands over her head and stretched again, this time like a cat being scratched behind the ears. He'd scratch her, all right, everywhere she itched.

After setting the condom onto the floor within easy reach, he began by unbuttoning her blouse, pushing aside her bra, and taking a nipple into his mouth to suck. Digging her fingers into his hair, she let out a low moan that vibrated in his blood. Damn, but he wanted this woman with a power that would frighten him if he had any sense. Fortunately, the centers of higher reason in his brain had blinked out the moment she'd opened those green eyes, still full of the confusion of sleep. Right this minute, he was operating out of more primitive urges to feel her wetness against his fingers and hear her cry out in climax.

After giving her other breast the same loving attentions, he raised himself on his elbow to gaze at her. Her eyes had the half-closed, dreamy look of a highly aroused woman. The flush on her cheeks extended down to her chest, and she'd parted her lips to bring in air. She made the perfect picture of abandon and of trust that he'd satisfy her. So lovely, his chest hurt as he stared at her.

"We'd better get rid of your panties," he said. "We wouldn't want them soaked."

She groaned. "Too late for that."

"I want to feel that for myself."

"Go ahead."

When he reached under her skirt, she lifted her hips to let him tug the silky material down and then pull them off her feet. She had, indeed, dampened the crotch, scenting it with her own perfume. An aphrodisiac that filled him with an almost uncontrollable need to bury himself inside her. But that would end things too quickly. Instead, he lay back down, stroking her skin upward from her knee, over her inner thigh, to the very place she wanted him the most. The lips felt swollen and hot, and as he pressed his fingertips to the seam between them, her nectar fell freely to coat them.

"By God, you're beautiful," he murmured.

"Do you think they know what we're doing back here?"

"Do you care?" He found her distended nub and rubbed it in a circular motion.

"Not while you're doing…oh!…that."

"I'm going to make you come."

"I know."

He lay and watched how her climb to the pinnacle played itself out on her face. A soft smile of bliss on her lips, crinkles at the corners of her eyes followed by sighs. All the while, the flush of arousal grew brighter on her fair skin until her chest was a rosy pink. She'd made herself completely vulnerable to him, trusting that he wouldn't disappoint her. He'd never in this world betray that trust, so he continued stroking her sensitive bud. Rolling and pressing rhythmically.

"Dev." She gasped. "Oh God!"

He worked her clit harder, calling up the storm. The power of her orgasm registered inside him, coiling in his gut. As her hips rose, he covered her mouth with his own and swallowed her cries. He could tell her later that he'd muffled them so the pilots couldn't hear, but in truth, he needed to share the moment with her, to let her know how deeply her response to his touch moved him.

After a bit, she went limp, her head back under his chin and her fingers splayed over his chest. He brought the hand he'd used to caress her up so that he could breathe the scent of her arousal. The fact that he'd drawn this from her—that she'd become wet for him—made his heart swell with pride. Amazing creature. Giving, yielding, and giving some more. In a just world, he could keep her with him forever, not only for a flight or the days ahead of them.

He would make love with her again. His body had made that decision for him. Even now, it craved release inside her. The strength of the need would be painful if he didn't know he'd soon find relief. Yes, he'd continue to know her intimately. He and his native land would show her a fairy tale until she had to return to her studies. He'd have to stay in Danislova and assume the duties of his birth. Because of his father's health, his days of freedom were over.

She stirred finally, much as she had from waking up. "That was amazing."

"You're amazing."

"More to come, I hope."

"We'll use that lovely gift you gave me," he said.

"I think you have a gift for me, too." She reached lower to his trousers. When she found the zipper and pulled it downward, he had to clench his teeth and fight for control. His cock felt as if it had been waiting for hours, so swollen the skin could barely contain it. When she reached inside and wrapped her fingers around the shaft, he groaned out of pure frustration.

"Take care," he said. "Or this will end before you want."

"I'll always take care with this." She pulled his member free of his clothing and stroked it from the base to the tip. "And you think I'm beautiful."

"You are, and you're going to make me wild in another moment."

"I think I want you wild."

Damn. He was going to explode. Right this minute. "All right. You get your wish."

After shoving his pants and boxers over his hips, he found the condom and managed to get it out of its wrapper. Within seconds, he'd put it on and had Felice on her back beneath him. She wrapped her legs around him, guiding him to her entrance, and with one thrust, he plunged into her.

For an instant, his mind registered one reality. *Home. Where I belong.* And then he was pounding into her. Fast and hard, his hips working on their own. He was being rough with her. Too rough, but he could not stop.

The walls of her sex clamped around his cock, her heat sinking into his flesh. She was wet, either still or again. No matter which, it meant she wanted him. She'd accepted the invasion, welcomed it.

Through the haze of his need, he barely sensed the scratch of her fingernails against his back. Her breath came harsh and fast in his ears.

"Dev, it's so good," she said. "Don't stop."

But he'd have to stop. Already, the climax was building in his sac. He couldn't slow down, couldn't make it last for her. He had to come.

"Yes," she cried. "Yes!"

And then, she was climaxing around him. Strong spasms that pulled at his cock, milking it. He let go of the last tether to sanity and allowed his own orgasm to come. It crashed through him, claiming his whole body as his cock released his seed until she'd drained him and he had no more to give.

For a few minutes, he blacked out, slipping into a semi-conscious state of utter satiation. Nothing penetrated except for the sound of her breathing and the scent of her skin. When he finally returned to the world, he discovered he was on top of her, crushing her with his weight. He never did that to a lover. Never. So he quickly rolled onto his side and pulled her against him.

"How much more of that half hour do you suppose we have left?" she asked.

"I hope a few minutes because I can't move."

"Have you ever used this couch before?"

She didn't say used it for what, but the meaning came through all the same. "Never. And even if I had, it wouldn't have been the same."

"I'm glad."

He tipped her head up so that she had to look him in the face. "Sex has never been like this for me."

"That makes me even gladder," she said with a smile that radiated joy.

He tucked her head under his chin again, and shut his eyes as the pain of reality stabbed at him. He would end up hurting her. It was too late now to prevent that, damn his selfishness. At least, he had the consolation that saying goodbye to her was going to break his own heart.

*

Danislova could have been the location for a child's story book. Once they'd barged their way through a clutch of photographers with fast-clicking lenses, the limousine with Dev's family crest took them through narrow streets that wound upward to the palace at the top of the highest hill in the city. Small shops stood side-by-side with houses that had to be hundreds of years old, and from time to time they'd pass a park or plaza. One sported an outdoor café and another an open market. Despite the pleasant weather, the distant mountains held caps of snow at the peaks.

Felice almost strained her neck trying to take it all in. Dev, on the other hand, ignored it all as he spoke into his cell phone in German. She smacked herself inwardly. Of course, he didn't notice the scenery. They'd come here because his father was ill.

"Any news?" she asked.

"He's doing well. They're already bringing him home."

"Thank heaven." At least, she didn't have to feel guilty for enjoying herself nor have to worry that the poor man had been on his death bead while she'd been having mind-blowing sex with his son on the plane.

"Will I get to meet him?" she asked.

"He'll insist on it. I'll do my best to make him behave himself."

She had to laugh at that. "You can order a king around?"

"Prince Royal. And no. No one tells my father what to do." He put his phone in his pocket and took her hand in his. "Thank you for coming."

"Thank you for asking me."

"It appears I won't need your moral support, after all, but I appreciated the diversion on the way here."

She laughed again. "Is that what they're calling it now?"

"Felice, I..." He took her chin between his thumb and forefinger, gazing at her with the same sad weight-of-the-world expression he'd had that day he'd taken her out of Marc's seminar.

"I know," she said. "Obligations."

"I was selfish to ask so much from you when I can't make any promises."

A lump formed in her throat. Obligations made some sense now. The man was a prince, the next in line to his country's throne. He didn't get to marry just anyone.

Marry? Why in hell was she thinking of marriage? Two weeks before Dev had been no more than the dorky but sweet guy who sat in the back of class wearing corduroy pants. The sex had obviously scrambled her brain.

"Promises aren't worth much, anyway. They get broken," she said. "Enjoy the present, and let the future take care of itself, I always say."

He stared at her as if he didn't believe her, which was fine because she'd never in her life said that.

"Something like that," she said.

"Fine." He lifted his hand and stroked her cheek with the backs of his fingers. "We'll let the future take care of itself."

Before she could brood on the fact that their future held nothing more than her reading about Prince Christian's wedding in the papers, the limo turned off the main road onto the drive that led up to the palace.

A close-up view did nothing to dispel the image of its luxury and history. Behind a high fence of metal posts painted in gold lay a circular courtyard with a marble fountain. Cherubs poured water into a reflecting pool while dolphins arced above the surface. Past all that stood the palace proper. Its polished grey stones gave way to arching windows, and gargoyles stared downward from their perches on the roof. A forest of chimneys spoke to dozens of fireplaces.

The view disappeared as they drove through a stone gateway and guard tower and re-emerged even more imposing as the limo brought them to the base of the grand staircase leading upward and into the magnificent building.

When the driver stopped and came around to open the door, Felice suddenly remembered what she was wearing. The skirt and casual top had seemed like a great idea when Dev had been a regular guy in jeans. He'd turned into a prince in a finely tailored suit. They didn't match.

"I can't go in there like this," she said.

"Why not? Is there something wrong?"

Because the driver stood less than six feet away, she leaned toward Dev's ear. "I'm not dressed correctly."

"We don't wear ball gowns and full dress uniforms all the time."

"Uniform?"

"Of course, I served in our army," he said. "I still retain my rank."

The driver neither moved nor made a noise, but a servant came down the palace steps and opened Dev's door. Now two of them were waiting for her to do something, and people might be watching from inside.

"You should have told me where I was going," she said.

"Why? So you could pack your tiara?"

"This isn't funny. I don't have anything right to wear."

"I'll take care of that." He caught her chin in his hand and turned her face to stare into his huge, brown eyes. "Do you trust me?"

"Well…sure."

"I can have the car take you back to the airport. The jet can fly you home."

Now, *that* was nowhere near the top of the list of things she wanted to happen. Not to leave this beautiful place without having seen any of it, nor to leave this man.

"You're right," she said. "I trust you."

He gave her chin a squeeze before releasing her and then waited for her to climb out first. Neither driver nor servant so much as lifted an eyebrow at her appearance. Of course, they were professionals and wouldn't let their opinions show on their faces.

As Dev put his hand at the small of her back and guided her up the stairs, the huge double doors opened to reveal a man in the stiff, dark clothing of a butler.

He bowed smartly as they approached. “Welcome home, Your Highness.”

“Thank you, Wilson,” Dev said. “This is Miss Larson.”

The man bowed again. “My lady.”

“Not lady,” she corrected. “Just miss.”

Like the others, he gave no overt reaction to her presence one way or the other. Just as well. She had no idea how to react, either.

“My brothers have arrived?” Dev asked.

“I’ve put them in the gold salon, Your Highness.”

“Thank you.” His hand settled itself on her back again, this time to lead her through an entryway made of marble flooring and dark wood walls. The ceiling soared to the top of the curving staircase, and a chandelier of brass and crystal dominated the ceiling. She could only marvel at it all until the realization hit that he might be taking her to meet his brothers.

“I can’t meet your family like this,” she said.

“They won’t care. Ulrich studies art. He’s probably covered with paint half the time.”

“Yeah, and you wear corduroy pants.” She stopped dead, not taking another step. “But you’re not wearing them now.”

“All right.” He pulled her into his arms. “We’ll get you settled first. You can meet them later.”

“What’s wrong with right now?” a male voice said from behind Dev. Felice jumped out of his embrace to find a man standing in a doorway with a second behind him in another room.

Dev practically launched himself at them, and soon, they were locked in a three-way hug like long-lost brothers. The brother part had to be correct, as they all had the same stature, although Dev had an inch or so on the other two. One had his dark complexion, while the other was pale and blonde, his eyes a soft blue. When they pried themselves apart, she had to admit they all made quite a feast for the eyes, with Dev the most handsome of them all.

"Aren't you going to introduce us?" the blond said.

"Felice, these are my brothers, Kurt and Ulrich. Kurt's the middle one."

"I'm the baby," the blond, Ulrich, said. "Our parents kept trying until they got it right."

"This beautiful lady is Felice Larson assholes," Dev said. "Don't get any ideas about her."

"What kind of ideas would we get?" Kurt put his hand over his heart in faked sincerity. "Based on what we just saw, it seems you have ideas enough for all of us."

"Let's not discuss this out in the hallway," Dev said.

He ushered them into what could only be the gold salon. Everything in the room came golden-hued or cream-colored. Damask upholstery covered antique chairs and settees. Far too nice to sit on, but that's what the three men did, anyway. Dev pulled her down onto a love seat next to him.

"So, are they teaching you foul language in the United States?" Kurt asked.

"There's plenty right here at home," Dev answered.

"Don't let Friedrich hear you use any of it," Ulrich said.

"Speaking of the old man, where is he now?" Dev asked.

"Grigori's bringing him home from the hospital," Kurt said.

Dev leaned forward, resting his elbows on his knees. "It was a stroke, then."

"A minor one. They treated it with the new drug," Kurt said. "He'll be fine."

"This time," Dev said.

"He can't last forever," Ulrich said softly.

A pall settled over the room. Their grim expressions told the story repeated everywhere when families had to face the loss of a beloved elder. This might be a palace and all the sons princes, but they clearly cared for their father as much as any child loved their parents.

"What is this? A wake?" a deep voice sounded from the doorway. "I'm not dead yet."

All three brothers went to their feet, and Felice joined them. Easily the most remarkable man she'd ever laid eyes on had entered the room. Despite his cane, he stood tall and straight. Like Dev and Kurt, he had dark skin. He also shared Dev's high cheekbones and strong jaw. But where Dev's hair was a dark brown, this man's shone white, which made quite a contrast with his busy black eyebrows and long lashes.

This had to be Dev's father, the king. No…Prince Royal. Friedrich. Should she bow, curtsey, or simply stand where she was? Suddenly, her hands felt huge and uncomfortable either in front of her or behind.

"You've done it again, old man," Dev said. "No woman ever looks at us with you in the room."

"Are you going to stand there like an ignoramus or introduce us?" Friedrich demanded.

"Father, may I present Miss Felice Larson."

"It's a pleasure to meet you, Your…" Felice said.

"Majesty," Dev whispered.

"Your Majesty." At that, she did curtsey, awkwardly. It only seemed the logical thing.

"Americans don't do that." Friedrich gestured with the hand that held his cane. "Do they?"

"No, sir…Majesty."

"Then, you needn't do it." He approached her, seeming to tower over her, even though he was no taller than any of his sons. "You're welcome in my home."

"Thank you." It took all her willpower not to curtsey again.

"Now, then. What do the lot of you have to say for yourselves?" Friedrich demanded.

"Let me get Felice situated before we start a long, family fight," Dev said.

"Do that. Find her a nice suite of rooms near my own. I'd best keep watch over her with the three of you around," Friedrich said.

"I'll do that," Dev said.

"And then get back here. It's been too damned long since I've seen you."

*

Felice absolutely took Dev's breath away. He'd always known that the palace staff could work miracles, but within hours, someone had picked out a gown that not only fit her perfectly but brought out the color of her eyes. The emerald satin bared one shoulder and yet remained modest. Rather than show off the swell of her breasts, the bodice focused attention on her graceful neck. Someone, most likely the maid they'd assigned her, had piled her hair in golden curls on the top of her head, letting one tendril hang along the side of her face to her throat.

She was, quite simply, stunning, and it took a few seconds for Dev to recover enough composure to rise with the others when she approached the table.

Rather than a large affair, they'd chosen to eat in the small, family dining room. No more than the VonRamsberg men, their advisor Grigori, and the vision that was Felice Larson. Dev pulled out the chair beside his to seat her. She wore no jewels except for small earrings that were probably her own. He'd have to fix that. He'd open the family vault and urge her to borrow whatever she liked. He'd have the jeweler from the city bring trays of diamonds and pearls and buy her whatever *he* liked. He'd do anything for this magnificent creature.

Anything, that was, but keep his hands off her. Despite his father and brothers looking on, he absolutely could not resist reaching behind her to touch the warm skin just above the back of her dress. In response, she gave him a tiny smile as she looked down at her silverware and shook her head so slightly the others might not notice.

His father noticed everything, though, and the lift of one of his eyebrows sent Dev the message that he'd better get himself under control. Grigori sat silently, watching. His expression gave no clue to his thoughts, but Dev could read him well enough. He was worried about Dev's interest in Felice. So, as much as his palms itched to explore more and more of her, he rested his napkin in his lap and did his best not to think of the way she'd moved beneath him on the cramped couch earlier in the day.

The soup course was leek and potato and delicious. For now, he'd indulge his taste buds. The other senses would come later when he could peel the gown off her.

"So, Miss Larson," he father began after a few spoonfuls of soup. "I understand you and my son are colleagues at the university."

"In the same lab, yes," she answered.

"And do you also study snakes that wind sideways?"

She cocked her head in confusion for a moment and then laughed. "Sidewinders. No, I don't."

Friedrich's eyes took on the twinkle that warned a test would follow. "Why not?"

"I don't want to spend my career chasing after rattlesnakes, I suppose," she said.

The twinkle grew even brighter. "You don't like them?"

"No woman likes snakes, father," Ulrich said.

She paused with her spoon halfway to her mouth. "Oh, but I do. They're fascinating creatures. Dev can tell you. That is, the prince. His—"

"Dev will do among us," Dev said. This wasn't easy for her. His father could be formidable under any circumstances. Worse, she found herself surrounded by royalty in a country where she knew none of the customs. He really had been selfish asking her to come with him. He'd make amends even if he had to do it morning, noon, and night.

"Dev's doing great research, Your Majesty," she said. "You must be very proud of him."

"I'm proud of him for any number of reasons," Friedrich said. "But I wonder why you don't work closely with him."

"I prefer not to study an animal that can kill me," she said.

Friedrich sat back in his chair as the footman took his soup away. "There, you see. The lady has more common sense than my son."

She set her spoon into the empty soup bowl and let the footman take them away. "It's usually that way with men and women, isn't it?"

"*Touché*, father," Ulrich said.

Friedrich hmphed in mock disapproval. "Women didn't talk to men in that way in my day."

"You know that's not true," Dev said. "Mother put you in your place many times."

Friedrich's expression softened, with a hint of sadness around his eyes. "That she did. You've won this point, Miss Larson."

"I didn't know this was a contest."

Ulrich laughed. "Always, Miss Larson."

"You, at least, will call me Felice, won't you?" she said.

"Of course." Ulrich lifted his wine glass toward her. "I'm looking forward to a warm friendship."

Something very like jealousy roiled in Dev's gut. His baby brother could charm the bees off a blossom. Women adored him, and he adored them right back. Dev touched Felice's shoulder, deliberately letting Ulrich know where things stood. Ulrich only chuckled. He'd been toying with Dev, as Dev would have known if he hadn't been so besotted with her.

"So what do you study, if not snakes?" Friedrich asked.

"Coyotes. I've been documenting the reduced populations and distribution. You see, when I was a child, you'd find coyotes in places like the Oakland hills. With the development up there…" She stopped mid-sentence. "I'm sorry. I'm lecturing."

"It's good to have passion about your work," Friedrich said.

They sat quietly while the fish course was served. When Felice tried hers, she let out an oh! of surprise. "This is wonderful. I don't think I've ever tasted anything like it."

"Caught a few hours ago in the stream that runs through our woods," Friedrich said.

Dev had fished that stream as a boy, and they'd often had this dish...a filet with a sauce made from the poaching liquid. It had a pleasant taste but nothing that deserved such elaborate praise.

"Do you eat stale fish in the United States?" Friedrich asked.

"No, father, but most people don't get it quite this fresh," Dev answered.

"My son will show you the stream and the woods," Friedrich said. "Or I will."

"I'd like that very much. In fact, I'd love to see all of Danislova. It's so…" She gestured as if groping for the right word. "…I don't know. 'Lovely' seems inadequate. Your people must be very happy to live here."

She couldn't realize it, but she'd said exactly the right words to win his father's heart. Friedrich's love of his country and people came second only to his love of his family.

"My son will take you wherever you want," Friedrich said. "All my sons are at your disposal."

"Happy to be," Kurt said. Ulrich lifted his wine glass again.

"Thank you all." A soft blush colored her cheeks. She seemed pleased, although flustered. The pleasure settled into Dev's chest, where he could share it with her. It felt good.

"Now then, what does your family think of my son spiriting you off to a foreign land?" Friedrich said.

"Oh, my." She brought her hand to her mouth. "I didn't call them."

Friedrich set down his fork and stared at her for a moment. "They don't know you're here?"

"With all the excitement…it just didn't...occur to me," she babbled.

"My children are grown men, and I know where they are all the time."

Oh no. The man could be building to a full-blown bluster. Dev and his brothers were used to it. Felice wasn't.

"I'll call them immediately," she said. "That is, when I figure out what time it is in Peru."

"Peru?" Friedrich said. "Why would they be in a place like that?"

"It's where they work. " Dev set his napkin on the table and prepared for a battle. "They're archeologists on site at a dig."

"That's all well and good, but it doesn't excuse them from taking care of their child," Friedrich said. "If I'd been lucky enough to have a daughter, I wouldn't let her run around the world without telling me. I can tell you that."

"Father, please don't upset yourself," Kurt said. "You're just home from the hospital."

"Who says I'm upset?" Friedrich demanded.

Dev stared at his father. He'd learned the imperious glare rather well by now, and his father quieted…some.

"The rest of your family, then. What about them?" Friedrich asked.

"I am the rest of my family, I'm afraid." Felice set her hands in her lap like a child who'd been scolded.

"You're an only child?" Friedrich said as if he'd never heard of such a thing.

She forced a laugh. "The product of some pills that didn't get to a dig site on time, I'm afraid."

Friedrich's back went ramrod straight. "They actually said such a thing to their daughter?"

"It's not our business, father," Kurt said softly.

"It's just a joke," Ulrich added.

"It's not funny," Friedrich declared. "A child should be treasured."

An awkward silence settled over them, broken only by the sounds of china settling on china as the footmen served the main course.

Felice still sat stiffly with her fingers clasped in her lap. With no care for what the others thought, Dev covered her them with his hand and squeezed.

"I didn't mean to offend," she said.

"I'm not offended at you, my dear," his father said finally. "Not the least little bit. You're parents are another matter. "

"Father, please, "Dev said.

"Very well. " Friedrich made a disapproving rumble in his throat. "While you're here, you'll be part of my family, Miss Larson."

CHAPTER FIVE

Evening had turned into night some time before. They'd eaten dinner, had some brandy—limiting Friedrich to not much more than a thimbleful—and retired for bed. Now, Dev sat in his sitting room, dressed in pajamas and robe, facing a dilemma that wasn't any real puzzle at all. What bed would he sleep in? Felice's or his own?

Unfortunately, Grigori had more or less the same problem on his mind, although he'd never try to discuss Dev's sex life. He would, however, have very definite opinions on any woman Dev might become involved with, and the possibility of Dev having a relationship with Felice had alarmed Grigori enough to prompt a meeting at this hour.

Always serious, tonight Grigori appeared downright dour. He hadn't changed from the dark suit he'd worn at dinner, but the fringe of hair that circled his bald head appeared ruffled, as though he'd run his fingers through it and then tried without success to smooth it back down. His bushy grey eyebrows were arched, nearly meeting over the bridge of his nose.

He hovered over Dev's armchair. "The American, Your Highness…"

"Miss Larson. What about her?"

"She's quite attractive."

Dev smiled up at Grigori. "She is, isn't she?"

"May I ask what your intentions are, concerning her?" Grigori stood completely still, his hands behind his back.

"Ah, well there you have me," Dev said. "I don't know."

Grigori blinked several times. "You don't know?"

That did sound ridiculous. It *was* ridiculous. If he were an ordinary man, free to make any decision about his life he cared to, he could simply answer that he planned to allow the relationship to deepen or not, letting it develop on its own. As heir to the throne, he didn't have any choice in whom he married, so he couldn't consider marriage an option.

He could have a temporary affair with Felice, or he could make her his long-term mistress. She deserved better than the second option. She deserved better than both, actually, but that second? Absolutely not. Too unfair to her and to Astrid or whatever woman he married. Hell and damnation.

"She can't be your Princess Royal, sir," Grigori said. "I hope you see that."

"I didn't say I was going to marry her." Although the thought did warm him inside. Waking up to her face every morning made a very pleasant prospect, indeed. One he could start enjoying while she stayed at the palace. Yes, her bedroom, not his. What sort of idiot had thought he could stay away from her after what they'd shared on their way here?

He rubbed his fingers over his mouth and chin and discovered he was smiling. He'd also grown some stubble. He'd have to shave for fear of rasping against her soft skin.

"What are you thinking, Your Highness?" Grigori asked.

"Nothing that concerns you."

"The future of Danislova concerns me very much. *Your* future concerns me very much, and that includes the proper match for you."

"For the love of God, why are you bothering me about this?" he said. "Marriage is for the future."

"Not very far off. You're at a prime age to marry. You'll have to succeed your father, and you'll need a royal family of your own." Grigori spoke quickly and with some vehemence as he always did when he delivered a lecture. "You'll need an heir."

"Fine. Astrid will be my wife, or someone else you and my father approve."

"Then, what about Miss Larson?"

"I don't know." Dev shot out of his chair. Instead of smashing something, he paced. Movement helped him think, but no matter which direction he went or which pieces of furniture he barely managed to avoid, no answer came to him. What about Felice, indeed? He shouldn't want her like this, shouldn't need her, but damn it, how was he supposed to keep his hands off a woman who stirred his passions as deeply as she did? How was he supposed to walk away from the sort of intimate union he'd always hoped for with a woman but had never found…until now?

"I don't know," he said more quietly. "I'll figure something out."

Grigori approached him and placed a hand on his shoulder. "I don't want to see you hurt."

"I know that."

"I don't want Miss Larson to suffer, either," Grigori said. "I'm not heartless."

"I know that, too." Dev stuffed his fists in the pockets of his robe.

"You bear a hard burden, as your father has and his father before him. Danislova demands everything from you. Can you give it?"

"Of course, I can. I want to."

"Then, guard your heart," Grigori said.

His heart. Well, yes, that. But right now another part of his anatomy was giving him the most fits where Felice was concerned. She'd gotten completely under his skin, and he could no sooner stay away from her than he could sprout wings and fly.

How ironic that he'd always expected his lovers to keep things light—making sure not to become too attached—and now he stood in danger of failing to take his own advice. He'd never had any trouble before, but Felice affected him differently than any woman had before.

Perhaps she moved him so deeply because she hadn't come to him as Prince Christian but as Dev. She hadn't given herself to a rich and powerful prince, perhaps in hopes of advancing herself socially. She'd offered her body to a man she believed to be painfully shy, maybe even a man who'd never lain with a woman before. And then she'd blossomed beneath him, parting her legs and accepting him inside her body with an abandon that matched his own.

"You need to guard her, too, Your Highness," Grigori said. "She must know from the outset that you're betrothed to someone else."

"Yes, yes, I'll guard her." He didn't promise to tell her about Astrid. If she realized their affair would end, why inflict all the details about another woman on her? He sure as hell didn't want to think about her with another man.

"Good then," Grigori said. "I'll leave you."

Dev nodded, dismissing his advisor. Already his mind had turned to finding his way into Felice's bedroom. Would she still be awake, and what would she be wearing? If she'd fallen asleep, he'd slip into her bed in much the way she'd done to him in his apartment. Then he'd rouse her with kisses and give her the sweetest dreams he could.

Grigori disappeared quietly, and Dev ran his hand over his chin again. Yes, a quick shave, and then he'd give his body what it craved.

*

Felice's father answered his cell phone on the fourth ring. In the late afternoon where he was, he could have responded more quickly, but that was dear old dad.

"Hi, sweetie. What's up?" His standard greeting with the usual note of excitement at hearing from her.

"Hi, dad," she said. "Nothing much. I wanted to let you know I'm in Europe with a friend from school."

"Europe, huh? Did you arrange that with your advisor?"

Marc. Another call she should make. "There wasn't time. My friend's father was sick, so I came along to lend him moral support."

"You're friend's a guy, then."

"Uh…yeah." The guy in question, or his reflection, appeared in her vanity mirror. Dev stepped over the threshold from her sitting room and approached where she sat. He wore a silk robe with silk pajamas showing from beneath. His collar was open, giving her a peek of his chest. He looked regal and sophisticated and sexy beyond belief.

"So, who is this guy?"

Somehow, telling her father that her graduate school bud was a crown prince felt like making up a fantasy. She hadn't become completely comfortable with the fairy tale herself.

"He's another student from Marc's group," she said. "He's from a country called Danislova."

"Hm...Danislova. Can't say it rings a bell."

Dev walked up to her and rested his hands on her shoulders, the warmth from his palms seeping into the naked one.

"It's a great place," she said. "You and mom would love it."

"Okay, but don't let the visit interfere with your work," her father said. "Your mother and I are both very proud of our little PhD."

Right. They'd been calling her that ever since she had a perfect grade point average in high school and had served as valedictorian.

"I'll check in with Marc and straighten things out," she said.

"Do that, sweetie."

Dev reached to her hair and removed the pins her maid had spent over half-an-hour sticking in. It fell free, one curl at a time, until he could spread it out over her shoulders. For a moment, he studied her in the mirror, and that hungry look she now recognized entered his eyes. Then he pushed her hair to one side and bent to place a kiss at the base of her throat.

She gasped and covered the phone with her hand. "What are you doing?"

"Playing," he answered. "Go on with your conversation. Pretend I'm not here."

Easy for him to say. No one was breathing against his neck in that sexy way of his. She set the phone back to her ear and did her best to concentrate on what her father was saying.

"I'm glad you called. We've have exciting news," her father said.

"Really?"

Dev chose that moment to kiss his way up to her ear and nibble on the lobe. She had to bite her lip to stifle a moan.

"We've found the king's palace this time," her father said. "We're almost one hundred per cent sure. I'm standing in the middle of it right now. Isn't that great? The palace!"

"Wow, dad. A palace. Sounds fascinating." And it would be if she weren't distracted by the gentle tug of Dev's teeth and the way his fingers massaged her shoulders.

"All the times we've thought we'd discovered this," her father said. "All the grant money. If we have it now, we'll never have to worry about funding."

"Tell him good-bye," Dev whispered into her ear.

She covered the phone again. "He's my father."

"He'll still be your father tomorrow. Tell him it's late and you have to go."

"You're impossible."

"I need you," Dev said.

He couldn't have said anything more efficient at curling her toes. A husky, caveman voice telling her he couldn't wait. Maybe she had spent enough time on the phone.

"Look, dad, I'd better go," she said into the phone.

"Okay. You take care, sweetie."

"I will."

"And check in with Marc asap," her father said.

"Tell him good-bye, or I will," Dev whispered.

"Is someone with you?" her father asked.

"Nope. Just the wind. Nothing."

The wind curled an arm around her and cupped a breast through the material of her gown. She pushed his hand away. "Cut that out."

"Sweetie?" came her father's voice from the phone.

"I'm sorry? You were saying?" she said.

Good-bye, dad, Dev mouthed. She glared at him. Then he reached for the phone and she nearly toppled over pulling it away from him.

"Bye, dad. Love you and mom," she almost shouted before cutting the connection. "Did your father teach you to be so rude?"

"Well you should bring up my father after you so thoroughly seduced him tonight."

She turned on her chair to face him. "I did no such thing."

"Metaphorically speaking." He kissed the tip of her nose. "You won him over completely."

"That's some metaphor, pal."

"You worked some magic on him," Dev said. "He never warms up that quickly to strangers."

She smiled inwardly. They'd had a tense few minutes at dinner until she realized he'd been upset *for* her rather than *with* her. After that, everything he said made him more and more charming. And dear. "I think he's magnificent."

"All women do, and he basks in their admiration." Dev kissed her softly. "He honestly likes you."

"I'm glad."

"It's your mother and father he disapproves of. I hope that was clear. He has very definite opinions on parenting."

"I realized that. It's sweet, actually."

"Sweet," Dev repeated. "Don't tell him that. He'll deny it."

As the warmth of feminine pride bloomed in her chest, she turned back to the mirror so she could study her own reflection with Dev's. He could only have come to her room for one thing. He'd be her lover again tonight, and studying his handsome face and body gave her a shiver of anticipation. She knew what he could do in bed, and they'd have all the time and room for him to do it. As she watched, he bent again and laid a path of kisses over her naked shoulder.

"I wanted to eat you all through dinner," he murmured against her skin. "I wanted to spread you out on the table and devour you."

"Your father would approve of that, I'm sure."

"It wouldn't matter. I wouldn't be able to control myself."

"What an animal." What started out as a chuckle ended up more like a groan as he eased her gown off the other shoulder and gave it the same treatment.

"You looked like dessert, you know?" he said. "You still do."

"I hope you'll soon look like the main course."

"Wicked woman," he whispered. "I've been swollen and ready for you since we kissed good-night in the hallway."

"Then what took you so long getting here?"

"I was trying to behave myself and not touch you." He moved her hair and laid a trail of caresses down the other side of her neck. "We are near my father's rooms, after all."

"I'll try to be quiet."

"And I'll do my best to make you loud." He took her hand and urged her to her feet.

Leaning into his large body felt so natural now that she'd slept in his arms twice. The silk of his robe was a whisper against her cheek. Beneath that, his heart beat in a steady rhythm, perfectly matched to her own. He tugged the zipper of her dress downward, its scratch the only sound other than their breathing. Then his fingers brushed over her spine. He could comfort or arouse, and the gentle stroking would soon turn into something more lethal and more perfect all at once. She'd given him so much power over her body. He'd own her heart soon as well. But then, he probably already did.

"It's a good thing I didn't know you weren't wearing a bra," he said. "I would have been erect all through dinner."

"I like it when you're erect." She shifted so she could place her palm against him. She found the now-familiar hardness, long and thick with the prominent head.

He let out a long ahhh of pleasure. "I'm sure my father has guessed our relationship."

"But we don't have to display it to him at the dinner table?"

"Discretion is the better part of valor," he said.

Dev's obligations again. His father couldn't completely approve of his son bringing home a nobody American, even if he acted gracious about the fact. She couldn't have Dev forever, so she'd best enjoy him fully while they could be together.

When he pushed her away so he could slide the dress over her shoulder and then down her body, his gaze drifted lower to her breasts. She'd never thought them particularly beautiful before. They were too small to attract the notice of most men, but Dev seemed entranced by them. Especially when he flicked his thumbs over the already hard nipples, as he did now, tightening them further. Under his expert touch, her flesh became super-sensitive, and the ache between her legs sharpened into a need that wouldn't go away on its own. She'd have his hands there and his cock, the shaft stretching her as he thrust. He'd make her come. He always did. Then she'd take his orgasm as proof that she could move him just as powerfully.

Only tonight would be different. She'd come to a decision waiting for him. They'd make love without reservation.

"Nothing between us tonight," she said.

For a moment his brows arched in confusion. "Felice…"

"No condom. I want to feel you inside me."

"We can't—"

She put her hand over his mouth to stop his words. "I'm on the pill. I won't get pregnant."

"You'd trust me that way?"

"I'd trust the prince, and I'd trust the nerd," she said. "I trust Dev."

"*Mein Schatz*."

He might not ever realize that he'd switched to German, but she understood that word well enough. He'd just called her his treasure.

She stepped out of the puddle of fabric that was her dress and kicked it aside so that she could step back into his embrace. Though layers of clothing still separated them—his robe and pajamas, her half-slip and panties—in a way, she was still more exposed than ever before. They wouldn't fumble for each other in the dark nor couple half clothed. They'd leave the light on so they could watch each other's faces at the moment of penetration, when his most intimate flesh would enter hers, making them one.

She tipped her head up for a kiss, and he complied. Their mouths met, lips parted as they began the dance in earnest. Taking his face in her hands, she rose up on tiptoe to demand more. Her tongue sought his and found it as his breathing grew labored and she could scarcely get air into her lungs. Arching against him, she pressed her body into his firmer one, her nipples poking at the muscles of his chest beneath the silk.

Suddenly, even the soft material formed an unacceptable barrier between them. By tugging at the belt of his robe, she had it open, and he shrugged out of it. The buttons of his top resisted opening, and she could not slow down to take them calmly. When his own fingers did no better, he pulled the garment over his head and threw it aside. Then, he pushed the bottoms down and stepped out of them, making him completely, utterly, gloriously naked.

This time when he took her into his arms, her breasts met his skin and his member pressed into her belly through the little clothing she still wore. She reached toward the waistband, but he covered her hand with his own and took over. Lowering himself, he took a few seconds to swirl his tongue around one nipple and then the other. Eventually, he was on his knees in front of her with her slip and panties at her feet. Placing her hand on his head, she stepped out of the last of her clothes.

Instead of rising to lead her to the bed, he reached around and pulled her toward him, burying his nose in the hairs that covered her sex.

"Do you know what your scent does to me?" he said.

"I can guess, but I'd rather you tell me."

"It makes me feel like the greatest lover in the world."

"What if I think you are?" she said.

"You've made me so hot. Let me see if I can do the same for you."

At that, he parted her legs and eased his face between them. Before she could brace herself, his tongue came out, parting her lips and landing directly onto her hot button.

The intensity of the caress sent shock waves through her body. This time, she put both hands on his head as he continued the gentle rasp against her clitoris. The world receded, leaving nothing but the sensations of her swollen petals parting for him and moisture—his and her own—coating her inner thighs.

It was heaven, and it was too much. Too much intimacy, too much vulnerability, too much honesty. And yet, she couldn't stop him, couldn't hold back the inevitable. So while her breaths turned to sighs and then gasps, she let him go on and on. Still stroking, still lapping at her.

Eventually, her knees buckled, and she swayed, almost falling. In an instant, he'd caught her, straightening and lifting her into his arms. Barely conscious of anything but the throbbing between her legs, she let him carry her to the bed and lay her across the turned down sheet. Then his mouth was back on her, and the firestorm built even higher. Close, so close. She strained for the orgasm at the same time she wished it away so that he could continue.

In the end, he pulled the bundle of nerve endings into his mouth, and she was lost. The flames rushed through her, spreading outward from her sex to consume all of her. A woman's voice shouted—her own—as the spasms started. They came one hard after the other until they built into one huge cataclysm. She continued crying out until she had no breath, and all throughout, Dev stayed with her, never stopping until she'd finished and sank into a puddle of satisfaction against the covers.

While she floated in bliss, he brought his body up next to hers and looped his arm around her waist. "Nothing gives a man more satisfaction than to have his lover climax like that."

Sweet of him, but she could think of a few things that would satisfy him. She'd do them, too, as soon as she could make her limbs function again.

Slowly, the world came back into focus, hazy around the edges at first. The feel of the smooth sheets beneath her, the pressure of Dev's arm. Finally, his face came into clear view as did the impression of his member against her thigh. He hadn't softened in the slightest, and he seemed to have grown a bit longer, although that illusion could have been the product of her lust-addled brain. If her love juices acted as an aphrodisiac for him, she'd see he got as much as he could handle.

The heat in the brown depths of his eyes and the evil curl to his lips told her he had more planned for her. Well, she had her own plans, and his could wait. Before he could launch another assault on her senses, she scooted down beside him and raised herself on one elbow.

With his impressive erection only inches from her mouth, she grasped the base with her free hand. He was so thick at the root, she could barely circle him with her fingers, but she pumped him, anyway, and bent to run her tongue around the head.

"*Gott*," he cried. "You don't have to do that."

"I want to. You're the main course, remember?"

"I didn't think you meant that literally."

"I don't like my food talking back to me," she said. "So, you just lie back and let me have my meal."

"You'll kill me, I swear."

"That's the general idea," she said.

"Not that way. I want to come inside you."

She tongued him again, this time flicking at the pucker at the tip.

"I mean it," he said. "Stop when I tell you to."

The head of his cock looked absolutely delicious, like a ripe fruit, so she sucked it into her mouth.

"Felice…" he shouted.

She released him and did her best not to chuckle. "All right, all right. I promise to stop when you tell me to."

She had no intention of making him come with her mouth, especially not the first time they did this without a condom. He'd be inside her, of course.

But she did plan to make him squirm the way he did to her. And she had the most beautiful joystick in all of creation to play with.

Grasping his shaft in her fist, she spread her lips over the head and worked her way downward. She couldn't take much more than the thick tip of him, he was so blessed big, but she did her best and continued pumping him.

"*Ach, gut*," he murmured. "Your pussy will feel like this around me."

Her pussy would take all of him, but it didn't have a tongue to circle the ridge around the head as she did now. And she wouldn't be able to reach to his sac while he was inside her. She did that, too, oh so gently feathering her fingertips over it.

He didn't say anything as she worked, at least not in words. His sighs and moans told the story of his rising arousal. He'd surrendered to having her mouth on his sex the same way she'd surrendered a few moments before. He'd ceded control so that she could give him pleasure, and she'd use every trick she could think of to make it beyond fabulous so that whatever happened between them, he'd never forget this night.

She continued working him, sucking his swollen flesh into her mouth and bobbing her head to take more. Then, she'd remove her lips and use her hand, stroking upward from the base. Each tiny twist at the tip earned her a gasp. Then she'd go back to swallowing him.

"Stop," he cried after a while. "Oh, God, stop."

She'd promised, so she removed her mouth. Now she threw a leg over him, bringing the entrance to her body above his cock. Parting her lips with one hand, she steadied his member with the other so she could lower herself onto him slowly.

His eyes were half-open as he watched his cock enter her. The moment dragged on in slow motion while the walls of her sex noted the passage of his hardness into her. She could only sigh at the pure, all-encompassing pleasure. A storm could have raged, shooting lightning down like spears of fury, and she wouldn't notice. The walls of the palace could crumble around them, and she wouldn't do anything that would separate their bodies.

They'd merged completely, with her sex impaled on his and his embedded inside her the way no other man had ever been.

They paused for a few heartbeats, gazing into each other's face, and then his eyes closed, and he began to move.

His thrusts sent her into a new heaven as she held herself upright to absorb the impact. This was no gentle coupling with slow and easy strokes to get things started. She'd made him too excited for that—too close to the edge of his control. The fact that she could do that to him…for him…gave her physical pleasure, and her sex responded to his roughness by becoming wet enough for their bodies to slap against each other with each passage.

Unable to hold still any longer, she rested her palms against his ribs so she could meet his upward thrusts with a rocking of her hips. In perfect synch with each other, they created a complex dance of thrust and retreat, back and forth. Her muscles gripped at him, seeking friction and finding it. He was the prince and the primitive male in heat. And he was her lover.

Then he did something that would end them both. He placed his hand at her pussy, found her clit, and pressed against it with his thumb. She'd come…soon and hard. He knew that. He'd come with her, and she knew that.

As she soared, nearing the precipice, she used her last free breath to call his name.

"Felice," he answered. "Oh, God, Felice."

The fury broke loose inside her…a climax so powerful it raged through every part of her. A thousand tiny suns exploded on the backs of her eyelids, and she stiffened, shuddering violently. The spasms started in her sex, grasping at him over and over.

With perfect clarity, she felt his orgasm claim him. Impossible, but true. She sensed the urgency as his hips jerked upward several times. She felt the rush of his semen as it left his cock. One large burst followed by several smaller ones. They'd truly merged into one being for these blinding moments, and they'd never be completely free from one another.

The thought followed her as she let herself float down onto his chest. It stayed with her, niggling from the back of her brain, as he wrapped his arms around her and took a deep breath. She couldn't have him, not really, but she couldn't face that while he was still embedded inside her and her sex still fluttered with aftershocks of her orgasm. For now, he was hers, and for now, that would have to do.

Chapter Six

An entire palace proved too much of a temptation for Felice to ignore. Every nook and corner had shown her a treasure, and she'd seen so little of the magnificence. Who could pass up an opportunity to explore when everyone else was asleep and she could pretend she owned the place and everything in it?

She probably could have worn slippers, but bare feet made no noise at all. She had had the sense to put a robe over her nightgown in case she encountered any drafts or, heaven forbid, people. She'd be careful not to touch anything but simply look and move through the space, so full of history and grandeur, as if it were her own.

The brass banister felt cool and smooth as she ran her palm along it, descending the grand staircase to the front entryway to the palace. The chandelier hung silently, its crystals now dark with no light to reflect. When she reached the bottom, she stepped onto the marble floor. Colder than the brass, it made the soles of her feet tingle, and yet, that only added to the excitement.

Because she'd seen the golden salon, she headed in the opposite direction to the other wing of the palace. All along the sides of the hallway stood objects that could have graced any museum. Low tables held huge vases, some filled with flowers. A suit of armor guarded one doorway. The man who'd worn it would be small, indeed, by today's standards…an inch or two shorter than she was.

Farther down, she came to a pair of large doors. They had to lead to something important, so she pushed one open a crack and stepped inside. She'd found a huge dining room with a table that could easily seat forty. No cloth covered it, as would be the case during a formal meal, and in the moonlight that spilled in from windows high up on the walls, the wood gave off a sheen. A huge fireplace stood at one end of the room and another on a side wall. They would have provided all the heat in earlier times. She could easily imagine a holiday dinner with logs ablaze and body heat filling the space with the warmth of the season. Women in flowing gowns of every color and men in stiff uniforms.

Portraits hung on the long wall opposite the fireplace. They depicted men and women in costumes from various eras. Some wore crowns, but all were dressed royally. As she walked along, she studied them until she came to the end. The last was Dev's father. The artist had captured him perfectly—the stern resolve softened by a light of tenderness in his eyes.

Dev had been right. If she wasn't careful, she'd end up falling for the man. That was silly, of course, but he still drew her as if he could fill some need she couldn't quite put words to.

Good grief. This country, this palace, and the men in it had her dreaming fairy tales. Well, why not? She blew Friedrich's picture a kiss and left the dining room to see what else she might find.

After passing a few more doors, she found one that stood open. It seemed to lead in to a library or study. A large leaded and mullioned window dominated most of one wall. The moonlight revealed bookshelves so tall they had rolling ladders to provide access to the ones on the top. A massive desk had papers strewed on top of it in haphazard piles. Someone, probably Friedrich, actually worked in here. She approached and studied the sheets that the moonlight made ghostly. She wouldn't snoop. She wouldn't be able to understand the German, anyway. Some imp in her dared her to get a look at his handwriting.

The moment she reached the front of the desk, the light came on, filling the room and for a moment blurring her vision. She turned to find the Prince Royal himself standing near the doorway.

"Do you find palace accounts interesting, Miss Larson?" he said.

"No sir…Your Majesty." Oh, shit, shit. "I was only…that is…I didn't touch anything, I swear."

He glanced around. "Everything seems to be the same as I left it."

"I wanted to explore," she continued babbling. "We don't have palaces in the United States, and yours is so beautiful."

He crossed his arms over his chest. "I see."

"I didn't damage anything, and I didn't take anything."

"Of course you didn't. My son has better judgment of people than to bring a thief into our home."

Her heart stopped its threatened nosedive into the vicinity of her stomach. "You'll forgive me then?"

"It doesn't seem there's anything to forgive," he said. "But I am curious. Did you find anything that interested you?"

"Oh my, yes." Okay, she was gushing, but the palace really held all kinds of fascinating things. "That suit of armor, for example, and all the portraits in the dining hall."

He gave her the same smile he had at dinner...at least before the eruption about her parents. As if she'd chosen exactly the right answer.

"Are they all rulers of Danislova?" she asked. "Even the women?"

"We've had ruling princesses, of course, but most of us have been men," he said. "Would you like a brief genealogy?"

"I would."

He stepped away from the door and indicated she should go ahead of him. When she did, they walked the short distance to the dining hall in silence. He held his hands behind him, the way high-born gentlemen did in novels, although he wore a robe and pajamas similar to Dev's and she had nothing on her feet. Not exactly Elizabeth Bennet and Mr. Darcy.

"So you like to prowl, Miss Larson," he said. "Prowl we shall."

"Do you often wake up in the middle of the night, Your Majesty?"

"All of us do. The men of my family are very light sleepers."

"That's odd. Dev always…" She stopped in her tracks. She'd just confessed that she and Dev had slept together. He must have guessed, but it wasn't something she particularly wanted to discuss with him.

He stopped beside her and cleared his throat. "Yes, well. I often slept like a dead man myself after my wife and I…"

"Of course." A truly awkward conversation, but he understood and hadn't objected. He certainly wasn't shy about making a fuss over something that displeased him.

At the dining hall, he opened the door and waited for her to go inside. This time when he turned on the lights she got a better view of the furnishings—the sideboards and endless table, all in highly polished wood, and the chairs lined up in rows.

The Prince Royal led her to the bank of paintings. "This first one is purported to be the likeness of Danemon, the first prince of Danislova."

The man in question looked absolutely fierce with a scar that ran from the corner of one eye down to his jaw just below his ear. His robes were hardly more than furs, as though civilization hadn't yet perfected clothing.

"According to legend, Danemon rallied the various tribes against the Romans and defeated them," he said.

"Beat the Romans?" she said. "Quite an accomplishment."

"The tribes asked him to rule them, and the country was founded."

"So long ago. What a rich history," she said.

He took her hand and curled her arm around his. "Your own country is young, but it has its own accomplishments."

"We try."

He chuckled, leading her toward another portrait. "This is Heinhold, the thirtieth Prince Royal. He was cousin to Marie Antoinette."

"Oh, my. I'm sorry for his loss."

"All of Europe's ruling families have tentacles into each other's," he said as he led her to another portrait. "And this fine fellow almost brought the whole house down in scandal."

The man in question was slender, in contrast with the stouter, earlier rulers, and even in his portrait an air of affectation came through.

"He had an affair with a notorious widow," Friedrich went on. "Nothing unusual there, I'm afraid, but he tried to have their son named Crown Prince, even though they'd never married."

"How did that end up?" she asked.

"The country found an acceptable heir in the German side of the family." He made a small bow. "My side of the family, and we've ruled here ever since."

"Then I'd say it ended up just fine."

"So these are some of our princes and princesses," he said. "There are more in various places in the castle and the national museum."

She walked to his likeness. "And here you are."

"My son's portrait will hang next to mine."

"Of course." That annoying sense of the puzzle pieces not fitting together returned. Dev belonged here, and she didn't. She didn't share his history, and she certainly wasn't princess material. Unfortunately, Marc's lab and the coyote population now felt like memories. Her academic work didn't quite hold the appeal that it had when she'd begun.

"Let me show you our greatest treasure." He winked at her and guided her to one of the sideboards. From inside, he produced a crystal decanter with a dark golden liquid inside.

"Whiskey?" she asked.

"Brandy. Made by the monks in a secluded valley between the mountains. Some of the blend goes back one hundred years." From a glass case, he retrieved two snifters and poured them each two fingers of the liquor. "I'm not allowed to drink it any longer."

"But you do."

He raised his glass in a toast. "Danislova."

"Danislova," she repeated and clinked her snifter against his. Though no expert on brandy, even she could tell this was the good stuff. It was smooth and complex all at once, with hints of honey and oak. She took another sip and let it roll around on her tongue.

"What are you doing, old man?" Dev entered the room. He'd put on his pajamas and robe and had had the sense to wear slippers. "You know you're not supposed to drink that."

"He isn't drinking it." Felice snatched the prince's glass from his hand. "They're both mine."

Dev's brow went up. "Really."

"Really," she said. "Your father was showing me the difference between vintages."

That was all nonsense, of course, as Dev would very well know. So to back up her claim, she downed Friedrich's drink in one gulp. Though smooth, the stuff *was* hard liquor, and it made her eyes water. She forged ahead, though, swallowing the rest of her own brandy. She did her best not to choke.

"Wonderful," she croaked as she handed the glasses to the prince. "I think I prefer the second over the first."

"Very perceptive, my dear." The prince winked again, which Dev couldn't miss. Dev shrugged. What else could he do? He wasn't Prince Royal…yet.

*

His father and his lover had formed some kind of unholy alliance. Dev might have felt left out if he weren't enjoying their company so thoroughly. Everything Friedrich showed her delighted her, and everything she said delighted him. So when the time came for the Prince Royal and his heir to make themselves visible in the city, his father demanded that Felice come along. He'd promised to show her Danislova, Friedrich insisted, and show her he would. The paparazzi would follow them, but that would happen, anyway. The palace guard would keep the leeches at a distance.

The jeweler knew them from previous visits and ushered them into a private room where tea and coffee in silver service awaited them. His father took coffee and sat back in his chair to watch as the jeweler brought trays of his finest pieces.

"This one's nice," Dev said as he picked a diamond and sapphire necklace. The stones were perfectly matched and shone brilliantly.

"You have an interesting definition of nice," Felice said.

He lifted it to her throat.

"Hey, what are you doing?" she said.

"I want to see how it looks on you."

"Why?" she said. "I'm not going to wear it."

"Why not? It's a perfectly fine necklace." Dev glanced at his father for help.

Friedrich set his cup on the table at his elbow. "This was your idea. Work it out yourself."

"I'm not going to borrow this from Herr…" she said.

"Schneider, ma'am," the jeweler said. "Is something wrong?"

"Not with you." She inclined her head toward Dev. "But if he thinks I'm going to borrow that necklace, he can think again."

"Who said anything about loaning it to you?" Dev said.

Her eyes widened in shock. "You weren't thinking of buying this for me."

"If I want you to have it, yes." For the love of God, what woman became angry because you wanted to give her something?

"No." She pushed his hand away from her neck. "I'd never wear it. It would only scare me to have the thing around."

"But—"

"Listen to her, son," Friedrich said. "Women know what they want in these matters."

"All right." Dev put the necklace back, but he had a bigger problem than that particular collection of gems. He needed to give her something that would make her eyes light up. The feeling was physical in the general vicinity of his heart. He'd like to give her the world, but failing that, some truly fine jewelry would do.

He blew out an exasperated breath. "You will accept something from me, I hope."

"I don't want to seem ungrateful." She glanced at Friedrich, and he nodded.

"All right," she said. "But nothing so…well…big."

"Something smaller," Herr Schneider said as he brought out a second tray.

The fellow was clever enough to have some simple designs with stones so magnificent the pieces would cost easily as much as the necklace. She might not realize that, and Dev could turn that to his advantage.

Near the center sat a large emerald on a golden chain so fine it almost disappeared. A pair of drop earrings contained two smaller emeralds the exact color of the larger stone.

He dangled the necklace near her face, and her eyes picked up the striking green of the emerald.

"Remarkable," Friedrich said softly.

"You will accept this," Dev said. "You must."

She took the emerald from him, placed it against her palm and stared at it. "It's beautiful."

"It's a perfect stone, ma'am," Schneider said. "A wonderful color and not a flaw in it."

"The earrings, too," Dev said. "I want to see them on you."

"I suppose I'd better," she said softly. "Thank you."

Other gifts must have given him this much pleasure. His mother had always gushed over things he'd given her, from the crude childhood paintings to the antique music box he'd found in a tiny shop in Vienna. Felice seemed as much awed by the fact that he'd chosen the emeralds specifically for her as by the gems themselves. She couldn't know how much more he'd have her take if he could.

“That’s it then?” his father asked.

“For now,” he answered.

Felice rolled her eyes at him, but she smiled, too.

“I’m not through adorning you yet.”

His father glanced away. They all knew this love affair had no future, but Friedrich clearly wouldn’t end it for him. That was Dev’s responsibility, and he’d shoulder it...only not quite yet.

For long seconds, no one spoke. Finally, Herr Schneider cleared his throat. “If that’s all, I’ll have these packaged for you. Shall I have them sent?”

“I’d like to take them with me, if that’s all right,” Felice said.

“Of course you will, my dear,” Friedrich said. “Herr Schneider will only need a minute.”

The jeweler rose and bowed briefly before taking the tray and leaving the room. Dev’s glance fell on something on the other tray and held.

“Father, would you take Felice to the car?” he said. “I’ll wait for the package.”

Neither of them questioned him, thank heaven. Friedrich rose and extended his arm to Felice, and the two of them left, thoroughly charmed with each other as usual. Dev stayed and stared at the ring that wouldn’t let him leave without it.

When Herr Schneider returned with a velvet bag holding his earlier purchases, Dev lifted the ring from the tray and rolled it between his thumb and forefinger. “This is quite old, isn’t it?”

“Indeed, Your Highness. The filigree was done by hand.”

It was very obviously a wedding band, rather ornate in style. With no gemstones, the value lay in the workmanship and its uniqueness. There could hardly be another like it in the world.

He had no reason to buy a wedding band. The new Princess Royal would wear the set his mother had worn and his grandmother before that on back through the generations. If he could get Felice to wear this one, she'd realize his feelings even if he couldn't follow through on them.

Yet somehow, that seemed even crueler than pretending they had nothing more between them than a casual affair. It was like half a promise and a demand that she love him all the while knowing he'd disappoint her.

There. He'd said the word, if only to himself. He loved her, and buying the ring would prove that. He ought to put it back. School his emotions more closely. He'd always managed before.

"Your Highness?" Herr Schneider prompted.

He handed the ring to the jeweler. "Have this sent to the palace to my attention."

Herr Schneider bowed and went about his business as Dev entered the main salon of the shop. His father and Felice hadn't left but stood at the front door, peering outside. When Dev joined them, he discovered the reason. At least a dozen of the leeches had pressed themselves against the palace guard and were trying to get past to gain entrance.

"We'll have to run the gauntlet, it appears," Friedrich said.

"Why are they doing this?" Felice asked.

"They got wind of you at the airport, and now they'll follow us everywhere," Dev answered.

"Me?" She put her hand on Dev's arm and stared into his face, her brows knitted in alarm. "They're doing all this because of me?"

"You and I have become an item."

"Bastards." She turned to the door and stared outside for a few more seconds. "I'll go out there and let them take all the pictures they want of my middle finger."

Friedrich had the good sense to put an arm around her and hold her back. Just then the door opened, and one of the palace guard slipped inside. "We can get you to the car if you're ready, Majesty."

"But they'll get what they want," Felice said.

"Keep moving and hold your head down," Dev said.

For a moment, she appeared willing to fight him, but in the end she gave him a thumbs up. The guard opened the door, and the three of them moved out and between two rows of more guards toward the car. Shutters clicked, and the paparazzi shouted at them in several languages. When they got half-way to their goal, one called out in English.

"Hey, miss," he shouted. "Over here."

Felice did what any normal human would. She stopped and looked in his direction. The reporters went into a frenzy of cries and cameras going off. After no more than a split second, one of the guards guided her away and into the car. Too late. They'd gotten good pictures of her.

Dev remained, staring at the bastard who'd called to her. He'd hated these types before, but he'd honest to God like to kill this one. He lunged in the fellow's direction, and the coward backed up, cringing. Dev couldn't get to him though, because another guard held him back. With more force than he would normally use on the Crown Prince, he pushed Dev toward the car.

Once Dev had taken his seat next to Felice, the driver maneuvered the vehicle through the crowd, which had now assembled itself around the windows and were trying to get more pictures.

Dev discovered he was still holding the velvet bag. If he'd lost it, he really would have to go back and beat the reporter to a bloody pulp. Instead, he handed it to Felice, and her smile made the whole ordeal worth the trouble.

*

The day Felice saw the stream that supplied the palace with fish, all four of the VonRamsberg men escorted her to a private picnic of cold chicken, freshly baked bread, cheese, and local smoked sausages. By the time they'd washed all that down with dark beer, she'd stuffed herself. As the warm afternoon sun beat down on the landscape around them, the small party took to the shade of the trees beside the water. Still, it all made her drowsy, and she stretched out on her back near where Dev sat dipping his bare feet in the cool currents.

Ulrich had disappeared somewhere, and the Price Royal sat in a folding chair watching his second son dangle a line into the water. Aside from an earlier dispute between the young men and their father about his diet, the hours had passed peacefully, and she couldn't help but imagine this scene had played out between the four of them many times over the years.

"I'll bet no one's caught Uncle Bert yet," Kurt said.

She rolled over and propped herself up on an elbow. "Uncle?"

Dev glanced over his shoulder at her. "A particularly large fish. It's escaped Kurt for years."

"He's gone on to fish heaven long ago," their father said. "Perfectly safe from you."

"I'll find him yet," Kurt said. "I'll eat him, too."

"I don't know how you can do that all the way from New York," Dev said.

"I'll do it before I leave," Kurt said.

With their father's health mended, all of them would depart. Unless, of course, Dev remained to assume his role as second in line behind his father. But Kurt and Ulrich had no such obligations and had lives elsewhere, as Felice did. She'd have to return to school eventually.

Maybe when the two younger princes said their good-byes, she'd take her cue and go, too. Her nights of falling asleep in Dev's arms and her mornings of waking to find his face near hers would end.

Grigori, the man who served as advisor to both Friedrich and Dev, appeared, hurrying down the path and stopping in front of the Prince Royal to bow and hand him an envelope. Dev's father had to break a heavy, wax seal to open the letter. The whole thing appeared very official and very serious.

"Damn and blast," Dev's father said. "He's invited himself for a state visit."

"Who, father?" Kurt asked.

"Vaclav. Who else?"

Dev groaned. "Not him."

"I'm afraid so, Your Highness," Grigori said. "He had a personal envoy deliver the note."

Felice sat up on the blanket. "Should I know who Vaclav is?"

"I'm sorry, my dear," Dev's father said. "He's a relation."

"Vaclav Marek, Archduke of Rosnia," Grigori corrected. "His Majesty's cousin."

Friedrich's bushy eyebrows rose. "Distant cousin."

"Did I hear someone mention Vaclav?" Ulrich appeared, carrying a handkerchief wrapped around something. When he bent to hand it to Felice she discovered it held wild berries.

"He's invited himself for a visit." Dev's father waved the letter toward his youngest son. Ulrich took it from him and read for a moment.

"The usual flowery rot," Ulrich said. "'Beloved cousin'…'desire to inform myself of your health'…'lift your spirits.'"

"Bah," Dev's father said. "The only spirits of mine he wants to lift are my brandy."

"Why is he coming now?" Kurt asked.

"He says my health and because the three of you are at home," Dev's father said. "But I suspect he's really interested in Miss Larson."

Felice put her hand on her chest. "Me?"

Dev sat beside her and placed a possessive hand on her shoulder. "He must have seen the pictures."

"I'm turning out to be kind of a pain in the butt, aren't I?"

"Nonsense, my dear," Dev's father said. "The sweetest fruit attracts the most flies."

Bless him. What a dear thing to say. It didn't change the fact that their lives would be a lot more peaceful if Dev hadn't invited her.

"I guess it can't be avoided," Ulrich said. "At least, there'll be a ball."

"You'll do anything for a party," Kurt said.

"Hey, brother. You wouldn't mind meeting a few women, would you?" Ulrich countered.

Kurt said nothing and went back to his fishing.

"A ball?" Felice repeated. The fairy tale aspects of this visit had been fun so far, but a ball might be taking things a little too far.

"Vaclav rules a small duchy to our north," Dev explained. "A visit from him is a state visit."

"Therefore, a ball," Ulrich said.

"Vaclav will arrive with all of his relatives and half of the population of his country," Dev's father said.

"You know you're exaggerating," Dev said.

"It'll seem that way," Friedrich grumbled. "The palace will be overrun because that mongrel wants to satisfy his curiosity."

Kurt reeled in his line and leaned the pole against a tree. "Why do you dislike him so much?"

"Because he tried to seduce my wife," Friedrich said, possibly more loudly than he'd meant to because he let out a huff and rested back in his chair. “He’ll probably try the same trick with Miss Larson.”

“With me?” She gaped at the Prince Royal in disbelief. “Surely, he’s too old…that is, I’m too young. He wouldn’t.”

“I wouldn’t put anything past him, my dear. Stay close to either me or my son,” Friedrich said.

“Well, there’s a lot to be done, and you won’t be doing it.” Ulrich folded the letter and handed it back to his father. “You’re too soon out of the hospital.”

“Of course not.” Grigori bristled. “I’ll take care of everything, consult with Wilson and cook. Have the rooms made up, set the menus, hire musicians and extra staff. His Majesty won’t lift a finger.”

“Thank you, Grigori.” As soon as Grigori had bowed and disappeared, the Prince Royal let out a disgusted huff. “The sooner Vaclav is here, the faster we can be rid of him.”

*

Of course, a ball required a ball gown, something more glorious than the ones she wore to dinner every night. The closet attached to Felice’s bedroom had been filling slowly with clothes more beautiful than she’d ever be able to afford on her own. Now, it threatened to overflow with dresses for every occasion—morning walks in the garden, afternoon formal teas, more dinners, even trips through the countryside, although Dev hadn’t taken her out of the palace since they’d faced the crush of reporters at the jewelry shop.

Then of course, the negligees took up their own corner. Silks and laces in the colors of gemstones. A new one arrived almost every day. Dev picked them out himself and took great delight in having her wear them so he could take them off her and lavish her with the greatest gift of all, his lovemaking.

Wearing nothing but her panties and bra, she stood in the midst of all of it, her head swimming. She'd have to search the deepest recesses to find anything of her own.

A soft tap came at the door. "The dressmaker's here, miss."

"I'll be right there," she called to Greta. At least, she knew how to find the drawers that held her underwear. She selected a slip, put it on, and went out into the bedroom. The small woman who'd measured her stood holding what looked like an avalanche of satin the color of sapphires. She took one look at Felice and launched into a tirade of German.

"The bra and slip," Greta translated. "Madame says your shoulders will be bare. You must change."

"Right." She dashed into the closet and searched through the drawers until she found a strapless bra and half-slip. The new slip felt normal enough, but the bra did amazing things to her breasts, pushing them upward and giving her more cleavage than she'd ever had before. The illusion wasn't strictly honest, but she didn't have time to worry about that now.

When she rejoined the others, the dressmaker grunted her approval and came toward Felice holding out that mass of lovely material. Felice had to bend to help the woman get it all over her head, and in a moment, the dress fell into place, and the woman had the zipper done in the back.

"Ach, so lovely," Greta said, clapping her hands together. "You must look at yourself in the mirror."

The dressmaker pointed toward a low stool, and Felice climbed up onto it, turning toward the full-length mirror on the far wall. "Lovely" she would have expected, but the gown turned her into something more remarkable than that. The bodice did nothing to mask the fullness of her breasts. From there, the satin hugged her ribs to her waist and then fell in a waterfall of deep blue to her feet. She could have been a princess or a figurine on the top of a music box.

While she'd been staring at her reflection, the dressmaker had produced a pair of matching shoes from one of her bags. Covered with the same material of the dress, they had low heels that, thank heaven, would allow her to walk normally. She let the woman help her on with them and then stood to allow the dressmaker pin up the hem.

What on earth would Dev and his family do with this creation once she'd left? Made especially for her body, it would have to be altered for anyone else. The sort of woman any of the princes would marry would hardly take hand-me-downs from an earlier lover. Dev would have to give the clothing away, but to whom? People seeking charity didn't need ball gowns and smart outfits for taking tea.

Suddenly, the dressmaker got to her feet, and Greta stood stiffly where she was.

"Your Highness," Greta said. "Miss Larson is being fitted."

"I can see that," Dev said from the entrance to the bedroom. Felice didn't have to see him or even really to hear him. She sensed every time he entered a room. He had a presence about him, and they'd become so...close. Intimate.

He walked around her and stopped a few feet away. A sharp intake of his breath told her he approved of the dress. Most likely, the bra, too.

"You may leave us," he said.

The dressmaker said a few words in German, and he answered. Finally, with a few curtseys, the two women left.

"What did you tell them?" Felice asked.

"I told them to come back in ten minutes to get the gown. I imagine I'll have you out of it by then."

"You didn't tell them that last part, I hope," she said.

"I'll let them figure it out for themselves." He took a step back as his gaze wandered over her. "Do you suppose it's bad luck for me to see you in this now?"

"I don't think so." She didn't follow that with *It's not a wedding dress*, but he had to be thinking that to have asked the question.

"Good. Because I can't take my eyes off you."

"Dev, you shouldn't buy me all these things."

He lifted an eyebrow. "Why? I have the money. I enjoy dressing you."

"I don't know. It's just so...wasteful."

"Not a waste." He walked to her, standing so close, his breath grazed the skin above the bodice of the gown. He tipped his head up toward hers, demanding a kiss. She didn't have to obey him, of course, but she could hardly refuse. So she pressed her lips to his. She didn't normally stand above him, so the stool gave her a different angle for taking his mouth. The novelty of his lips beneath hers gave her reason to explore, and soon she was tasting every curve and corner of him.

As the kiss deepened into something more intimate, more urgent, he lifted her off the stool. When her feet hit the floor, her folded her into an embrace that had her breasts pressed against his chest. They'd looked full before, and now they seemed to swell and become more sensitive. His breath came fast and hard as he placed the side of his face against hers and reached behind to work on the zipper of her gown.

The satin fell slowly downward. Faster when he moved to give it room. It made a pile around her feet, and even though he had her well on the way to complete sexual excitement, she couldn't let anything happen to the gorgeous creation. She stepped carefully out of it, scooped it up, and laid it across the bed. The dressmaker might want the shoes, too, so Felice stepped out of them before walking back into Dev's embrace.

"They'll be back any minute," she whispered.

"I don't care." He undid the clasp of her bra and pulled the garment from between their bodies. "Do you?"

"I don't want them to find us like this."

"Like this?" While one of his hands covered a breast, he bent to take the nipple of the other one into his mouth. The moisture, the suction…God, the heat of him…brought her sex to life. Her clit throbbed while moisture collected between her thighs.

"Dev, really." Lord, she could hardly talk. Already. "We can't have them find us going at it on the bed."

"The closet, then."

"You can't be serious."

"Deadly serious." His hand burrowed under the waistband of the slip and then into her panties. He found her hard nub immediately, his finger tip circling over it.

"Dev!" Damn it, he was going to make her come, and the dressmaker with her stern little black dress and sterner face would intrude just as the climax hit.

Sure enough, there was a knock on the door and an impatient call in German.

"The closet," he whispered and led her there on shaky legs.

Once inside, he guided her back against a wall and pulled the door nearly closed.

"Come in," he called.

"You can't mean…"

He pressed a finger over her lips and closed the door quietly. Then, unbelievably, he slid his hand back into her panties and between the lips of her sex.

Her clit didn't notice that two women were just on the other side of the door. It just wanted more. When he touched it, she nearly jumped out of her skin. She had to bite her lip to hold in a whimper. He had to have lost his mind. He knew her response well enough now to realize how close he'd brought her to orgasm. Even if he didn't, the wetness coating his fingers would tell the story. Whatever those women were thinking about His Highness who'd summoned them into the room and then disappeared...with his female houseguest, no less...it couldn't compare to the shock they'd get if he made her scream as she came.

The infernal fumbling on the other side of the door continued, along with conversation in German. So did the constant flick, flick, flick of his finger. When she couldn't stand another moment of the torture, she bit him on the neck. Not hard enough to leave a mark…probably...but enough to get his attention. It worked. He removed his hand from her pussy. She took in air in gulps, leaning against the wall for support.

Whatever insane game he was playing, he hadn't finished. He bent, sweeping her slip and panties off her together. When she stepped out of them, she was completely naked. Then, he unzipped his fly and pushed his pants and shorts over his hips.

The sounds seemed deafening in the small enclosure. The women on the other side seemed to take no notice, though, but just continued packing and whatever the hell else they were doing.

Now, Dev pressed her against the wall again, and his cock, so heavy and hot, pushed against her belly. Every inch of her body craved him, right down to the roots of her hair. Surely, if he plunged into her and started thrusting, they'd hear. Why, in God's name, wouldn't they go away?

Finally, they did. The voices grew fainter, and the door between her bedroom and sitting room closed.

"Are they…" she whispered.

He held up a finger to silence her, cocked his head, and listened for a moment. “They’re gone.”

“What in hell is wrong with you?”

“What’s always wrong with me when I’m around you?” He flexed his hips, pushing his solid member into her flesh.

“You almost made me come, for crying out loud.”

“Almost? That can be fixed.” He crouched low enough for the tip of his cock to press for entrance into her pussy. He was going to take her up against a wall. Suddenly, that seemed like the most logical thing in the world, so she spread her legs. In a heartbeat, he wrapped them around his waist and straightened, driving himself inside her.

“God, yes,” she cried. “Fuck me. Just fuck me.”

He did, and how. He moved like a wild man, slamming into her. She’d never been penetrated so deeply nor filled so completely. And every thrust jostled against her clit, relighting the fire that hadn’t gone out but only needed his loving to burst into flame.

She clung to his shoulders, angling her hips to find just the right position. A little more...a little more...and there!

“Yesssss.” The word came out like steam escaping. Unnatural. Not her own voice at all. “Don’t stop.”

His answer came out as a growl and he continued pummeling her. The climax hit with bone-jarring power. She hung onto him for dear life as it gripped her squeezing the air from her lungs. Then, the spasms started at the entrance to her womb, coursing outward around the cock that still moved inside her. When she could breathe again, she let out a loud cry. His voice joined hers as he stiffened, shuddering in her arms. After a few more savage thrusts, he came, too, finding his release inside her.

When the madness had passed, he still held her until his cock softened. Then he lowered her slowly and let his head slump onto her shoulder. After a few deep breaths, he laughed softly. “I’ll never look at this closet the way I used to.”

Chapter Seven

Over the next week, the palace went crazy. Everywhere Felice went, she disturbed someone on the staff either polishing something, instructing someone else how to polish something, or just generally making the already spotless and beautiful rooms even more magnificent. Maids hustled along the hallways, their arms full of linens. Footmen carried silver and trays of glassware. They mostly stuck to the servants' passages, but you couldn't miss nearly stumbling over one from time to time, and the person would scurry off with mumbled apologies in German or Russian. State visits did a lot of good for the local unemployment rate and economy, it seemed, but for Felice, the whole affair made moving around awkward.

So, she wasn't entirely surprised when she happened on the front hallway full of luggage. From her place on the top of the grand staircase, she stared down at dozens of suitcases and even a trunk. It all looked as if the neighbors had decided the grass was greener over here and were moving in for good.

Of course, a gaggle of footmen had assembled to dispense with it all, Wilson supervising their maneuvers with the air of a field marshal. He caught a glimpse of her and bowed.

"Is there something I can do for you, miss?" he asked.

"No, I was just…" Damn, couldn't she light anyplace without being in the way? "I'm sorry I disturbed you."

He gave her a harried smile. "Thank you."

Before she could turn to go, the most unusual little man entered from outside. He wore a full-length cape, although the weather wasn't the least bit cold. When he flung it off and handed it to Wilson, he revealed a scarlet satin vest and white shirt with the sort of flowing sleeves actors used to wear in old swashbuckling movies. He patted hair so black the color had to have come out of a bottle, especially given his pale skin and small, blue eyes.

Grigori appeared below, dressed in his usual somber clothing. He approached the visitor and bowed sharply. "Your Grace, welcome. The Prince Royal is occupied at present, so he's sent me to greet you and make sure you and your retinue are well received."

"My dear cousin Friedrich is well?" the man asked.

"Very well, we thank the Lord," Grigori answered.

"Then…" The man lifted a brow in a small signal of disapproval.

"The prince is eager to see you, sir, most eager." Grigori raised his hands in a supplicating gesture. "He's been, um, detained."

Light dawned finally. This must be Vaclav, the distant cousin Friedrich disliked so much. Instead of greeting Vaclav himself, Friedrich had sent Grigori. A bit of a snub and one read correctly on the receiving end. She'd do best to avoid the fellow, so she took a quiet step backward.

No good, though. Vaclav glanced upward and found her. “My, but what’s this vision?”

“I-I’m sorry.” Lord, but she was stuttering. “I didn’t mean to stare.”

“Oh, but what man doesn’t bask in the admiration of a beautiful woman?” He put his hand over his heart. “Especially a humble man like myself.”

“Sure. Um, great.”

“Do come down, or I shall have to come up to you.”

“I’m afraid we haven’t time for that,” Grigori said. “Allow me to take you to His Majesty.”

Vaclav waved Grigori off. “But you said he’d been detained.”

By now, the footmen had rid the hallway of luggage, and only Grigori and Vaclav remained. She hesitated at the top of the staircase. Any escape she made now would appear rude, and Vaclav had already taken offense at having a mere advisor as a welcoming committee.

With no real choice in the matter, she descended the stairs and went to him, extending her hand. He took it, and instead of shaking, he brought it to his lips for a kiss that was a little too sloppy. His fingers dazzled with numerous rings, each holding what looked like a valuable gemstone. For a guy who claimed to be humble, he sure wore a lot of bling.

“I am Vaclav, Archduke of Rosnia,” he said. “Your humble servant.”

“I’m Felice Larson.” She could easily come to share the Prince Royal’s opinion of this man. She hadn’t read an old novel in decades, but the word “popinjay” sprung to mind.

“Ah, the American,” he declared, although he surely must have guessed her nationality from her accent. “I do love your people. So forthright and uncomplicated, so…how shall I put this…wholesome.”

“We’re corn-fed, that’s for sure.”

He cocked his head and studied her. Either his English wasn't as good as it sounded or he didn't process humor very well. But then, his expression didn't display the same intelligence as Friedrich and his sons did. That could make a person humor-impaired.

"We eat wholesome food," she explained.

"And with such pleasing results." His gaze traveled up to her head and downward, hesitating at her chest long enough to qualify as leering.

"Hey, you must be tired after your trip," she said. "Why don't I see if I can find De…"

A sly light in his eyes told her he was smart enough to realize she'd almost called Dev by the name his family did. He would have twirled his handlebar mustache if he'd had one.

"That is, the Prince Royal will want to know you're here," she said.

"Exactly." Grigori tried to step between them, but Vaclav waved him away again.

"His butler will have told him," Vaclav said. "Why don't you and I visit for a while until he calls for us?"

She was no expert in protocol, but most people didn't have heart-to-hearts in front entry halls, no matter how beautiful. "Here?"

"We can find somewhere more intimate," he said.

"Here's fine."

Before she had to do any serious plotting on how to get away from him, the doors opened again, and a whole stream of people came in. Men and women, young and old, and all dressed in vibrant colors similar to those the archduke wore. They looked and sounded like a flock of fluttering birds as they clustered around her. Grigori did his best to deflect them, addressing the group in German but was drowned out by a Babel of languages, including Russian. A small man with a pointed goatee took her hand in both of his and pumped it with more than a little enthusiasm and then pulled forward a woman even shorter than himself for introductions she couldn't understand. A female child of nine or ten wormed her way between the two of them and stared up at Felice out of huge, blue eyes.

Felice bent toward her. "Hello."

The little girl curtseyed, holding her skirt out to either side of her. "*Vous êtes très belle, mademoiselle*."

"*Merci. Je ne parle pas Français*." And that exhausted what little French she'd ever learned. With any luck, she'd convinced them to move along to a language she could at least stumble through. Unfortunately, no one here would likely speak Spanish.

Vaclav loudly clapped his hands together several times. "This is Miss Larson, our dear Cousin Christian's bosom friend."

"Would you mind dropping the bosom part?" she said.

Vaclav glanced around at his retinue, ignoring Felice. "You'll all get to talk to her later."

They'd better all speak some English, or the conversations wouldn't last for long.

"Well, well, well. What are you all doing out here?" The Prince Royal appeared from the corridor that led to his library.

"Beloved Friedrich." Vaclav went directly to the prince, took Friedrich's face between his palms and kissed both of Friedrich's cheeks. He went up on tiptoe to do it, and Friedrich had to bend, but the archduke managed his show of devotion well enough to have the others cooing with approval.

"Yes, yes. That's all well and good." Friedrich hmphed in a dismissive manner. "Grigori, have you assigned them all rooms?"

Grigori bowed. "I have, Your Majesty."

"Then you should all go and find them. You can dissect Miss Larson at dinner." Friedrich held out his arm toward Felice, and she gladly took it and allowed him to lead her away.

"Now you've met them," Friedrich said softly as they walked down the hallway. "We'll both need some of that brandy before the day is out."

*

Dev watched in admiration as Felice did better than hold her own at her first formal dinner. Friedrich had seated her between the Bürgermeister and one of their Rosnian cousins, a young university student of nineteen. She'd managed a few guffaws from Herr Schmidt. Of course, that became easier as footmen refilled the man's wine glass. The young man on her other side had obviously fallen in love with her over the fish course and now hung on her every word, ignoring his meal.

"You really should stop staring at her," their family friend, Lady Marta said.

"Hm?" He turned to glance at her where she sat on his right.

Nearly his mother's age, Marta took the opportunity of dressing in an elegant but understated way in hopes of catching Friedrich's eye. If Dev's father had been seeking a new wife, he could have done worse than this lady with the streaks of grey in her hair and dimples in her cheeks.

"The American," Marta said. "The way you gaze at her gives you away."

"I suppose it does."

"Does Friedrich know how you feel?" she asked.

"He must have guessed by now."

Marta laid a hand on his. "The two of you will do what's right."

She was no doubt speaking about Dev and his father, but she could have easily meant Dev and Felice. They'd all have to figure out the right thing and do it. Sadly, that wouldn't likely feel like the right thing.

Herr Schmidt roared with laughter now and slapped his fingers against the table hard enough to rattle his china. Felice laughed, too, her hand over her mouth and her cheeks a deep pink. Either she or the Bürgermeister must have told an off color joke, and the student on her other side had turned crimson. Felice had worn a modest gown—a ruffled affair in pink that showed off the healthy glow of her skin. Only Dev knew what lay beneath all that fabric and how she responded to the right touch in the right places.

So Vaclav had no damned reason to lean across the table toward her, the lecherous glint still in his eyes.

"My dear," he said. "You must tell us all the joke that has Herr Schmidt so amused."

"We'll let that be our secret, won't we, Herr Schmidt?" she said.

"It was about a man…" Herr Schmidt's voice broke with laughter. "He was from a place…what was it called again?"

"Nantucket," Felice answered.

Oh dear Lord. Their little group in Marc's lab knew a dozen of those limericks, but no one else around the table had ever heard one, at least not until Herr Schmidt.

"Nantucket?" Vaclav repeated.

"It's in Massachusetts," Dev said.

Ulrich nearly choked on his wine, and Friedrich's eyebrow rose in menace from where he sat at the end of the table.

"It's the home of the American Revolution," Dev went on. That wasn't exactly inaccurate if you left out Virginia, Valley Forge, and a dozen or so other places.

"That explains that then." Vaclav forced a laugh. "Very entertaining. You'll share more such jokes with us, Miss Larson."

"That's the only one I know." She picked up her fork and turned her attention to the sachertorte the footman had just placed in front of her.

"Is this your first visit to Danislova, Miss Larson?" Marta asked.

"It is," Felice answered.

"What have you seen?" Marta said.

"Well…" Felice glanced toward Friedrich for guidance.

Friedrich wiped his mouth with his napkin and set it aside. "We've hardly been outside the palace grounds. The vultures circle constantly."

"Surely you can control your own people," Vaclav said.

Friedrich bristled. He had little use for Vaclav to begin with and, now that Dev had watched the fool ogle Felice, he could understand why.

"They aren't Danislovan," Friedrich said. "We don't behave like that."

"Then you should shoo them off," Vaclav said. "That's what I'd do in Rosnia."

Vaclav didn't mention that his little duchy hardly merited such attention from the international gossip press. But even he couldn't be dense enough not to miss the subtle insult against the way Friedrich ran his country.

"The palace guard keeps them at bay," Friedrich said. "I can't arrest them if they haven't committed a crime."

"Sad. Our Miss Larson is doomed to be a hothouse flower," Vaclav said.

This time Dev bristled. In fact, he did a slow burn. Miss Larson didn't belong to Vaclav in any sense of the word "our." And his family could get her all the fresh air they wanted, as long as she returned to his bed every night. Or to hers, as the case might be.

"I might serve as her guide," Vaclav said. "I know Danislova almost as well as you do."

"My sons and I can guide her well enough." This time Friedrich's voice held more than a little cold steel in it. He'd tolerated enough from his cousin, and sparks would fly if Vaclav continued.

"It's been a long time since I've seen the Danislovan countryside," Lady Marta said. "Why don't we all have an outing?"

Murmurs of agreement went around the table as tensions eased. Dev's shoulders lowered to their normal place, and Felice took an almost audible breath.

"I'd like that very much," she said.

"We'll visit the high valley," Friedrich said. "See what the monks have been brewing."

"You mean distilling, don't you father?" Kurt said.

"Brewing, distilling. It's been too long since I've visited my monks. We'll go tomorrow." Friedrich rose. "Now gentlemen. The billiard room for brandy and cigars?"

The men also got to their feet, even the college student, although he gave Felice one more longing gaze before following the others. Dev stood, as well, and damn him if he didn't let his eyes linger on her, too, before heading off to make sure his father indulged in neither brandy nor a cigar.

*

With only a few hours' notice, the palace staff managed to pack for a party of nearly thirty, prepare refreshments for the long drive, and fuel a line of cars and have them waiting outside the palace entrance by the time Friedrich's guests had assembled themselves after breakfast. Dev hadn't thought much about what his father's people could accomplish until he'd taken responsibility for getting himself to class and feeding himself afterwards. All these people had merely had to tumble out of bed, allow their maids and valets to dress them, and fill their stomachs. They'd hardly notice the small miracle that had taken place all around them.

Dev went outside and down the stairs to where Wilson stood in front of the line of ponderous Bentleys and Rollses. He bent toward the Wilson's ear. "Have my car brought 'round."

"Of course, Your Highness." Wilson went down the line of cars to the last driver and repeated the order. When the man headed off in the direction of the garages, Dev smiled to himself. A plan had taken shape in his head as he'd lain cuddled-up, spoon fashion with Felice. She'd see the Danislovan countryside, all right, but she'd see it the way he wanted her to, without any obligation to entertain local dignitaries with naughty limericks and without Vaclav's lecherous gaze following her wherever she went.

When the others flowed over the steps like a waterfall of babbling aristocracy and packed themselves into cars, he hung back, waiting for her. She appeared, wearing slacks, a blouse of silk the color of champagne, and a light blazer. More and more comfortable in her surroundings, she carried herself with subtle dignity. If an observer had had to pick out the American graduate student from this crowd, he'd very likely choose a young woman from Vaclav's relations, not Felice. Though awkward at first, she'd slipped into the role of royalty easily, and if by accident of birth she had come from a noble family, she could easily rule by his side.

She came down the steps and stood beside him. "We'll make quite a procession."

"Wait until the palace guard have joined us."

Her eyes widened. "Black vans?"

"With tinted windows. Only until they've guided us out of the city."

"Does your father need all that protection?"

"Not at all. He'll be riding in an open car with Vaclav and my brothers so he can wave at his people."

"Then why all the security?"

"Our privacy," he said. "And then, Vaclav loves to make a production of everything he does."

She twined her fingers through his and tugged playfully at his hand. "Will you ride with your brothers?"

"I'd rather stay with the intriguing young woman I saw in the papers."

She groaned. "Those papers. What a pain."

"That's why we have security."

"Okay." She checked out the line of heavy cars and sighed. "Which one will we take?"

"None."

Just then, a driver brought his Lamborghini around. A two-seat convertible, it could hide effectively alongside one of the guard's black vans until they'd lost the paparazzi. He'd put the top down later.

Even among a collection of royalty and the wealthy, the car caused an audible reaction. It earned him a gasp from Felice.

"Ohmigod, is that yours?" she said.

"For today, it's ours." And tomorrow and maybe a few more days after that, if his plan worked.

"Holy sh…cow."

"You can drive it later, if you want." He'd never made that offer before. His brothers and father could buy their own cars, and he'd never felt close enough to anyone else to trust them with his baby. The expression on Felice's face—like a child who'd received a pony for Christmas—made him insanely proud of himself. He'd sit beside her as she took the Lamborghini down winding roads. He'd hear her laughter and share her joy.

For now, he took her arm and led her to the Lamborghini. The driver climbed out but left the motor idling. When the man moved to open the passenger door for Felice, Dev waved him away and did it himself. With a sigh of appreciation, she settled herself into the seat and rubbed her palms over the butter-soft leather. “Even standing still, it’s fast.”

Dev caught a passing footman. “Have Miss Larson’s and my things put in this car.”

The man bowed and went off to do as ordered. Still holding her door open, he bent toward her. “You packed enough for overnight, I hope.”

“More than enough. Greta would have filled three bags if I’d let her.”

“Good. You’ll need it.”

When she opened her mouth to demand an explanation, he shut the door carefully and jogged around to the other side. After getting into the car, he buckled up and waited for their luggage.

“Where is everyone going to stay?” she asked. “The monks can’t play host to all these people.”

“We have a hunting lodge nearby, and there’s an inn in the village. Everyone’s been alerted we’re coming. A few may end up in monastic cells.”

She laughed. “Not Vaclav.”

“No, not Vaclav.”

Several cases thunked into the trunk of the Lamborghini, and then the hood went down and latched. The footman appeared at Dev’s window, holding a small bag. “This one won’t fit, Your Highness. Should I put it in another car?”

“I’ll take it.” The bag in question turned out to be a small one of the type women need for cosmetics. Felice wouldn’t have to preen where they were headed, but it might hold something she needed. He handed it to her. “Put it behind the seat, won’t you?”

She did. The thing didn't fit easily, but she wedged it in. When the palace guard's vans took their place around the passenger cars, the caravan headed off.

*

Felice fell asleep a few minutes after the luxurious but heavy picnic and so missed Dev's break for freedom. As he'd planned, he hung back to find a place at the end of the stream of cars, and so when the rest of them turned left at the crossroads, he went right. As soon as the large cars had fallen out of sight, he'd sent a text message to Ulrich to let him know they'd escaped. Then he'd gunned the engine, accomplishing two things. He could finally let the Lamborghini do what it was designed for, and he could get the hell away.

Through all the speed and the rumble of the engine, Felice didn't wake, and on the straight roads, he could glance over to her. He'd watched her sleep before, of course, but somehow, this was different. It showed she trusted him to keep her safe. It proved she could make herself vulnerable, letting him take her wherever he pleased. It made her his.

If there was a male hormone for protectiveness, it was coursing through his blood stream right now. His woman…younger, smaller, and not as physically strong as he was. His to cherish and provide for. His to worship when she risked her life to give him children. His to keep until they grew old and weak together. His to selfishly pray the Almighty took him first because life without her was too bleak to contemplate.

They'd never have that except in his imagination, but he could pretend for as long as he could stay away from his duties.

He turned a curve and almost plowed through a herd of sheep crossing the road. The animals closest had enough sense to scatter, but he still had to slam on the brakes to keep from hitting them.

That, and all the baa-ing, woke Felice up. Rubbing her eyes, she sat straight in her seat and stared at the moving cloud of wool blocking their path.

"Hey, where are the others?" she said.

"On their way to the monastery, I imagine."

"And we're not?"

The shepherd appeared, shooing his flock ahead of him with a staff. His jaw dropped when he saw the car, and he hastily removed his cap and made a half-bow in Dev's direction. The fellow might not have realized his sheep had almost had the honor of being run over by the Crown Prince, but he clearly recognized wealth. He called an apology in the local dialect, a tongue Dev deciphered with a bit of effort, and then he urged his animals forward until they'd all entered the meadow on the other side of the road.

Dev set the car in gear, but Felice put her hand over his to stop him.

"Not just yet," she said. "I want to take everything in. It's like nothing I've ever seen before."

She had a point. Because of the car's speed and the fun of driving it, Dev had hardly noticed the scenery. At this altitude, the air was cool, the forests dark, and the meadows perpetually full of wildflowers. Though the trees didn't grow very tall here, they clung together enough to create a sort of cathedral ceiling overhead. They'd just passed from that deep shade into afternoon sunlight that slanted across the grasses and threatened to turn the puffy clouds to fire.

"Oh Dev," she said. "How can you ever bear to leave this place?"

"You truly love it."

"Every inch." She nestled her head on his shoulder. "Thank you for bringing me here."

The moment had come…the gesture he'd rehearsed, even knowing it was madness and would only make things worse for them when reality intruded. Still, he hadn't been able to leave the filigree ring behind, telling himself he could simply keep it in his pocket through the trip and put it away when he got home.

Deep inside, he'd known that if she gave him an opening, he'd take it, and she'd just said the magic words. They'd escaped reality for a while, and he could at least pretend he was at liberty to make her his forever. If she'd indulge him in this fantasy, they could play at the part of young lovers on the verge of a future together. The dream would end in a few days, but he'd always have the memories to cherish when his life became more laden with responsibilities.

Reaching into his pocket, he found the box easily and handed it to her without a word.

"More jewelry?" she said. "You have to stop buying me things."

"Open it."

When she did, she jerked upward, sitting straight again as she stared into the box. For long seconds, neither of them said anything while Dev held his breath and his heart hammered in his chest.

"Dev," she said finally. "Why would you give a wedding band to a woman you can't marry?"

"I'm taking you somewhere special, Felice. A place not even my family ever thinks of. While we're there, I hope…" He grasped at the empty air in front of him, searching for words. "We could pretend. For a few days."

"I see," she said softly.

"Besides I wanted to give you something symbolic," he said. "It's not a family heirloom. I got it when we bought the emeralds. Look, you can wear it on your right hand or on a chain around your neck. Just please wear it."

Damn the world, he was babbling. He'd rehearsed—how he'd give the ring to her as a pretty thing he wanted her to have. He'd counted all the ways she could wear his wedding ring and yet not wear it. None of them disguised his feelings or his intent.

In the end, he took the ring from her and slid it onto the third finger of her right hand, not the left. It fit perfectly, sliding past the knuckle with enough resistance to make it secure. When he'd finished, Felice stared at it, biting her lip.

"I hope you know how I feel about you," he said.

She stared straight ahead of her through the windshield. "Not a good idea, Dev."

It wasn't. It was a terrible idea, but the words wouldn't stay in his head. "I love you, Felice. No matter what happens between us, I'll always love you."

She made a tiny choking sound in her throat. "I love you, too, Prince Christian."

"Oh, *mein Schatz*." He kissed her, pulling her across the seat as far at the safety belt would allow. He didn't need her naked or sitting in his lap for this caress. He only had to taste her, feel her lips yield under his. Innocent contact would seal their love for now. Lust could come later.

Her fingers dug into the light fabric of his jacket, curling like a cat's paws, as if by digging into his flesh she'd never have to let him go. In fact, she'd already taken possession of him more effectively than any physical restraint.

Though the kiss was innocent, it nevertheless had his heart racing from the enormity of what it meant. He'd given his heart to a woman he couldn't keep. Eventually, she'd go home, and he'd remain here. So far away that the tie that held them together would snap. Then he'd truly lose something beautiful. Something he'd never get back.

She pulled away first, placing her palm against the side of his face. "Oh Dev, what are we going to do?"

"I don't know...that thing you said before, that we can let the future take care of itself."

"That was a load of crap, and you know it."

Only she could look desirable while saying a word like "crap." Just another thing he loved about her—that she didn't take herself seriously when everything and everybody else around him was stiff and formal. Exactly what he'd gone to the United States to get away from, and now, he'd brought a piece of America home.

"That load of crap is all I have to offer, I'm afraid," he said.

"I'll let you know if I think of anything better." She leaned back in her seat, ending the moment. It hadn't truly gone away, though. Things were changed between them. No going back.

"Let's not let the future get in the way of enjoying the present."

"Right." She pumped her fist in the air. "Onward to…say, where are you taking me, anyway?"

"You'll see. Want to drive?"

"Boy howdy."

As eager as she was, she jumped out of the car and dashed around. Dev had to climb over the gearshift before she physically pushed him over it, potentially causing some damage that could ruin parts of their vacation. Eventually, they were safely seated, and she started the engine and put it into gear. With a bit of a lurch, they took off toward Dev's favorite place in the world.

CHAPTER EIGHT

You could have knocked Felice over with a feather. When they pulled up at the small inn across the square of the tiny hamlet's church, she expected that the car would get some attention. It made sense that people would come streaming out of the buildings to get a look at the person driving it. But they really shouldn't surround him like a long-lost child, clapping him on the back and presenting their children for kisses. One older lady threw herself into Dev's arms, grasped his face, and smacked her lips against one cheek and then the other. Felice hung back and watched it all, catching a German word here and there but not enough to tell what in hell was going on.

Dev pulled himself out of the throng enough to grab her hand. "Welcome to Vogelsheim. Come on. Let me introduce you."

The crowd looked at her with curiosity for a moment. Until Dev put his arm around her and addressed them in German. Something about her being American. It worked because they went to patting her back and shaking her hand, and that same lady crushed Felice against her plump bosom.

"What did you tell them?" she said over the woman's shoulder.

"That you're American and very nice and you'll love them as I do."

"Doesn't appear I get any choice in the matter," she said.

Dev laughed, a deep, hearty sound that came from his center. Then he recited names as he touched or pointed at people. She'd never remember a quarter of them. In fact, the only one that registered in long term memory was Frau Baumgarten, she of the smacking lips and soft boobs.

The same Frau Baumgarten shooed them inside the inn in much the same manner that shepherd had marshaled his sheep. The whole town must have followed, crowding into the combination tap room and restaurant. Frau Baumgarten disappeared into the back somewhere, and a squat man with a round belly whom Dev introduced as Herr Baumgarten came from behind the bar to serve them steins of beer that could double as bath tubs.

Felice smiled and nodded before remembering she knew the German for thank you. "*Danke sehr*."

You would have thought she'd awarded Herr Baumgarten the Braumeister of the Year award, so bright was his grin. He clapped Dev on the shoulder in a way one would not normally do to an heir to the throne and said a few words before going back to his station.

"What did he say?" she asked.

"He said you're pretty and if you like his beer I should keep you."

She hefted her stein with both hands and took a drink. Dark and malty, the brew could make a beer drinker out of her. She hoisted the heavy mug in a toast toward Herr Baumgarten. "*Ganz gut*."

The whole room erupted into applause at that declaration. They'd been watching her, waiting to see how she'd react to the local beer.

"It seems I said the right thing," she said.

"You have a positive knack for that." He took a long draft of his beer and wiped the suds off his mouth with the back of his hand. "A valuable trait for someone who has to get along with people and not something that can be taught."

Frau Baumgarten emerged from what must have been the kitchen, carrying two plates loaded down with food. She set them, along with silverware and napkins, in front of Dev and Felice and put her hands on her hips. "You eat now."

"We will." Dev glanced at Felice. "I hope you like sauerkraut."

"Sure…on hot dogs." Felice studied her meal. Next to a pile of sausages stood a mound of sauerkraut. She'd never had to face a huge serving of pickled cabbage before. What would all these nice people think if she rejected it? She took a tentative bite as complete silence settled over the room. The whole crowd was holding their breath, and several dozen gazes burned into the back of her neck. The first taste was mild, not at all sour, so she took another, bigger bite. "Hey, this is really good."

Frau Baumgarten nodded and left again as more cheers filled the room. She'd passed another test. If only her orals had been this easy.

She shoveled some more sauerkraut into her mouth and chewed. "What does she put in here?"

"Onions," Dev said. "And…um…bacon fat."

"Oh God, I'll blow up like a balloon." She wiped her mouth with her napkin. "I can't eat all this, and I'll never finish the beer."

"Don't worry. I'll tell them you're worried about your girlish figure." He leaned toward her. "A figure I'm planning to explore at leisure tonight."

"They'll let us stay in one room?"

"We're all friends. They'll understand."

"You want to explain all this?" She made a circular gesture with her fork, indicating the room and all the people in it.

"I happened on this village one afternoon when the Lamborghini broke down. It took several days for the people to find someone to work on it. They had to get a mechanic from two towns over. First Frau Baumgarten adopted me and then the others."

"They must have known who you are."

"They did. We kept our distance for a while. Until the rectory caught fire and I helped to put it out before it spread to the church."

He stopped eating for a moment, sat back in his chair and gazed around him. A look of contentment settled over his features. She'd seen him happy before, but she couldn't really say she'd seen him at peace.

"That night we were all covered with soot, and you couldn't tell who was the prince and who was the baker. In a day, I became a member of this village. I can be myself here."

"Is that why you came to study in America and pretended to be a dork?" she asked.

"I was doing fairly well at it until you let yourself into my bed."

She leaned over and clapped her hand onto his mouth. Laughing, he pushed it away. "They won't understand, and if they do, they won't say anything. It's part of our relationship. They have a special place in the heart of the man who'll be their sovereign, and I have total freedom and privacy."

"Sounds like a good deal."

"It is. Now eat some of your knackwurst, or Frau Baumgarten will think you don't like her cooking."

"We can't have that." She dug in as if she hadn't eaten at a picnic a few hours before. It all tasted so good, and the beer accompanied it perfectly.

Maybe the mountain air had affected her, sharpening her senses and whetting her appetite. Maybe the expression on Dev's face—contentment and complete ease—allowed her to relax surrounded by strangers who somehow already felt like friends. Or just maybe the ring he'd placed on her finger told her she belonged with him, sharing his love for his country and his people.

Love. He loved her. Even if the words had meant nothing, he couldn't have faked the light in his eyes nor the tenderness of his kiss. He'd won a piece of her with his lovemaking that first night in his apartment. He'd taken more and more with every touch. Now he owned her completely. She returned his love with a ferocity that terrified her. How would she put all the pieces back together when the time came to leave?

She brought herself back to the present to discover him helping himself to some of her sausage. He'd finished his own meal, not leaving so much as a shred of sauerkraut on his plate and now was eating hers.

He stopped with his fork halfway to his mouth, and gave her a shy smile. "You did say you couldn't eat it all."

For a brief moment, he was Dev, the guy who loved reptiles. Not a prince at all. Just a man…the one she'd fallen in love with.

"Take anything you want," she said softly.

He popped the bit of knackwurst into his mouth and chewed quickly. Then he set his fork down and stretched. “I could use a nap. How about you?”

“Nap, huh?”

“Long day. Long drive.” The light in his eyes turned to heat. She knew that look, and it turned her molten inside.

“I drove part of the way,” she said.

“Then you must be tired, too.”

“I am.”

“We’ll go to our room.” He rose and held his hand down to her.

While she’d been preoccupied, the crowd had thinned out, leaving only a group of men in the corner who seemed more interested in their beer steins than other goings-on in the taproom. So she took his hand and let him lead her toward a staircase in the back. On the way, he stopped near the bar, reached underneath and produced a key. Herr Baumgarten watched out of the corner of his eye, smiled, and busied himself in polishing wine glasses.

*

Felice lay staring at the beamed ceiling while Dev performed his magic with her body, his mouth hot at the curve where her neck met her shoulder, his hands along her sides, molding her curves into his hardness. They’d settled deep into the soft mattress. It would serve as their nest. Smaller by an order of magnitude than her bed at the palace, this one wouldn’t allow them to stray more than an inch from each other. There was something definitely to be said for that.

Moving lower, he captured one breast in his hand while stroking the other with his tongue. The gentle rasping against her sensitive skin, even on the underside, had her heart pounding and her blood rushing in her ears. Arching her back, she reached above her head and curled her fingers around brass posts of the headboard. She could have pulled him up for a kiss so she could gaze into his eyes. She could have glanced down at the top of his head, loving him while he set her flesh ablaze. Instead, she lay as through a prisoner, her wrists tied, unable to protest as he worked his will on her. Complete surrender.

When he sucked the nipple into his mouth, clamping his lips down on it, her vision blurred. How many wooden beams stretched above her? Five? Six? Could she even count with his breath scalding her skin?

He moved to the other breast, leaving the first nipple moist in the cool air. The contrast with the heat of his mouth made the peak tingle. Already, her clit responded, even though he hadn't touched it. The sense of fullness, the ache, the dampness. If she pressed her legs together, she could create friction there, but how much sweeter to lie as his captive, letting her desire for him bloom.

When he released the second nipple, she couldn't hold back a groan. Of frustration, yes. His caress had felt so damned good. But the sound also held a plea in it. *Make me shatter. Dev, put your mouth there. I need to come. I need...I need...*

She didn't have to tell him, at least not in words. Her ragged breathing spoke volumes. It filled the room as her arousal grew more urgent, punctuated by cries that escaped against her will.

He eased himself along her body, his flesh whispering over hers. His hands stayed behind to cup her breasts, his fingers tugging at the nipples and making them stiffen even more. He murmured something in German against her belly. The huskiness of his voice blurred the words, but the meaning came through. He was taking possession of her. It wasn't a request or an order but a simple statement of fact.

Clutching the brass so tightly the ring he'd given her dug into her skin, she braced herself for what would come. The ultimate kiss. So intimate, and so miraculous when Dev did it. When he parted her legs, she imagined her ankles bound as her hands were. Attached to the foot of the bed. She couldn't move unless he allowed it. She could beg for mercy, but he wouldn't grant it. She'd have to lie here and take whatever he dished out.

When he brushed her pussy lips, she whimpered. Too gentle, too light. She ached for something to fill her, to shove itself inside her and force her to come. Instead, he continued his gentle torture, grazing the swollen petals and lingering over the hypersensitive bud.

Still too tentative, he eased her petals apart and slid a finger into her. Gritting her teeth, she stretched against her imaginary bonds while her hips moved, urging him on. She'd coated her inner thighs with moisture now, and his finger made wet noises as it moved inside her. He continued his gentle torture until she was panting, taking in air in gasps.

"Dev, please!" She hadn't meant to beg, but the last thread of her control had snapped. "Please."

As her cry echoed in her ears, he removed his hand from her pussy, clasped her hips and brought her against his face. His tongue found her bud immediately and stroked it with one long swipe. She could let loose now and allow the orgasm to claim her, but she fought it off, arching her back and holding herself rigid. This was too good to rush, and so she found the strength to let him continue. Vision deserted her. She might have closed her eyes, but even if she hadn't, the beams above would have disappeared. Nothing existed except the pressure of his tongue against her clit as he sent her higher and higher, closer to…

Another flick of his tongue, and another and another and she lost her battle. The orgasm built and swelled inside her and then burst, radiating through her. She shouted as her whole body convulsed with it. Powerful contractions coursed through her sex, and all through the chaos, he continued caressing her, drawing more and more out of her until she sagged against the bed, weak and trembling.

For long moments—time that couldn't be measured—she lay unmoving. Breath came more easily now as she rocked on a sea of contentment. The presence of his cheek against one thigh while his hand rested on the other came through dimly. Finally, she had enough strength to reach down and tangle her fingers in his hair.

In a heartbeat, he rose up over her. Briefly, his gaze met hers, seeking permission. The intensity took her breath away. He wanted her as fiercely as she just had him. He needed her as badly, but he held himself back to make sure she was ready. The knowledge created a lump in her throat, and she smiled past it.

"Yes, my love," she whispered.

With one swift movement of his hips, he embedded himself inside her, drawing a gasp of surprise and pleasure from her.

He held himself completely still. "Am I hurting you?"

"Never." She touched his face. "I forget sometimes how big you are."

"Then I'd better remind you frequently."

He began moving. Not in tentative first thrusts but in the rhythm of a man already past niceties. Pulling nearly out and then surging in again. This time, she clutched his shoulders to hold him against her so that she could savor the feel of his firmness against her everywhere.

"It seems I can never go slowly with you," he said.

"I don't want you to."

He groaned. "You deserve a gentle lover."

"I have the best lover in the world," she said. Honestly, how could he think she'd want anyone but him?

"I'm glad you think so because I'm about to lose control."

"Dev?"

"Hm?"

"Shut up," she said.

He groaned and obeyed. Wrapping her legs around him, she lifted her hips to take him deeper. As he went faster, each thrust impaling her, she covered his neck and shoulders with kisses. Every place she could reach she tasted, savoring the saltiness of his skin and breathing in the clean scent of the man she loved. Surely, two people had never been more perfectly joined, so attuned to the rhythms of give and take, thrust and retreat. Her heart beat next to his, thumping as if it would burst. And then, she was soaring with him, caught up in the moment and sharing his rising excitement.

When he flipped them over so that he lay against the bed with her straddling him, she took over, sliding up and down on his cock so that their bodies slapped together. Go slowly? How could he have entertained such idiocy? She rode him mercilessly, her hands on his abdomen for leverage so that she could get the deepest angle.

"Felice?" he whispered.

"I thought I told you to shut up."

"Yes, ma'am."

God, it was incredible, like flying. As much as she demanded, he gave, his hips moving upward to meet her. Then he reached down to the place where they were joined, and his thumb found her most sensitive flesh—that tiny bundle of nerve endings that could push her over the edge. After no more than a few seconds, she was coming again. Fast and hard...so different from the last time and so identically perfect. While the walls of her pussy clamped down on his cock, he continued stroking her.

She released a hoarse cry as the orgasm washed through her. Just when it ended, he gave a vicious twist of his hips, rolling her onto her back without pulling out of her.

His own madness possessed him as he continued thrusting savagely. Suddenly, she seemed a small thing in the face of his passion. She held his shoulders and clung to him, reaching deep into their connection so that she could experience his ecstasy with him. She sensed the exact moment the orgasm pushed everything from his mind, even her. She felt the first release of semen as it left him and entered her. The others followed, so that by the time his shout filled the room, he'd already finished except for the last few milliseconds of bliss.

When the climax had passed and he collapsed on top of her, it had drained her, too. She could only stroke his back and listen to his breath soften as he recovered.

When he tried to move off her, she held him right where he was. "Where do you think you're going?"

"I must be crushing you."

"The mattress is soft. I'm just fine," she said.

"A considerate man doesn't make his lover bear his weight."

"Yeah, and smart-mouthed Americans don't tell a crown prince to shut up," she said. "But I just did."

He chuckled, but it came out like a groan. "How shall I punish you? Throw you in a dungeon?"

"Why don't you chain me to your bed?"

"Not a bad idea, but I *am* getting off you." He did roll off her then, but the size of the bed didn't let him get far. So while she burrowed her face into his chest, he pulled the covers up around them, and she went to sleep with the sound of his heartbeat in her ears.

*

Felice felt pleasantly sore after that amazing night of lovemaking. She didn't wake Dev. Heaven knew he needed his sleep as hard as he'd worked to give her pleasure, so she moved silently to pull her nightgown over her head and top it with her robe. Then, she grabbed her make-up case and went out into the hallway to make her way to the bathroom.

The morning sun warmed the room, so after she threw the lock, she pushed the curtains on the window aside and glanced out at the village below. She really ought to pinch herself. Everything was picture perfect, directly from a movie or a porcelain plate. The ancient church ruled over the town square, and tiny, old wooden houses clustered together, sporting flowers in window boxes.

When she opened the window a breeze of air so clean it made her lightheaded washed over her. Birds twittered, and a cowbell sounded in the distance. This had to be Europe's version of Shangri La, exotic, forgotten, and mystical. In another minute, she'd start singing and a sparrow would land on the sill to chirp in harmony.

Silly, silly, silly. Still she couldn't stop grinning. Before she let loose in song and ruined eardrums for miles, she closed the window and turned her attention to the mirror. A woman in love stared back at her. A bit baggy under the eyes from lack of sleep and evidence of a love bite on her neck, but definitely smitten to the point of goofiness.

Oh my God, how had all this happened? Within a period of weeks, she'd gone from graduate student leading a humdrum life of the regular grind…seminars, research, reading journal articles until the words swam before her eyes...to sex therapist for the supposed virgin guy-geek of their group, to whisked away to a foreign paradise, to head over heels in love with the crown prince. He loved her back. You couldn't mistake the look on his face when he gave her the ring or to the catch in his voice when he confessed his feelings. The handsomest, most romantic man in the world, and the best lover, and he wanted her. Yes, she should definitely pinch herself. Instead, she'd brush her teeth.

She set the case on the sink and opened it, but instead of finding her toothbrush and paste on the top where she'd put them, she discovered an envelope with "Felice" written on it in a masculine hand. Not Dev's. She'd seen that often enough.

After opening the envelope and unfolding the note inside, she scanned to the signature at the bottom. "Your friend, Vaclav."

Oh, great. What did that bozo have to say?

"My dear Felice,

"Now that the cat's away from the palace, the mice shall play."

She re-read those lines. He must have heard the English expression but misunderstood it.

"Come to my room tonight," it went on. "I'll leave my door open for you."

"Oh, yeah, right," she said. "I hope you're still there waiting for me. Holding your breath."

The lecher had assumed they'd both end up in the same place, probably in the hunting lodge Dev had mentioned. He thought he could lure her to his room for a little of the old in-and-out. What a disgusting thought.

"You'll want the experienced touch of an older man," the next paragraph said. "I can show you such delights."

"Ewwww." She crumpled the paper into a ball and tossed it into the wastebasket. But she couldn't leave it there. Someone else would find it, probably Frau Baumgarten. So Felice fished it out again and looked for some other way to dispose of it. Nothing seemed safe short of burning it, but she didn't have any matches, so she stuffed it back into the case where it sat like a giant paper turd.

Well, shit. She'd have to have to read the whole thing eventually. What if the asshole was truly mental and dangerous? What if he'd issued some kind of threat? Giving it to Dev to read would only make him angry, so she'd better take care of this herself.

She unwadded the paper enough to make it legible and picked up where she'd left off.

"My cousin Christian can't offer you a future. He's betrothed to a young noblewoman."

The word hit her right in the chest, knocking the wind out of her. Betrothed. She sat on the edge of the tub to absorb the impact.

His obligations included a fiancée—a real person. A noblewoman, the perfect match for a crown prince—beautiful and sophisticated and European. She probably spoke seven languages and never farted.

Felice glanced at the letter again.

"The young woman adores my cousin and will make him an excellent wife. I am unencumbered and free to offer myself to you," it continued.

"You nasty, old bastard," she said. "You don't want to marry me, you only want to..."

She stopped herself before the words got out of her mouth. Some things should never be said aloud. Even on the preposterous chance that the old fool would consider her marriage material, she wouldn't have any of it.

"Come to me tonight," the note ended. "I'm waiting for you."

"Get stuffed, asshole," she said as she crumpled the note again and put it in her case, this time moving things around to lay it on the bottom.

Well, that took a little of the magic out of the situation. Reality had a way of doing that. A young noblewoman and Prince Christian. Dev, the man she loved, got lost in the shuffle. He'd fulfill his obligations, shutting her out. It was only a matter of time.

Correction. It was only a matter of time if she stuck around. He hadn't invited her here to live with him and his family. Technically, she could have gone home as soon as they found out his father was all right. Friedrich had invited her to see his country, and now, she was seeing it. When they got back to the palace, she'd have to figure out how long to continue the charade. For now, she'd make the most of what she had, and when the end came, she'd leave.

*

When Dev finally opened his eyes, the sunlight was pouring between Frau Baumgarten's lace curtains in a way that told him he'd slept hours past his normal rising time. Or rather, he'd stayed in bed. How much of that time he'd spent in sleep was another question all together.

He flopped onto his back and finally registered the fact that he was alone. He ought to find out where Felice had gathered the strength to get out of bed and see if he could borrow some. His whole body had a supple worn-out feeling to it. Not unpleasant. Actually, more relaxing than anything else. He'd had quite a work-out. Some demon must have possessed him. He'd never performed like that. It seemed every hour or so one of them had wakened the other to make love, and his body had managed each time. Twice in the middle of the night and again just before dawn, he'd buried himself in her warmth and heard her moans and cries.

After a good stretch, he swung his legs over the side of the bed and sat up. So far, so good. Glancing around, he took in all the details of the Baumgarten's best room. Tiny by palace standards, it still gleamed with the polish of the old wood and the brass of the bed. At the other end, the ceiling slanted under the house's eaves. The same wardrobe he always used stood against one wall, the full-length mirror in a frame next to it. One arm chair and a bedside table with a lamp completed the furniture. He'd often lit a fire in the small hearth so he could watch it flicker. He'd do that again the next time he made love with Felice.

An objective observer would say nothing had changed here since his last visit. But something had. Felice had made it all different. He'd always come here as a single soul, adrift. He had a role at the palace. He'd lived that role his entire life except for his brief freedom in the United States. It had completed him. Without it, he was just Dev. Now and here, he was half of Dev and Felice.

He'd better go and find his other half. Heaven only knew what she was doing in a strange town in a foreign country where most of the people didn't speak her language.

He found his clothes where she must have draped them over the arm chair. For a moment, he considered padding downstairs in bare feet to look for her, but he did need to maintain some dignity. So he dressed completely and finger-combed his hair before stepping into the hallway.

As soon as he did, a cloud of baking smells wafted up to him from the floor below. Yeast and cinnamon and other spices he couldn't identify. His stomach rumbled, reminding him they hadn't left the room except for short visits to the bathroom down the hall. He hadn't eaten since that plate of sausage and sauerkraut. He could only hope Felice had something to do with those smells, because he was going to check them out before setting out to find her anywhere else.

He skipped down the stairs as fast as their narrowness allowed and dashed through the taproom to the kitchen entrance. Sure enough, she was there, just pulling a tray of pastries from the oven.

"There you are, sleepy head," she said as she set the tray onto the huge work table. "I thought you'd never wake up."

He could only stare and take in this new incarnation of the woman he loved. She wore casual clothes—a blouse and slacks—but she'd tied up her hair and covered it with a scarf the same way Frau Baumgarten did when she baked. She'd put an apron on over her clothing, and a good thing, too, because it had patches of flour on it and spots of grease or oil. In fact, she was a beautiful, green-eyed mess.

"Frau Baumgarten has been teaching me how to bake," she declared. "It's fascinating, really, although I only understand about half of what I'm doing."

The frau in question stood at the stove, stirring a pot. At the mention of her name, she glanced at him with a knowing expression and moved to the coffee pot. "*Guten Morgen.*"

"*Morgen*," he answered.

She poured coffee into a china cup and set it on the work table near him. Then she produced a pitcher of heavy cream from the refrigerator and put it and a spoon nearby.

Felice held up a pastry. "These are called butter…"

"*Butterknoten*," Frau Baumgarten supplied.

"Butter knots," Dev translated.

"They're tied and curled in several different ways, and they're delicious," Felice said. "I love cooking. I've never had a chance to learn."

"I'm sure Frau Baumgarten can fix that."

Frau Baumgarten gave him the same sly smile and went back to the stove.

"I'd better have one of your creations with my coffee." After pouring cream into the cup and stirring, he reached out for one of the rolls.

Felice batted his hand away. "You're supposed to have this one."

She selected a pastry from the tray she'd just removed from the oven. It must have retained some of its heat because she dropped it quickly in front of his cup. Dev stared down at the familiar shape—two strands of dough woven together and glazed with honey.

"Did Frau Baumgarten tell you what this figure means?" he asked.

"She just said to give this one to you," Felice said. "Is something wrong?"

"Our sweet hausfrau is too clever by half. It's a love knot."

Felice put her fingers over her mouth. "Love…"

"A bride makes them for her husband on her first morning in their new home," Dev said.

Felice moved to snatch the bun away from him, but he got it first. For a moment, they stared at each other, and the only sound in the room came from Frau Baumgarten's wooden spoon hitting the side of the pot.

"I'm going to save this one," he said finally.

"It's food, Dev. You can't save it. It'll go bad."

"I'm going to save it nevertheless," he said. "Give me another one to eat. I'm hungry."

Felice did—a perfectly innocent shape this time that didn't mean anything that he knew of. It was full of butter and all the spices he'd smelled from upstairs.

"Delicious," he mumbled around the morsel in his mouth. The sweet cream in the coffee made the whole experience something you didn't report to your doctor, but he'd never tasted anything better.

"You keep the Fräulein," Frau Baumgarten said without moving her gaze from her pot. "She's good for you."

"I certainly will for as long as I can," Dev answered.

Frau Baumgarten turned and brandished her spoon like a weapon. "Good baker. Good wife."

At that, Felice's pale skin turned a bright pink, highlighting a dusting of flour on one cheek. "Please, you must understand."

"*Ich verstehe*," Frau Baumgarten said. "He's happy now."

"I'm always happy when I'm here," Dev said.

"Not like now." After one more flourish of the spoon, Frau Baumgarten went back to her cooking. "Keep her."

"As you say," Dev said. "If you're quite through with the Fräulein, I'll borrow her for the day."

Frau Baumgarten dismissed them with a wave of her hand, but before he left with Felice, he grabbed the love knot. She could say all she wanted about the thing being perishable. He planned to keep it. End of discussion.

Chapter Nine

The whole town turned out for the fest. Though Dev had told Felice that the folks here would use any excuse for a party, she knew darned well after watching them that his arrival was a very special occasion, indeed. And why not? As crown prince, he'd succeed Friedrich to the throne. The Crown Prince might not rank up there with the Prince of Wales in the world of international royalty, but he mattered here.

The people had filled the town square with hundreds of lanterns, each giving off a glow that merged into enough light to show off the colorful costumes of the region. One might have felt the evening too cool for short *Lederhosen*, but the men never stopped dancing long enough to get cold. The constant jumping and slap, slap of palms against leather made for an almost dizzying display. Still, she couldn't have taken her eyes off it all. She might have recorded it on her cell phone, but that felt much too twenty-first century for this celebration. And modern electronics didn't fit at all with the peasant skirt and blouse Frau Baumgarten had found for her nor with the ribbons and flowers in her hair.

Dev ambled up to her and handed her a glass of wine. "It's local and rather sweet, I'm afraid."

She took a sip. "It's fruity, not sweet, you silly man. It's delicious."

"Always the diplomat." He pulled her to his side and planted a kiss on her cheek. "I should make you ambassador to somewhere."

"I'm only speaking the truth. Everything about Danislova is perfect."

"Hardly perfect." He smiled when he said it. He might pretend modesty, but if he puffed out his chest any farther, he'd resemble a pigeon.

"Absolutely perfect, especially the royal family." She clinked her glass against his and then raised it to her lips to drink.

He took a sip of his own wine and savored it, a thoughtful expression on his face. "We'll have to go back tomorrow, you know."

"The ball?"

"It's only a few days away," he said. "We'll be needed at home."

Yes, indeed. They'd have to leave. Nothing this magical could last forever. But then, she'd have the prospect of a royal ball to console her. "Will your father be angry at us for taking off?"

"Annoyed, perhaps." He shrugged. "I've done it before."

"He won't be worried about you, then."

"Not particularly. Vaclav will be furious he didn't get a chance to seduce you."

Vaclav had done his best with that note. Luckily, she hadn't been anywhere near the creep when she'd read it. She could tell Dev all about that, but why ruin this beautiful evening? "He wouldn't try anything at the palace with the others all around us, would he?"

"He might. He's as silly as he is lecherous. But let's not talk about him." He stepped behind her and pulled her back against him. They stood that way for a while, not talking but watching the dancers as Dev's warmth surrounded her.

After a moment, he sighed. "So, tell me, pretty lady, what are we going to do about your education?"

A twinge of guilt settled into her stomach. She hadn't thought a whit about her studies or research. The idea of a doctorate and an academic career had lost its appeal. But to be totally honest with herself, she had to admit it never had felt like a real ambition so much as something she ought to do because her parents had chosen it for her. "Their little PhD" and all that. If she never went on another research trip or wrote another journal article, her life wouldn't lose one tiny bit of its luster.

"What about your education?" she asked.

He rested his chin on her shoulder. "I'm mostly done. I can finish from here. Although I am sorry I'll never watch another rattler side wind down a sand dune."

Anyone rational would laugh at that last statement, but his wistful tone said he meant it. He really did care about his research while hers was little more than a way to avoid engaging in the real world.

As odd as it might seem, the fantasy she was living now seemed more authentic than what she'd had at home. People were so generous and loving here, even the ruler of the country. She fit here. Everything just felt right. Something else to miss when she left. Someday, she really had to have a talk with herself about what she wanted to do when she grew up.

"You look wonderful, by the way," Dev said.

"No *Lederhosen* for you?"

"God, no," he said. "And I'm not trying that dance, either."

"What a sorry excuse for a monarch you are."

"There's only one place I'm interested in ruling right now." He pressed his mouth to her ear. "Your heart and, of course, your bed."

The men had paired off for another dance in the center of the square, and this time, the women joined them. The little band started up a slower melody, and the women formed a large circle around the men. One young girl separated herself from the crowd and came up to Felice, her hand outstretched in an invitation. Dev took her glass. "You've been summoned."

"But I don't know how to do it."

The girl laughed and extended her hand again, this time more emphatically. Dev gave her a nudge, and the next thing she knew she'd joined the circle and was stumbling over her feet in an effort to learn the steps. The dance turned out to be far simpler than what the men were doing with their leaping, and soon Felice was keeping up with the others. Breathing hard, she circled while lantern light flickered and the colors of the costumes blurred. For a split second, she caught a view of Dev's smile before moving on to a glimpse of the church, to the women handing out plates of food, and to the winemaker giving away his merchandise for the celebration.

By the time the dance ended, she was quite out of breath and gasping. The other girls and women laughed and applauded her. She joined the laughter and could have fallen in a heap for lack of oxygen if Dev hadn't come up and put an arm around her.

"Do you know what the altitude is here?" he asked.

"Let me guess." *Breathe, breathe.* "Mountains?"

"I'm out of breath from watching." He gave her ribs a squeeze. "The others were taking things easy, but not you."

"I was having fun."

"And so you went all out, as you do with everything," he said. "Including seducing virgins."

She clapped her hand over his mouth, but she couldn't do anything to dim the wicked twinkle in his eyes. He nipped at her fingers until she pulled her hand away.

"No one heard, and if they did, they wouldn't understand, oh Princess of the Three Condoms," he said.

"Shhh, the priest is coming this way."

"*Ach*, and he speaks English." Dev turned toward the man who no doubt headed the local church. In black clothing and white clerical collar, he could hardly be anything else. His gaze fell on Dev's hand where it had settled on her hip. She tried to step away, but Dev held her where she was.

"Father Wilhelm." Dev finally released her so that he could shake the priest's hand. "Have you met Miss Larson?"

The priest gave her a smart bow. "I haven't, but I've heard a great deal about her."

"Good, I hope," she said.

"The town has taken to you as we did His Highness," Father Wilhelm said. "He helped to save the church. Did he tell you that?"

"He did."

The priest arched a brow. "So then I'll see you there on Sunday?"

"I'm afraid we'll be gone by then," Dev answered.

Though the sounds of the fest continued, a small silence settled over the three of them. The priest couldn't approve of their relationship, without benefit of clergy as it was. He didn't say anything, and his features remained neutral. Royalty and some services in fighting fires seemed to earn Dev a small dispensation, obviously.

"Well," the priest said after a moment. "I wish you a safe trip home and a swift return here, with Miss Larson, if the Lord grants us the pleasure."

He lingered on the "miss" a bit. That might have been the result of German syntax, or it might have been disapproval. Whichever, he smiled before melting away into the crowd.

"I hope that wasn't too awkward for you," Dev said.

She shrugged. "I guess the rest of the town likes me."

Dev took her hand. "He does, too. It's his profession to disapprove of things."

"Well, we won't be around much longer to ruffle his piety."

Dev stared out over the party, which showed no sign of slowing down. "No, we won't."

*

The morning after the fest, Dev sat on a bench in the town square with a flock of birds gathered at his feet and the remains of the now stale love knot in his hands. The townspeople had cleared away everything before they'd headed off to bed, and now he was the only one stirring in the village. Or rather, one of the two. The door to the inn opened, and Felice stepped out wearing slacks and a sweater against the cool mountain air. No longer the Fräulein who'd danced so easily with the others, she'd transformed herself into the American young woman who'd return to graduate school soon.

She glanced at his hands and stopped for a moment as recognition dawned. If he'd gotten out of bed earlier, he might have completed the process of destroying her gift without her knowledge.

She walked toward him, scattering birds as she went, and sat beside him. For a moment, he couldn't look at her but stared at the broken pastry. "You were right. It's perishable. But I couldn't throw it away like trash."

She held out her hand. "Give me some."

He did, and they sat, tossing pieces to the birds, which had floated back down when she sat. Neither of them spoke as, piece by piece, her handiwork disappeared. When they finished, she clapped her hands together to free them of the last crumbs. “We can’t leave without saying good-bye to Frau Baumgarten. She’d never forgive me.”

Likely Felice would never see Frau Baumgarten again, so forgiveness was hardly an issue. They both knew that, but he wouldn’t say it to anyone but himself.

“She’ll only make a fuss and pack us a huge basket of food to take with us,” he said.

“She’s already doing it,” she said. “She was in the process when I left her, and Herr Baumgarten is adding some bottles of his beer.”

“Then I suppose it can’t be avoided.”

“Dev.” She put her hand on his arm. “Thank you for bringing me here. I’ll never forget it.”

“Thank you for coming, not just here but to Danislova.” *Thank you for loving me.* He ought to say it. He’d already confessed his love for her. They hadn’t hidden anything from each other about the reality of their situation. But every time he said the words they felt like another nail or another brick in building a foundation that would have to be crumbled later on—that much more emotional violence they’d inflict on each other when they parted. She knew how he felt, and if she had any doubt, he’d demonstrate for her with his lovemaking in the short time they had left.

“It’s hard to describe, but I have such a sense of home here.” She gripped the bench in her fists and leaned forward, avoiding eye contact. “This town, your family, even Vaclav, who’s like the crazy uncle.”

“You don’t have a crazy uncle?”

"My father has two brothers, a physicist and a research biochemist. We never see them. Everyone's too busy."

"But surely, your family…" He let his voice trail off. She was an only child, and her parents traveled constantly. "What about your home?"

"We have a very nice house in Northern California. That's where I go on holidays."

"You're all alone there, aren't you?" He caught her chin in his hand and turned her head to face him. "Tell me."

"It's not a big deal. I went to the best schools, had everything I needed. I traveled to their digs sometimes, and they usually came home for Christmas."

"Usually?"

"December is summer in South America," she said. "Prime time for excavation."

His father had seen this aspect of her with no more than the information that she hadn't called her parents to tell them she'd gone off to Europe with a man they didn't know. He'd been so busy enjoying her body he'd hardly scratched the surface of Felice Larson as a person.

He'd thought himself isolated from other people because of his royalty. True, he couldn't move about as freely as normal people and couldn't make friends without wondering if the person truly liked him or only his wealth and privilege. But he'd had his family growing up—the fights with his brothers over silly nothings, the stern love of his father and the softer adoration of his mother. Felice had had phone calls, or not.

"You'll always be welcome in Danislova," he said.

"I know. That means a lot."

She could come back years from now, bringing her husband and children. He'd probably be married to

Astrid with a son or daughter of his own. Would the feelings flare between them after years apart? Would his body crave hers constantly as it did now? Would she still wear his ring?

"We probably should be going before all the others are up and we have dozens of good-byes to make," he said.

"I'll see how Frau Baumgarten is doing." They got up and strolled hand-in-hand toward the inn. When she went inside, he let down the top of the Lamborghini. After starting the engine, he pulled up to the front door and let the motor idle while he waited. In only a moment, Felice appeared with both Baumgartens, all three of them carrying bundles. They stowed it all in the car somehow, and Frau Baumgarten bent to kiss his cheeks the way she always did in greetings and farewells.

Felice stood nearby for a little bit, apparently hesitant to take her seat. In the end, she went to first Frau Baumgarten and then her husband and got a hug from each of them.

When she finally joined him in the car and he put it into gear and rumbled out of the village, she stared straight ahead, biting her lip. For a few seconds, her chin trembled before a deceptive expression of calm settled over her features.

*

With the state of chaos at the palace, Dev almost managed to sneak himself and Felice into their rooms without alerting his father to their presence. He'd planned to have a private talk with Friedrich to soothe the old man's feathers, but best laid plans and all that. And who else to release the bugle's cry to alert the household that the prodigal had returned other than Vaclav?

"My dear cousin." Vaclav descended the formal staircase as quickly as his short legs would allow and launched himself at Dev, catching him in a hug that brooked no resistance. "We've all worried ourselves into our sick beds."

"No need." Dev finally managed to extricate himself from Vaclav's affection. "We're fine, as you can see."

"Miss Larson." Vaclav attached himself to Felice. "What a cad he was to spirit you away when we were just getting to know you."

"I'm back now." She stared over Vaclav's shoulder toward Dev, begging with her eyes for help. Before Dev could stop him, Vaclav pressed a wet kiss to her cheek.

Dev hauled Vaclav off her. "That's enough concern for today, thank you."

"My heart nearly stopped when you went missing." To illustrate, Vaclav let his hands flutter over his chest. "I wanted to search for you right then, but your brother said you run away from time to time and you'd be fine."

"They were right, and now if you don't mind…" He took Felice's arm and attempted to lead her around Vaclav, but Vaclav was having none of it.

"I consulted with your father every day. 'Call out the guards,' said I. 'The prince must be found.' But did he listen to me?" Vaclav waved a finger in the air. "This is not how we do things in Rosnia."

"I'm sure. I apologize sincerely. Now would you please let us…"

"So there you are finally." His father's voice boomed from the hallway nearby. "You took the devil's own time coming back."

"We're here now," Dev said. "Did we miss anything important?"

"I'm not going to discuss family business standing in a hallway." Friedrich swept his arm in the general direction of his library. "Come along, and don't dally."

With that, the Prince Royal walked off. Dev kept a hand on Felice's arm and took her with him rather than leave her to Vaclav's tender mercies. When they reached the library, Friedrich had already seated himself in the throne-like chair behind his desk. A decanter of brandy...untouched by all appearances...stood on a side table. Dev's father glanced at it and then shot Dev a look that warned him to say nothing about it. So he didn't but guided Felice to a chair and stood behind her.

"You chose a fine time to run away and leave me with a palace full of relatives." Friedrich pronounced the last word the way one might say "halfwits."

"That seems a perfect occasion to get out of Dodge," Dev said.

Friedrich's regal eyebrow went up in a regal display of displeasure. "You'll be speaking cowboy now?"

"It's just an expression."

"I'd like to know where in hell you were," Friedrich said.

"And I'd rather not tell you." Dev placed his hands on the back of Felice's chair to brace himself for the inevitable argument. His father never took it well that he needed to get away sometimes. Friedrich had reigned so long he had little memory of life as a private person. He lived every moment of every day as the monarch. Dev would, too, when he assumed the throne. His secret visits to Vogelsheim would end then but not before.

"You two haven't been in Paris stirring up gossip, I hope," Friedrich said.

"We never left Danislova."

"No scandal sheets, then?" Friedrich rested back against his chair and laced his fingers together over his stomach.

"No."

"How was I supposed to know you were safe?" Friedrich said.

"I sent a text to Ulrich. Look, we've been through this before. I wanted to show Felice Danislova. Can you blame me?"

The storm clouds vanished from his father's face. "Did you enjoy it, my dear?"

"Very much, sir. I've seldom seen such beautiful country or such wonderful people."

"Then I suppose it was worth leaving me with all the relatives."

"You had Kurt and Ulrich," Dev said. "They could buffer you from the others."

"They're going to leave," Friedrich said.

"When?" Dev asked.

"Right after Vaclav does." Friedrich straightened a pile of books on his desk as if it were an important task and not something to help him avoid meeting Dev's gaze. "They have their own lives elsewhere."

"Of course," Dev said.

All the air seemed to whoosh out of the room, although Dev managed to keep breathing, barely. They'd come to the discussion of leave takings and who would be staying and who wouldn't. No wonder his father had seemed so upset on confronting them in the hallway. He hated not having his children nearby, even though he encouraged them all in their life paths and had appointed Kurt to his post at the UN.

"And you?" Friedrich glanced up at Dev.

"I'll be staying here." He didn't add that he'd be preparing to take his father's place. Preparing for his death.

"What about your snakes that wind sideways?" Friedrich said.

"I'll do my dissertation here. I might have to take one trip to tie up the formalities."

"Good." Friedrich let out a slow breath.

Felice reached up to put her hand over Dev's. "Kurt will be flying to New York, right?"

"That's where his work is," Friedrich answered.

"Maybe that'll be a good time for me to go back to the states." She made the statement so matter-of-factly. *Yes, of course. If the royal jet is going my way, I'll hitch a ride.* More power to her. Dev couldn't have pushed the words past his lips. At the moment, he could hardly stand under the weight of reality and had to take strength from the touch of her fingers against his.

"If you wish, my dear," his father said from somewhere distant and down a dark tunnel.

She was going to leave him. He'd known that she would. They'd both realized from the first that this relationship had no future. How could he have let things go so far? He'd done himself no favors, but what really twisted his gut was that he'd hurt her. She'd return to…what? An empty apartment near campus with no one to greet her but a cat? An even emptier house in northern California? To a dig in a foreign country where at least she'd have her parents' attention for part of the time?

He had everything, and she had nothing. Correction. He had everything but the woman he loved with all his heart.

"I think I'll go lie down for a while." She rose, outwardly as steady as he was unsteady, as composed as he was fragile. "It's been a long day."

A day that had started with them destroying the love knot together.

Friedrich got to his feet, too. "Is there anything you need, my dear?"

"No." Her voice almost broke. "I suddenly seem to have a slight headache. I'm sure I'll be fine by dinner. Until then...if you wouldn't mind…"

"Anything at all," Friedrich said. "You only have to ask."

"Just a little quiet." She gave Dev a smile that faltered at the corners. "And privacy."

She was pulling away already, and he had to let her go. He had to help her, be strong for her sake. Not tell her that she'd take part of him with her and that he'd bleed inside when she did. Not beg her to stay and become even more entangled with his life.

"I'll take you to your room." Dev moved to her side.

She held out a hand to fend him off. "No need. I can find it. I'll see you at dinner."

No. He would not let her simply back away from him. Not yet. Not until the last possible moment. He put his arms around her, and though she put up a half-hearted resistance, he took her lips in a kiss. Not a prelude to lovemaking nor a possession but a simple connection. His father could look on or not, as he wanted. Friedrich knew where things stood between them. But she could not abandon him. Not yet.

After a bit, she pulled away, her hand covering her mouth and her eyes wide above her fingers. After one glance at his father, she nearly turned and ran from the room.

"Felice," he called after her.

"Don't, son. Let her go."

"But I love her."

"I know," his father said. "That changes nothing."

*

Dev sat staring into the fire his valet had started in his bedroom. The weather didn't require a blaze to keep him warm, but it fit his mood. So did the snifter of his father's brandy that dangled from his fingers. He should be dressing for dinner, and he would in a minute or two. Right now, he watched the flames twine together and apart and enjoyed being alone with his thoughts.

"Enjoyed" was the wrong word, obviously because all his thoughts ran to life continuing on here without

Felice. “Indulge” might fit better or even “wallow.” He could easily sit here until he fell asleep and then crawl into bed alone. But that would leave Felice to face dinner without him. She’d have to paste on a smile, and he wouldn’t be there to touch her hand and lend her whatever strength he had. He couldn’t allow that. Another minute or two, and he’d get up, finish dressing and go downstairs.

At least, he’d planned to do that until a hand came down on his shoulder. He jumped, nearly dropping the brandy. “What the…”

“I’m sorry,” Felice’s voice came from behind him. “I didn’t mean to startle you.”

“I didn’t hear you come in. I was...thinking.”

“So that’s your word for it.” She came around the chair and slithered into his lap. He could only stare at her for the miracle she was. So open and giving when he’d led them into this emotional morass.

She hadn’t finished dressing, either, and wore a robe over some underclothes. Her lips were soft and full, as tempting as usual, but her eyes appeared puffy and red.

“You’ve been crying,” he said.

“That’s my word for it.”

“I’m sorry, love,” he said. “I’m so sorry.”

She looped her arms around his neck. “I got myself into this. I kissed the frog.”

“Frog?”

“The fairy tale about the damsel who kissed the frog and won a prince,” she said. “I’d do it again in a heartbeat.”

“You’re far braver than I. I think I’ll guard my heart from now on.”

“Oh, no. You mustn’t.” For a moment her chin wobbled, and she seemed ready to cry again. He’d done this to her. He’d broken his most solemn obligation as a man—to protect the woman he loved, to keep her safe from harm. And now he was the one who'd caused the pain.

"Please don't, my darling. Please don't cry."

"You'll love again, Dev. We both will. That's how we're made."

"Not like this," he said softly.

"No." She tucked her head under his chin, and he felt moisture against his neck. "Not like this."

He held her for the longest time. Not rocking her or stroking her but just keeping his arms around her. The old clock in his sitting room ticked, occasionally interrupted by a hiss or crackle from the fireplace. He'd never made love to her in front of a fire in their little room in Vogelsheim. He could do it now, if she wasn't too upset. His cock would cooperate. It always wanted her and was already stiffening at the thought of joining with her.

Sex probably wasn't wise. They shouldn't strengthen the bonds that held them together any further. But damn it all to hell, he had her for a few more days. He'd never keep his hands off her for that long.

In the end, she made the decision for him. Her fingers went to work on the buttons of his shirt, carefully opening them as if she'd premeditated every move. He held his breath, not moving, and let her continue, while his member grew thick and hard in anticipation. When her lips brushed his neck, he let out a sigh. He'd never realized how sensitive that flesh was until she'd caressed him on the plane. He'd always thought that men had skin there while women had perfumed velvet. She'd awakened every nerve ending, and she was doing it again now.

"You're certain of this?" he asked.

"Dead certain," she answered. "I think we should spend every minute we have left making love."

"That might prove awkward at the ball."

Now that she had his shirt open, she ran her hands inside and splayed her fingers over his chest. "Screw the ball. Let's skip it."

"And miss seeing you in that dress?"

She laughed softly. "That dress did have a dramatic effect on you, didn't it?"

"Your hands are having the same effect right now."

"Glad I haven't lost my touch," she said.

"Never." Although she'd started this, he'd take over now. This time, finally, he'd take things slowly and make their lovemaking last. He'd intended to so many times and let his control slip. Not this evening, not when his time with her had a limit to it and the fire would light her skin.

He set the brandy on the table next to him and eased her hands aside so he could tug her robe open and press his lips to the hollow above her collarbone. As he kissed her shoulder and then proceeded up her throat, devouring her inch by inch, he reached around her and fumbled for the fastening of her bra. It resisted, but he continued, and by the time his mouth had reached her jaw, the hooks gave way, and her breasts fell free. Now he could cup them. Savor their weight and feel the nipples stiffen against his palms.

She lifted his head from her jaw and held it away from her, staring into his face. Her eyes seemed huge. No longer filled with moisture. Pupil's dilated and the irises as green as the fields she'd loved so much in the mountains. Her lips were parted, soft and moist, and her breath came in shallow puffs.

"God, I want you," she whispered.

"Love," he corrected. "Not lust."

"I love you."

The words pierced his heart. Shards of joy that left pain in their wake. The pain would have to wait. There would be plenty of time for it later. Right now, his woman had become aroused, and he needed to satisfy her.

So he lowered them both to the floor and claimed her mouth with all the bottled up emotion inside him. Each movement of her lips beneath his tugged at something inside him. A flash of a memory of another time they'd kissed, the sound of her laughter in the recesses of his mind. A tiny part of what would become his cherished past, the knowledge that he was capable of love great enough to blind him.

With every bit of skill he had, he set about to turn her into a creature of female needs and wants. He helped her to sit up so that she could ease her arms out of the sleeves of her robe. He guided the straps of her bra off her and tossed the scrap of a garment aside. After that, he slid her panties down her legs and discarded them, too, leaving her naked and ready for him. Then he set about loving her using every bit of knowledge he'd gained of what could make her wild with wanting him.

Because she preferred his mouth at her nipples rather than his fingers, he ran his tongue around one before closing his lips around the peak. Still, he massaged her flesh until he'd won a low, sweet moan from her. When he'd finished with that breast, he moved to the other one, lavishing the same attention until the sounds of her cooing filled his ears. Clearly impatient now, she slid her fingers into his hair, holding him against her as if he'd leave her if she released him. Not a chance.

While he continued sucking, he spread his hands over her ribs and then to her sides, massaging her flesh. She always went limp and pliant when he did that, and she didn't fail him now. She relaxed completely, opening herself to him and anything he cared to do to her. He cared for a very great deal.

Lifting his head, he gazed into her face and found the mask of a woman who'd retreated into her own pleasure.

She took shallow breaths into her mouth, and her eyes were closed. The firelight kissed her skin, adding a glow to the flush of arousal. He couldn't take his eyes off her, not even as he stripped out of his clothes. Because she'd opened his shirt, that came off easily. Then shoes and socks followed and finally his pants and boxers.

This time when he resumed loving her, he started at her feet. He stroked her instep while planting a kiss at the inside of her ankle. After repeating the caresses on the other foot, he moved to her knee and stroked the tender skin at the back. She let out a gasp, telling him he'd found a sensitive spot, so he repeated the process on her other knee and listened as her breaths came faster. And now, her thighs…the long expanses of flesh that led to heaven. She was so smooth here, so powder soft, he couldn't hold back but nipped and sucked and kissed her, first on one leg and then the other.

She let out a whimper and dug her fingers into his hair again, pressing into his scalp. Her patience was running out, obviously. She knew where he was headed and wanted him there. But he'd take his time, making her insane with wanting him so that when he finally took her, he'd give her pleasure like she'd never had before.

Still, he inched closer to her pretty puss and the very seat of her arousal. He brushed his fingers over the petals of her sex, and they came away damp with her nectar.

She'd grown wet for him, and the message zinged along his nerve endings right to his cock. As much as he'd planned to tease her and make her wait for him, that meant he also had to put off his own indulgence. His shaft would have to wait to feel her muscles clamp down on it. The head would have to wait to feel her climax around it. And right now, he desperately needed both.

He touched her again, this time letting his finger rest against the seam of her pussy lips.

"Yes," she whispered. "I'm ready."

"I'm not."

"I swear I'll kill you."

"I don't doubt that one bit." Pressing gently, he slid a finger inside her. Her muscles gripped it eagerly, and she sucked in a loud breath.

"Good," she said. "More."

If she wanted more, he'd give it to her. His thumb found her clit and rubbed it. She responded immediately, her hips moving as if seeking yet more contact. Well, he could do that, too.

He moved his hand and buried his face in her muff. This time, he used his tongue to explore her stiff bud. He lapped at it and enjoyed the tiny release of moisture that told him she was approaching her climax. He still wouldn't rush the foreplay, though. In the years to come, there would be nights when he'd lie alone and aching for her. Then he could remember this moment and the joy he'd taken at pushing her past her own boundaries. He kept on stroking her with his tongue until the pitch of her cries told him she'd come soon. So he stopped, breathing evenly to bank his own excitement.

"Dev?" she called. "What are you do—"

He stroked her clit again, just a few times before stopping again. She fairly growled out of frustration. Hell, even he could feel it in his balls. She couldn't endure any more, and neither could he. So after one more touch, a lingering caress right at the tip of her, he pushed himself up, took his place, and drove himself into her.

She exploded immediately, her whole body vibrating, as her pussy went wild around him. He held himself still, enduring the shocks. Not thrusting. Doing nothing to bring on his answering orgasm. Her spasms—and the knowledge that he'd made her come—usually sent him over the edge, but he'd wait her out. Once her urgency had passed, he could spend the time he'd wanted buried inside her. Going easy at first until neither of them could stand that and he'd have to push her harder.

She let out a groan and melted back against the carpet. For long moments, he did nothing but drink in the sight of her. Her eyes remained closed and her lips parted. A perfect picture of feminine bliss. He couldn't help but grin back at her.

After a while, she lifted her hand to his face. "I swear, you know my body better than I do."

"It's been my very great pleasure to learn." And a privilege. He'd always feel honored that she'd opened herself so completely to him. He made a small movement inside her, a test to see how she'd react.

Her eyes opened. "You haven't come yet."

"And I don't plan to for a while."

"We're going to have to dress for dinner eventually."

"Let them wait," he said. "Let them wonder what we're doing."

A wicked light entered her eyes. "Even Vaclav?"

"Especially Vaclav. I ought to bite you to mark you as mine. He might understand that."

"You wouldn't." She squirmed beneath him, but not enough to seriously try to get away. The futile attempt was playful, though. If she wanted play, he'd give it to her.

He made a more serious move then, a slow slide and thrust. In response, she sucked in a deep breath and let it out slowly. "That is so good."

"I'm going to spend an hour doing it."

"I'll never last. I'm still sensitive after that amazing orgasm."

"Is that a good thing or bad?" He withdrew and then pushed deeper into her.

"Oh." She released a high-pitched whimper. "Good. Definitely good."

She'd climax again. He'd guessed as much, but hearing it from her lips made the knowledge all the sweeter. He thrust again, a long slow glide forward, retreating, and then entering again.

"Such luxury. " She wound her arms around his neck, taking in a deep breath and letting it out slowly. "I feel I should be doing something for you."

"Believe me, you are." He continued in a steady rhythm. He couldn't make this go on for an hour, of course, but he could make them feel as if time had passed. This would be one of those memories a couple carried with them into advanced age. *Do you remember that afternoon in your bedroom? You were drinking brandy, and I snuck up on you. You'd lit a fire.*

Yes, my love, I remember.

The fact that they'd never share those memories mattered not at all. All he cared about in these perfect moments was that she lay beneath him and that her inner walls accepted the stroking of his swollen shaft. He'd make this wonderful for her, and she'd reward him with the ultimate—her complete surrender to another orgasm that he'd give her.

As the fire continued to warm them, their bodies moved together. She rose to meet him, and he kept thrusting. She slipped her hands under his arms and up to his back where her nails scraped against his flesh. Her signal that she wanted him, needed him to take her to the place where stars would shower down on both of them.

He'd do that for her, of course. So, he went faster. Straining, pushing, giving her everything he had. With a rising cry, she climaxed. And the orgasm glittered brighter than stars, more beautiful than music, more mystical than heaven. He couldn't help but respond by driving into her frantically and following her.

He came with every part of him from the balls of his feet to the top of his head. Semen streamed out of him and into her as his shout joined hers. *My woman, my other half, mine.*

When it ended, she held him against her, not allowing him to roll off or pull their bodies apart. If there were any justice in the world, they could lie like this forever.

CHAPTER TEN

The ball was a chaos of sounds, lights, and swirling colors, but after Felice‘s time in Danislova and especially in the palace, she could make some sense of it all. Felice stood off to one side, a flute of champagne in her gloved hand, and watched the crowd. By now, she recognized many of the revelers. Others, who knew? She could only hope she could tell the difference between people she ought to know and those she didn't.

She still had to pinch herself to prove it was all real. She hadn't worn a formal since high school, and this dress outclassed her wildest dreams. The emeralds sparkled at her throat and ears. Dev had sent a note to ask her to wear them. He had last minute business and would catch up with her in the ballroom.

"You're looking most spectacularly beautiful tonight, my dear."

She knew that voice by now. The unctuous roll of the r's told her Vaclav had arrived. She turned to find him just behind her. Over the fine white tie attire all the men had on, he wore a floor length cape with red silk lining.

It made him resemble a cross between an old-fashioned stage magician and Dracula.

She gave him a pleasant but not encouraging smile, which was a hell of a lot more than he deserved, the bastard. “This is quite a party.”

“Made all the more delightful by your presence.” His eyes traveled to her bosom and stayed there. “I hope I may have the pleasure of a dance with you.”

“I’m not much of a dancer, I’m afraid.”

“But the waltz.” He put his hand over his heart. “As they say in my country…”

At that, he launched into something Slavic that might have been random sounds for all she could recognize them.

“Well, as they say in my country,” she replied. “Don't count your chickens until they‘re hatched...”

He‘d never understand that, of course, but it might keep the silly lecher busy figuring it out while she made her escape. “You’ll pardon me.”

Without waiting to see what Vaclav would do with her gem of American wisdom, she put her glass on a waiter’s tray and walked away to lose herself in crowd of strangers. Different languages were flying everywhere. Occasionally, she’d catch a phrase in German, but otherwise, she was totally lost. With any luck, she’d find the Bürgermeister and they could trade a few more limericks.

“Ah, there you are, Miss Larson.” An older woman fell into step beside her and took her arm. “I did want to get to know you better, and we’ll all be leaving in a day or two.”

Felice searched her memory for a name and identity to put with this lady’s face. She was actually quite lovely, with the grey in her hair and the wrinkles at the corners of her eyes promoting her from merely beautiful to striking. She’d come in Vaclav’s party. Lady Martha, or no…Marta. Felice breathed an inner sigh of relief at remembering.

"I'm sorry you can't stay longer," she said, although the point was moot. She'd be leaving herself soon. But she would *not* think of that tonight.

"Has Vaclav made himself a complete pest yet?" Lady Marta asked.

"I'm not with him all the time, so he can't irritate me 24/7."

Lady Marta laughed. "You Americans have such colorful ways of putting things."

"Don't we though?"

"If Vaclav becomes too forward, do what I always do. Slap him."

"Hit him?"

"He loves drama more than anything," Lady Marta said. "It'll give him something to console himself with when he realizes he can't have his way with you."

"I'll bear that in mind." In reality, she'd keep away from him as best she could. She *didn't* love drama.

"So, have you enjoyed your stay in Danislova?" Lady Marta asked. "I hope you got to visit the countryside. We missed you at the monastery."

A pointed reference to the fact that she and Dev disappeared. Well, she didn't have to pick up on it. "And how were the good monks? In perfect health, I hope."

"The monks were fine. The brandy was fine. The accommodations were ghastly."

"I'm sorry."

Lady Marta stopped walking and turned to face Felice. "Oh dear. I'm being coy and making a mess of things."

Compared to the awkward conversations Vaclav created wherever he went, this one hardly qualified as a mess. But maybe if she held her tongue, Lady Marta would explain herself.

"VonRamsberg men. There's no one else quite like them in the world, and believe me, I've traveled and seen a good deal of what civilization has to offer."

"Lady Marta…"

"Please, don't say a word. I don't want to know any details." Lady Marta straightened a curl that didn't need straightening. "As much as I admire Friedrich, he's going to be difficult about you and his son."

Difficult? More like impossible, but that hardly mattered because Dev wouldn't defy his father. They were both dedicated to this country and would put personal considerations aside, no matter how much that might hurt. Surely, Lady Marta could see that.

"You must be even more determined than he is," Lady Marta went on. "Fight him. He'll respect that."

"I know you're trying to help, but I really can't discuss this." Especially not surrounded by a horde of strangers and near strangers.

"I wouldn't press you, but we might not have another chance to talk." Lady Marta took her hands and squeezed them. "I've come up against Friedrich's stubbornness. It's formidable, but I haven't given up, and you shouldn't, either."

"Lady Marta, I don't understand." What could she say? It all seemed so mysterious, and yet also important. "Your situation doesn't involve me."

"Doesn't it?" Lady Marta glanced across the room. Someone had just entered, and a murmur had gone up.

Felice turned in that direction and instantly understood. Dev had come in, and every woman in the room had taken note. How could they not?

Without doubt, he made the most magnificent image of a man she'd ever seen or could even imagine. He wore the dress uniform of an officer, complete with gold braid, epaulets, and medals decorating his chest. Finely tailored, it fit him perfectly, setting off the width of his shoulders and his narrow waist and hips. He stood tall and straight, a sword dangling at his side as his gaze swept the room and fell on her. His deep brown eyes glowed, and the flash of his smile made a contrast with his dark skin.

Lady Marta gave Felice's fingers one last squeeze. "Remember what I said."

"I will." Although the rest of the evening up to this point had fled the moment she'd set eyes on Dev. She'd known for some time that he was an honest-to-goodness prince. Now he was her fairy tale prince, as well. The answer to every woman's dream, and he was headed her way.

When he got to within a few feet of her, he stopped and stared the same way she was doing to him. The people around them might have thought it peculiar how they were standing there, not saying a word but simply taking in the sight of each other. Who could care about a thing like that at a time like this?

Finally, he closed the distance and bowed. "May I have the honor of this dance?"

"Is someone playing music?"

"An entire salon orchestra." He held out his hand. "Come on."

She let him lead her onto the dance floor and put his arm around her. There was, indeed, music. A waltz, thank heaven. She knew the steps to that. If she hadn't, she would have learned quickly because Dev made the perfect partner. With his fingers splayed at the small of her back, he held her firmly—close but not too close—and guided her as they rocked and turned in time with the tune. What had seemed like a riot of color now became a blur as they went around and around. It all left her a bit breathless, in no small part because of the man who held her in his arms.

"You wore the emeralds," he said.

"Of course."

"And my ring."

She hadn't taken it off since he'd given it to her, as he surely must have known. Maybe when she got home, she'd stash it away with other keepsakes that she could happen on again years later. Maybe then she'd smile when she found it and remembered this night. Until she left him, the ring would remain on her finger.

"You're absolutely stunning," he said.

"You stun pretty well your-own-self," she said. "Every woman here wants you."

The corner of his mouth went up in a smile. "You think so?"

"Didn't you hear the gasp when you entered the room?"

"I was too busy looking for you."

They danced for a bit without talking, swirling with more abandon. Dev somehow kept them from colliding with other couples, allowing her the freedom to fly within his embrace. Tonight, she'd replay every moment of this evening in her mind's eye until she'd memorized the taste of the champagne, the sound of the violins, and the feel of his uniform under her palm. After he'd fallen asleep beside her, no longer the prince but the human male her body had mated with, she'd make sure that she'd never, ever forget how she'd felt as the princess in the sapphire gown and the emeralds. She'd never forget everything he'd given her.

It had to end, though. Finally, the orchestra played the last strains of the waltz, and they all stopped dancing to applaud. Dev tucked her arm around his and led her from the dance floor. "Shall we find something to eat or drink?"

"If you say so."

"Toast points with wild mushrooms and cream, perhaps?" he said. "A mound of caviar or something equally exotic?"

"And to think I once thought you were a socially inept dork."

He bent his mouth toward her ear. "You thought I was a virgin, too."

"I don't think I'll ever live that down."

"In a way I was."

"You were what, big brother?" Ulrich had sidled up to them. He wore the same formal dress the other men had on. White tie and tailcoat. Trousers with a silk trim along the side of the leg. Lady Marta had been correct about VonRamsberg men. Ulrich made almost as splendid an example of maleness as Dev did. She could easily have fallen for him, with his blond good looks, if she hadn't met his brother first.

"I was a pest," Dev said. "Just like you're being now."

"I?" Ulrich managed to look wounded while still keeping a twinkle in his eye. "You're the one monopolizing the most beautiful woman in the room."

"And I intend to continue," Dev said. "Now why don't you go and find Miss Larson some food?"

Ulrich flagged down a passing waiter. "My good man, would you do us a favor and bring the lady a plate of the best from the buffet?"

"Very good, sir." The man bowed and moved off, presumably to find her something with a mound of caviar on top.

"There," Ulrich said. "You see how that's done?"

"Now, little brother, there must be a flock of women waiting for you," Dev said.

"They can wait." Ulrich touched her elbow. "Come on, Felice. Wouldn't you like to dance with a man who won't crush your toes?"

She had to laugh. The two of them were adorable. They didn't dislike each other in the least. Dev even trusted Ulrich enough to let him know when they'd dumped the others and headed off for their adventure in Vogelsheim. And wasn't it fun to have two such handsome men "fighting" over her?

"There, you see? Your smile means you want to dance with me," Ulrich declared. That only made her laugh harder.

"Done." Ulrich took her hand and guided her toward the dance floor.

"What about her food?" Dev called after them.

"You eat it," Ulrich answered over his shoulder.

Ulrich danced almost as well as his brother, and soon, she was enjoying herself again as they waltzed among the others.

"I'm glad Dev met you," Ulrich said. "He takes things far too seriously."

"That's his job, isn't it, as heir apparent?"

"He isn't the sovereign yet. He needs to have more fun."

"And you know all about fun,"

"I have one brother practicing to be a head of state and another at the UN." He grinned, all mischief and charm. "I live in Italy and study art."

"And eat good food and drink good wine."

"Always." He bent her over his arm in a dip and then pulled her back up. When she got her bearings, she discovered that a man had joined them and was tapping Ulrich's shoulder. Vaclav.

"The lady promised me this dance," Vaclav lied.

Before she could protest, Ulrich pulled her closer. "I'm sorry, dear cousin, but my bother ordered me to keep the lady to myself and return her to him directly."

"Could Danislova truly be so miserly?" Vaclav said. "Our countries have a long tradition of bosom friendship."

Again with the bosom—an interesting choice of words, given how much interest the man had in hers. The fellow was already puffing himself up, building to the sort of drama Lady Marta said he enjoyed.

"As Danislova's closest ally and brother-in-arms, I must insist," Vaclav said.

"You'd best take that up with Dev. He's standing right over there." Ulrich gestured with his chin to where Dev watched them from the side of the crowd.

"Nonsense. The lady will dance with me, won't she?" Vaclav said.

Oh for heaven's sake. The little creep was not going to give up until she let him put his paws on her. She touched Ulrich's arm. "It's not worth letting him make a scene."

Ulrich bowed and let Vaclav take his place. As Ulrich blended back into the crowd, Vaclav put his hand at her back, and they were off. Vaclav didn't actually slobber over her as she might have feared, but his fingers did tend to wander lower, toward her buttocks.

"Now then, my dear, we must arrange for your visit to my country," he said.

"I'm afraid I won't have time. I'll be returning to the United States in a few days."

She'd honestly surprised him with that news if she could read the rise of his eyebrows correctly.

"So soon?" he said. "Surely, you could find a few weeks for us."

"I have an education to pursue. I've already taken too much time off."

"But I had thought…you were intent on staying here."

"You thought wrong."

"Ahhh," Vaclav said. The syllable held some meaning to him she'd probably be better off not pursuing. His hand snuck downward to the entirely wrong place, and she reached behind to move it back up.

"Do you mean to say that Cousin Christian's charms have faded?" he said.

"It means I have a life on the other side of the Atlantic." He'd probably like to pursue the invitation in that note now that he thought she'd rejected Dev. She could reject every other man in the world, and she still wouldn't want this one. But she wasn't going to dignify that atrocity in her cosmetics case by pretending it even existed. If he wanted to bring it up, he'd have to admit that he'd put it there.

He didn't do that, but he tried to pull her closer again, and this time her breasts nearly brushed his chest. She pushed him away with enough force to tell him to cut the crap out. At least, she hoped so. You couldn't tell for sure what penetrated that thick skull.

Finally, Dev showed up at Vaclav's elbow. Though you couldn't call the expression on his face rage or fury, it sure qualified as determination. And he was wearing a sword.

"I'll take over from here," he said as he nudged Vaclav aside.

"Do save me another dance later on," Vaclav said more or less over Dev's shoulder, or more like around it. Dev had blocked him out pretty well.

"I'll put you on my dance card," she said.

"You don't have a dance card," Dev said as he moved them away to renew the waltz.

"Gee, do you think he noticed?"

"I never understood before why my father disliked him so intensely," Dev said. "If he behaved this way with my mother, it's a wonder he's still alive."

"I suppose you could still kill him. Is that sword real?"

"Don't tempt me."

They danced until the song ended, undisturbed by small, insignificant lechers. Dev held her close, but she would have preferred to crawl further into his arms. The evening was a dream, and if she could work magic to make it last forever, she would. When the last strains of the waltz faded, they turned to face the orchestra and applaud. Dev stopped with his hands still together, and his expression fell from a smile to surprise and not of the pleasant kind.

"I don't believe it," he said. "Astrid."

She followed his gaze and discovered that he was staring at a young woman who stood beside his father. Even Friedrich seemed stunned at her presence, worry creasing his forehead. Grigori stood on her other side, and his expression was even grimmer.

"I *am* going to kill him," Dev said softly.

"Your father?"

"Vaclav," he said. "I'm sorry. Please forgive me."

With that, he walked off in the direction of his father and the woman. Astrid.

She was a perfect, little jewel of a woman, the sort who'd made Felice feel like a big clod in high school. Her jet black hair hung in thick curls down her back, creating a stark contrast to the pale skin of her arms. Blue eyes filled much of her face, and her mouth took up the rest that a button nose didn't. She wore a gown of crimson satin that hugged her slender body, and she stared up at Dev as if he were the sun, the moon, and the stars. In return, Dev kissed her fingers, but he seemed to be staring right through her.

A man came up beside her. Kurt touched her elbow and stood there in silence.

"Who is she?" Felice whispered.

"Astrid delaCroix," he answered. "Dev's betrothed."

Of course. Certainly, no other woman would take Dev from her side, and no other woman would stand between Dev and Friedrich as if she owned the two of them. All feeling left Felice's body, as though she was suddenly full of cotton balls. No, one sensation remained—cold that sank deep into her bones.

"Is she a terrible shrew? Maybe a gold-digger? Shallow and silly?"

"She's a lovely person. You'd like each other."

"That figures." So, she had no real reason to hate the woman, although if she tried, she could manage pretty well.

"Can I get you some champagne?" Kurt asked. "Or perhaps some brandy."

"Nothing. Just take me to a chair." As Kurt took her arm and led her away, she did her best to keep her feet moving. If he hadn't been there, she would have fallen into a heap.

This was the moment she'd never scrub from her memory. The relationship, love, arrangement…whatever she had with Dev…ended right now.

*

He'd never make love to Felice again. Dev's fiancée had just surprised him with another woman in his arms, and he could only concentrate on the fact that he'd never make love to that other woman again. Worse, Astrid clearly knew what was going on in his mind. Perhaps not the details. Please, not the details. But she'd recognized their situation instantly, and now she stood in a side parlor—empty of people except for the two of them, thank heaven—and stared out a window into the dark.

"We weren't expecting you," he said.

"Obviously," she said to the panes of glass.

"What prompted you to come?"

"A note from Vaclav."

Damn the man. Bad enough that he'd schemed to get Felice into his bed. He'd dragged Astrid into his plans, too, even though he'd known it would hurt her. There had to be some way to teach the man a lesson.

"That's an excuse. I would have come eventually." Astrid turned and leaned against the windowsill. "You two have been in the papers."

"I've been in the tabloids before."

"It's different this time. The new pictures are…" She gestured as if trying to snatch words out of the air. "They're full of feeling somehow. The two of you radiate intimacy."

"How could we radiate anything in pictures taken through crowds in a matter of seconds?" He did his best to conjure up what she might have seen. The photographers had caught them at the airport just after they'd first arrived. He and Felice hadn't truly been in love with each other then, or at least, they hadn't realized it. However they had *made* love a few hours earlier, and Felice had given him the condom in the jewel box. He certainly could have appeared charmed by her and the gesture.

Then, they'd been caught leaving the jewelry shop. He'd bought her the emeralds…and the ring. He'd loved her when he'd purchased that for her.

"You're not trying to deny it, then," Astrid said.

Say something. You have to say something, and fast. But nothing came to him that wouldn't make him sound like the cad and bastard he truly was. He couldn't dishonor both women by denying his love for Felice. And yet, he couldn't confess it and hurt Astrid with the details. Nor would he discuss his and Felice's relationship with another person.

In the end, he settled for the simple truth. "Nothing has changed between you and me."

Her mouth dropped open. "How can you say that?"

"Because it hasn't. Felice is leaving in a few days. You and I will be married as we planned," he said. "In fact, it's time we set a date."

"I don't believe you." She lifted her arm and pointed in the general direction of the ballroom. "You'd discuss our wedding when the woman you love is only feet away?"

"It doesn't matter." Damn, but it did. He'd never make love with Felice again, and that mattered very, very much.

"I'd say the fact that the man I'm marrying is in love with someone else is rather important."

"Nothing has changed, I tell you." Wonderful. Now he was shouting at Astrid. She hadn't created this mess.

She stood like a statue, staring at him, part confusion and part hurt.

"Ours was never a love match," he said. "There was always a possibility this could happen. You might have fallen in love instead of me."

"If I had, I would have told you about it. You wouldn't have had to see it in the papers and then be summoned by a relative to confirm the truth."

"Vaclav. He needs to pay for this."

"If I'd fallen in love. I would have asked to be released so you could find someone who could devote herself to you."

"I can still devote myself to you."

He reached for her, but she pulled away, wrapping her arms around herself in a defensive gesture.

"I can, Astrid. I swear it to you."

"You'd try," she said. "You're a good man."

He could have laughed at that last statement if the situation weren't so miserable. He'd taken up with another woman, established the sort of relationship that would normally lead to marriage and children until death did them part, and now the woman he should have done all that with called him a good man. He'd betrayed his fiancée, his father, and his duty, and God help him, he'd walk away from all of them if he had any choice. Instead, Felice would go away in a day or two, and he'd never make love to her again. He couldn't with Astrid staying under the same roof.

"You're not going to get over her, are you?" Astrid asked softly.

"Of course, I will. People can get over anything." With those words, he'd betrayed Felice, perhaps even more deeply than anything he'd done to Astrid. He'd denied his love for her, made it sound trivial when it was the most profound emotion he'd ever felt. He deserved every bit of the misery cutting through him now.

"We'll be married the same way my parents were," he said. "We'll have children, and they'll bring us closer together. We'll be happy."

All the things he'd told himself over the years when he'd contemplated marrying someone he didn't love. How hollow they sounded now.

"I don't think so." Astrid continued hugging herself as if she'd fly apart if she let go. "I don't think I want that kind of marriage."

"For the love of God, what kind of marriage did you think you were going to get?"

She recoiled, taking a step back, and no wonder. Until this evening he'd never raised his voice to her. He'd never had any reason to.

"Please." He spread his arms. "Please come to me and don't look like that."

"Like what?"

"I don't know. As if you're going to cry."

"I'm not." She was biting her lip, and her blue eyes had misted over.

"Please," he repeated.

Finally, she stepped into his arms, and he held her while she trembled like a trapped bird.

"I always hoped you'd come to love me," she said against his shoulder.

"I can. I will."

"The way you love her."

He didn't say anything to that. He wouldn't lie to her. They would come to love each other, but not with the same passion he shared with Felice.

"We'll make things work," he said as he rubbed her back. "I promise you. I'll be the best husband in the world. You'll see."

At that, she did begin to cry. Softly, her shoulders shaking. He could have run himself through with his own sword, but that would spare him the punishment of living without Felice. He deserved that and more for hurting both women.

No, he'd keep his promise. He'd marry Astrid, and he'd make her happy. He'd had his happiness, and look at where it had gotten them all.

CHAPTER ELEVEN

Dev caught the little bastard a few mornings after the ball. He had to wait a long time in the corridor outside Vaclav's suite to do it because the man always needed his beauty sleep. But somehow Dev found the patience when he'd rather have pounded Vaclav's face into a pulp before Vaclav had awakened. Vaclav was his elder and the ruler of his own country, so Dev mustered what little respect he could for the worm and would simply issue some threats and watch him squirm.

The minute Sleeping Beauty stuck his nose out his door, Dev caught him by the back of his collar, yanked him up, and stared him in the eyes. So much for respect.

"We have something to discuss."

"My dear cousin Christian." Vaclav tried to pull himself free, but Dev hung on as he charged down the corridor to his own rooms, dragging Vaclav along with him.

"What are you doing?" Vaclav said. "I demand that you release me."

"You demand nothing until we get a few things straightened out." They arrived at Dev's suite, and Dev opened the door and shoved Vaclav into his sitting room. He released his dear cousin long enough to slam the door and then turned on him.

"Okay, pal, your fun and games are over." Odd how Americanisms came in handy on occasions like this. Probably because of the violence of their films and television shows. If he knew any gangsta, he could throw that in, too. And they'd stick to English, which would put Vaclav at a further disadvantage.

"Fun? Games?" Vaclav straightened his clothing and tried to look offended. "I don't know what you mean."

"You've been putting the moves on Miss Larson, and I don't like it." He bent to stick his nose in Vaclav's face. "In fact, I'm ending it right now."

"Just an innocent dance." Vaclav gave him a phony smile.

"You had your hand all over her butt."

"It meant nothing. She wasn't harmed. And the note—just a joke."

"Note?" Dev said.

"No note." Vaclav let out a string of ha-has that he probably meant to sound like a laugh. "None at all. Ha-ha."

"Tell me about the note, or I'll wrap my fingers around your throat and force it out of you."

"So violent. This isn't like you. You were always the good son. Obedient. Dignified."

"Note!" Dev bellowed.

"Nothing. I slipped it in her case before we went to the country. Just a joke. Nothing at all. Ha-ha."

"What…did…it…say?"

"It said how much I admired her," Vaclav said.

"And…"

"And how I'd enjoy a…what shall I call it...a private interview. A few moments."

A few moments to put his hands all over Felice and follow that up with something worse. Bastard.

"And…" Dev prompted.

"And that you were engaged and couldn't marry her." Vaclav stood a little straighter and stared back at Dev. "That was all true."

"And you didn't care if you hurt her?"

"Is it I who hurt her?" Vaclav said.

That set Dev back as he'd thrown the same accusation at himself over and over through the past sleepless nights. Still, this was none of Vaclav's business, and he'd made things worse with his meddling.

Felice must have found the note while they were in Vogelsheim and said nothing. It had to have clouded all the joy they had there. She hadn't shared the knowledge with him but had kept the sadness to herself. The image of the two of them sitting on that bench feeding the love knot to the birds crowded back on him. No wonder she'd seemed tearful as they'd left Vogelsheim. She'd been focused on the fact that she'd never go back.

"When that didn't get you what you wanted, you wrote to Astrid," he said.

"She needed to know what her fiancé was doing." By now, Vaclav had recovered sufficiently to summon up some moral outrage. "She had that right."

"Maybe, but you had to rub her nose in it," Dev said. "She hadn't done anything wrong."

"I knew you would fix things with her. You have, haven't you?"

He had, more or less. He'd reassured her that their plans hadn't changed. He'd even set a date to set a date—a time in the near future when things had settled down for their families to get together to make plans. And he'd hardly had a glimpse of Felice since the ball. They ate dinner at the long table, seated as far as possible from each other, thanks to his father. The rest of the day she disappeared. He'd gone back to sleeping in his own room. Here, as a matter of fact.

"There, you see?" Vaclav declared. "Miss Larson is no longer your concern."

"She is as long as she's a guest in my father's palace, and you'll treat her with respect."

"Of course, I respect her. She's a beautiful woman. I'm a connoisseur. What can I say?"

Dev grabbed him by the collar and shoved him up against the door. "You can say good-bye to the next hand you put on her because you'll lose it to my sword. And don't manhandle any other woman, either."

Vaclav's eyes widened. "My poor dear Christian—"

"And cut the 'dear' crap. I'm not your dear anything."

"You've lost your mind. Such threats. Your father never behaved like this."

"You mean when you tried to seduce his wife, my mother?"

"What?" Vaclav squeaked. "Who could have told you such a thing? I would never…"

"Listen up. My father's European. Civilized. I, on the other hand, have lived in America and know American ways, and I'm not bringing a knife to a gunfight."

"Guns?" Vaclav waved his hands around. "The Lord deliver us. Guns!"

"Guns. Big ones. Everyone in the United States has one, and I have…" What? What did Americans call their guns? "A Glock, and an Uzi."

"Uzi?" All the color drained out of Vaclav's face.

"It'll blow a hole in your head the size of a baseball."

"Please, no. No guns. I'm just a humble soul. I've learned my lesson."

Heaven only knew how long that lesson would stick, but it might take for long enough to get Felice away safely.

"So, just remember, whenever you see me I might be packing heat." Did they say "packing heat" anymore, or was that from one of the old movies? Well, if he didn't know that, Vaclav wouldn't have any clue.

"Very well." Vaclav held his hands up in a gesture that was half surrender and half warding Dev off. "No more fun and games, as you put it. In fact, I think it's time we returned to Rosnia. I have business to attend to. Very pressing matters. Yes, we'll be leaving. Today. Good-bye to you, dear cousin."

That concluded, Vaclav let himself out, and Dev allowed him to leave. The patter of his footsteps down the hallway told Dev he was running.

*

The bed was too damned big without Dev in it. No matter how Felice turned and twisted, she couldn't get comfortable. They'd been shoved together in the room in Vogelsheim, and she'd slept like a baby. Without Dev's head on the pillow next to hers and his arms around her, she couldn't cast off a chill.

She rolled over, clutching his pillow to her chest. A few more hours, and she could go home. She only had to hold herself together that long, and she'd be back in her apartment where she could scream and cry and kick things until she got her head screwed back on straight. The cat could listen to it all. She could soak Sneakers in tears, but she'd start to mend. As soon as breathing no longer hurt, she'd get back to school. She'd select a committee and schedule her orals, and that would put everything else on the back burner for months.

It was a great plan. One that would work. She only had to find a way to walk away from this palace and this country, a place she'd come to love as if she'd been born here. How absolutely bleak to set foot on that jet, knowing that she'd never see Danislova again. And worse, that if she ever did lay eyes on Dev in the future, it would be in newspapers or maybe a broadcast of a royal wedding.

God, this was going to absolutely rip her apart. But she'd do it because she had to, and then, she'd come out on the other side. What didn't kill you made you stronger, right?

Groaning, she turned on the bedside lamp and glanced at the clock. Only half-past one—long hours to pass before she could get up, have a quick breakfast, and leave. If Kurt wasn't ready, she could hide as she'd been doing. A palace with gardens and a forest around it made a great place to avoid the man you loved and his fiancée. If she took a book, she could stay away from everyone. If she had a book right now, she could read until she fell asleep.

She got up, slipped on her robe, and went barefoot to explore the palace much as she had on her first night here. That night Friedrich had surprised her in the dining hall. Tonight, she'd head toward the music room down the other hallway. She'd noticed some bookshelves there. One might hold something interesting to read.

She navigated the hallway easily enough and let herself down the formal staircase. Again, she marveled at the beauty of the palace. The daytime held too many distractions to notice the highly polished woods and oriental carpets. Alone, she could re-enter the fairy tale she'd lived since arriving here, if only for a few moments.

She turned and headed down the hallway toward the music room and found light spilling from the inside. Had the staff left a lamp on, or was someone in there? She tiptoed up to the doorway and peeked inside. Friedrich stood with his back toward her, damn it, so she retreated.

"Come in," he called.

He couldn't have heard her. She hadn't made any noise in her bare feet.

"I know you're out there," he said. "I can hear you breathing."

She walked to the threshold. "I don't see how."

He turned and spotted her but didn't appear the least surprised. "All the men in my family have heightened senses. They kept us alive in past times."

"What are you doing here? I thought you'd be in your library." If anywhere. He should have been in bed, as she should.

"I was, but someone took my brandy. I thought to find some in here." He turned away from her and opened a cabinet. "Eureka."

"Maybe you're not supposed to be drinking it."

"Bah. Don't tell me you're going to start acting like my sons."

She wasn't going to start acting like anything but out of here, so she didn't say anything but watched him remove a decanter from the cabinet and hold it up for her to see. "Come in, come in. We'll share some."

She entered the room, aware of her bare feet and night clothes. Friedrich also wore a robe and pajamas, but his looked more formal, as if someone pressed them. His pants did have a crease, so they'd obviously seen an iron, while her night gown was rumpled.

Friedrich set the decanter of brandy on top of the grand piano and pulled out the stopper. "See if you can find some glasses."

"Sure." A high shelf in the same cabinet held rows of glassware. She selected two snifters and took them to Friedrich. The whole thing took her back to a night in her early childhood when she'd crept downstairs to find her father having a snack in the kitchen. He'd set her a place, made her a peanut butter and jelly sandwich and poured her a glass of milk. It had been their secret because her mother disapproved of eating after bedtime, and the experience had stuck with her like something from the kind of dream that made you wake up smiling.

It had never happened again, but now, she was repeating it with a near stranger half a world away. No, not a stranger. She'd be leaving two men she cared about behind.

Friedrich handed her a snifter with more than a splash of brandy in it. "Perhaps we won't be interrupted this time, and you can tell me what you think of my monks' handiwork."

She took a sip. "As delicious as I remember it."

"Let's sit down and spend a few minutes together."

Most of the chairs were straight-backed and arranged for a recital, but in the corner stood a pair of armchairs with a low table between them. Friedrich lowered himself into one and groaned with pleasure. She took the other seat and dug her toes into the plush carpet.

They sat in silence for long moments, and that felt as good as the giggles over the PB&J had. The brandy was fine, the setting splendid, and the man across from her stern and yet very dear.

After a minute, he cleared his throat. "I'm very sorry for what my family has done to you."

"You mean opened your home to me, treated me like a princess, and dressed me like one?"

"Let's not try to keep secrets from each other," he said. "I know that you and my son are in love."

"Yes, well." Stupid, empty words, but nothing else came to mind that wouldn't make her cry. She'd managed to avoid that, at least most of the time. So she stared at her brandy and drew a finger around the edge of the glass.

"I want you to know that under other circumstances, I'd be honored to have you as a daughter," Friedrich said. "Things would be different with Kurt or Ulrich."

"Is one of them available?"

"Please, Felice. This isn't a joking matter."

Her head snapped up at the sound of her name. He'd never used it, but only "Miss Larson" or "my dear." She'd never called him anything other than "Your Majesty."

"This all brings such…" His voice trailed off, and he looked away, as if not seeing the room around them. "…memories."

She'd shut up for whatever followed, and she sure as hell wasn't going to use any wisecracks. She sat, holding her breath and waiting for him to continue.

"I'll tell you something I've never told my sons," he said. "My wife knew, of course."

"I won't repeat it. I promise."

He leaned over the table and patted her hand. "I know you won't."

He took a drink of his brandy and then lifted his glass to stare at the amber liquid for a moment. "I was in love once. Twice, of course, counting my wife, Cecile. I did adore her. Truly."

"I'm sure you did."

"But there was another woman before. The same as you and Christian. I knew there was no future in it, but I became involved so quickly, I hardly felt it happening. Until it was too late."

"That's what happened with us."

"Once you're in love like that, you'll do anything to keep the other person with you, right up until the very last minute," he said.

"And the longer you stay together, the more deeply you become involved," she said.

He squeezed his eyes shut in an expression that looked like pain for a second or two and then opened them again. "I watched it happening with you two. I should have done something."

"I don't know what you could have done." She'd probably fallen for Dev when he'd made such beautiful love to her on the plane. Maybe earlier. Who saved condoms in a jewel box, for pity's sake?

"I have to thank you for ending things," Friedrich said. "If my son feels the same way I did, he probably couldn't have found the strength."

"How did you?"

"My parents died, and everything became chaos. I was Prince Royal and had to return to the palace," he said. "I married my betrothed. I had to go through all that and my grief for my mother and father without the woman I loved."

How terrible that must have been. She couldn't imagine enduring something like that, and he thought her strong. How she'd love to touch him—his face, his hand, or just his arm. But she didn't have permission, really, so she clutched her snifter tightly.

"Eventually, things settled out, and since then, I've been the most fortunate man alive."

"That'll happen for Dev. He will be happy, won't he?" There wouldn't be any point of ending their relationship if marrying Astrid would ruin his life. "Your wife worshipped you, didn't she?"

"Not at first. She was a virgin and terrified. When she finally relaxed enough to…" He cleared his throat. "…enjoy being married, we got along. And then my son was born."

"Yes," she said. "That would bring you together."

"It's a soul jarring experience to hold your child for the first time. You'll find out."

"Astrid can give Dev his children." God, it hurt to say that, no matter how true.

He took some more of his brandy and then rocked the snifter back and forth, making the liquid film the inside of the glass. "She's a sweet girl. They'll get on well together."

"Then, that's how things should be." Felice brought her glass to her lips and finished her brandy, tipping her head back to get the last drops. It was very, very good. Maybe it would help her sleep.

"I hope you can forgive the ramblings of a selfish old man."

To hell with permission. She leaned over and put her hand on his arm. "How selfish?"

"To tell you my story so you'll agree to accept what's happening to you," he said.

"I do accept it." *No, I don't, damn it*. "I always knew I'd have to leave."

He covered her fingers with his. "I'd very much like for you to come back when…you're up to it. You're always welcome to consider this your home."

"Thank you." She would not cry. Would. Not.

He lifted her fingers to his lips. "You should be in bed."

"What about you?"

"I'll go along in a few minutes," he said.

She set her glass on the table and rose. "No more brandy."

He hmphed. "No more brandy."

"Good night." Before her common sense stopped her, she bent and placed a kiss on his forehead and then left. One last time she turned to look at him where he sat in his chair staring off into space.

*

He'd done the right thing. Every cell in Friedrich's body told him he'd had no choice. His family and Astrid's had political and business alliances for generations. She was the perfect match for his son. They'd make each other happy. What else did he need to know?

So, why was he standing outside Felice Larson's suite of rooms, imagining he could hear her cry inside? It had to be a trick of his senses. The sound of a woman's misery couldn't carry all the way out here through two rooms and two closed doors.

He'd done the right thing.

In his own life, he'd suffered the loss of his mother and father and Pamela all in one day, but he'd recovered. He'd thought about Pamela over the years. So many times remembering the feel of her in his arms. But he'd moved past that. There had been Cecile and Danislova and his duty to consider. Always his duty.

He'd loved his wife, his children, his people. He'd had the honor of serving his country by leading it and the privilege to live in this palace built by his ancestors. Christian would have all that, and he'd feel as blessed as he, Friedrich, had felt. He'd done the right thing, damn it.

So why couldn't he get the image of Pamela on that last day out of his mind? She'd been so brave, holding back her tears as the car waited for him out on the street below her apartment—the place where they'd spent so many hours in each other's embrace. She'd told him that he had to leave, that there were more important things at stake than their happiness. She'd said that she'd always love him and begged him not to forget her.

Forget her? Ha! He could still remember the spill of golden curls that framed her face, the cashmere dress that clung to her body, the way she'd clutched a handkerchief in her fist, squeezing it, releasing it, and squeezing it again. He should have been her comfort. Instead, he was breaking her heart, and she was telling him to do the right thing. And he'd never seen her again after that day.

Maybe if Felice had tried to cling to Christian, he could have dismissed her as overly emotional and not understanding what was involved here. He could paint her in his mind as selfish, perhaps even a manipulator after money and status. But no. She was brave as Pamela had been.

Oh God, was she crying? Had he heard something, or was his mind fooling him? He lifted his hand to knock and thought better of it. He might wake her now that she'd finally fallen asleep. If she was awake, what comfort could he give her? Nothing but platitudes and empty assurances that this would pass. Better to leave her alone.

He took a step away and nudged something with his foot. It turned out to be a cellular phone, and he bent to pick it up. The device didn't resemble the ones his sons or Grigori carried. It probably belonged to Felice, and she'd dropped it here.

Friedrich knew enough about these phones to open it and check the contacts. There was the name of the academic advisor she shared with Christian, some women's names, most likely friends, and one entry "dad." That gave him an idea. Maybe he could do something to help her, after all.

Friedrich made his way to his own suite, let himself into his sitting room, and turned on a lamp. After sitting down at his writing table, he pressed the button for "dad" and waited for the call to go through to South America.

"Hi, sweetie," a male voice answered. "What's up? It's kind of late for you to be calling."

He hadn't stopped to figure the time difference. Who cared about that? "Professor Larson?"

"Hey, who is this? Why do you have my daughter's phone?"

"This is Friedrich, Prince Royal of Danislova. Your daughter is a guest in my home."

“Yeah, she told me about that. Is she okay? Why are you calling instead of her? Has something happened to her?”

“She’s fine.” A bit of a lie there, but they’d get to that as soon as her father calmed down. “Please don’t worry.”

At the other end, Larson took a breath. “As long as she’s all right.”

“I found her cell phone and thought you and I should talk.”

“Now? It’s ten o’clock here. Her mother and I have a big day tomorrow.”

“I regret that,” Friedrich said. “But this was my first opportunity.”

“Go ahead and talk then.” Larson yawned.

“I’m afraid my son and I have hurt your daughter,” Friedrich said. “Rather badly.”

“Hurt? How? What do you mean by hurt?”

“She and my son became involved.” *Tell the truth, curse you.* “They fell in love.”

“What’s wrong with that? Isn’t my little girl good enough for you?”

“Please don’t misunderstand.” How did you explain royal obligations to an American? “Felice is a wonderful young woman, but my son is the Crown Prince. His marriage was arranged long ago.”

“Marriage, huh? That serious?”

Of course that serious, you idiot. He didn’t say it, though. That wouldn’t get them anywhere. “My son and your daughter fell in love, and now they have to part, and they’re both very hurt.”

“Yeah, that’s bad.”

“Thank you for not being angry with me,” Friedrich said.

“No point getting mad,” Larson said. “These things happen.”

"She needs her parents with her now. She needs her father."

Nothing came from the other end of the line but silence. Friedrich waited as long as his patience would allow.

"Did you hear me?" he asked finally.

"Sure. It's just…I don't see how that can happen. We're in Peru on an important dig."

"I'll send a plane for you. Tell me which is the closest airport."

"You don't understand. I'm on a grant and have to stay to finish the work."

"Your wife, then," Friedrich said.

"She's the other lead investigator."

The realization began to dawn. Neither of them were going to do anything to help their daughter. He'd feared they didn't much value their roles as parents, but he hadn't thought they'd leave her to deal with something like this all alone.

"You might at least meet her in the United States. Surely, one of you can cut short your expedition," Friedrich said.

That won him silence and finally a frustrated sigh from the other end. God help him, if he could crawl through the lines or bounce off the satellite or whatever made these phones work, he'd throttle the man on the other end. Had he no idea how it felt to lose someone you dearly loved? Had he no conception of his responsibilities as a parent?

"I guess we could juggle a few things around," Larson said finally. "It'd take some doing, and I'm not sure how soon one of us could get away."

"Then do it," Friedrich ordered. "Your daughter needs you."

"Tell you what. Have her give me a call. She and her mother and I can work things out."

Friedrich held the phone away from his face and scowled at it for a moment before putting it back to his ear. "I'll do that."

"Felice is a resilient kid," Larson said. "She'll get through this."

For a moment, Friedrich contemplated lecturing the fool on the difference between childhood crushes and the sort of bond their children had formed. But honestly, he'd already wasted his breath on this conversation, and the hour was growing ridiculously late.

"Very well, Professor Larson. Handle things your way, but handle them."

With nothing else to say and nothing further he wanted to hear, he cut off the connection. He sat for a while, clutching the phone. After a bit, he set it on the desk so he wouldn't throw it at the wall.

This wouldn't do. Not for a minute. He had no solution to the problem, but he knew in his bones that he wouldn't let this stand.

CHAPTER TWELVE

She couldn't find her damned cell phone. Felice stood in the entryway of Friedrich's palace, surrounded by an army of suitcases—all holding the clothing Greta had packed for her. She was ready to go. She'd steeled herself for this moment, and until a few minutes ago, she'd held herself together pretty well, and now she had to wait while the staff searched for her stupid cell phone.

"Why don't we leave without it?" she said to Kurt, who'd stood beside her since she'd descended the stairs to find all of this…stuff...waiting to tag along with her to the United States.

"There's no rush," he said. "The plane won't leave without us."

"I don't need all of this," she said, gesturing to the suitcases. "Why did Greta pack it all?"

"My father will want you to have it."

She wouldn't have a limit to her luggage on a private jet, but she'd have to figure out a way to get it from the airport to her apartment. Even if Kurt had arranged for a car, she'd still have to unpack it all, and each piece would only bring up a painful memory of her time here.

Maybe she could stack it, unopened, in her closet. Or get a storage locker somewhere.

"Are you sure you don't want to say good-bye to my father?" Kurt asked.

"I did say good-bye to him." That conversation over brandy and the kiss she'd planted on his forehead would serve as a farewell.

"And my brother?" Kurt added softly.

She didn't answer, but bit her lip to keep it from quivering. Dev was the absolute last person in the world she wanted to see right now. If she did, she'd probably end up bawling and creeping into his arms to make a fool of herself.

"As you wish." Kurt touched her elbow. "I'll call for our car. We'll wait a few more minutes and then leave."

She nodded, and he went outside, leaving her to hold her breath until she could get the hell out of here.

Only fate didn't seem to have planned a simple exit. Another servant appeared with more luggage. Surely, that couldn't be hers, too.

No, Astrid came down the staircase. The woman who would end up marrying Dev. Could this day get any better?

Astrid glanced around as though she hadn't expected to encounter anyone else. She looked up at Felice. "You're leaving?"

"Well, yeah."

"Not because of me, I hope."

Surely, she didn't have to explain things to Astrid. The woman couldn't be that dense.

"It is rather awkward having us both here," she said.

"You needn't worry about that. I'm not staying," Astrid said.

Of course, the extra luggage would belong to Astrid, who wore a pants suit—very elegant but comfortable for travel. They stood and stared at each other for long moments, and then Astrid lifted her fingers to her mouth and her eyes grew damp.

After a moment, Astrid swiped at her eyes and lifted her chin. “I’m not coming back.”

“But you and Dev…that is…Prince Christian.”

“You don’t have to pretend with me. I know about your relationship.”

“Our relationship doesn’t matter.” Felice did what she could to stiffen her spine in resolve. “The two of you will be married.”

“No.” Astrid said the word with enough force to make it a command. “He doesn’t love me, and I won’t marry a man who doesn’t.”

“Tradition—”

“Hang tradition. I would think that an American, of all people, would understand that marriage without love is unacceptable.”

“Astrid, whether you marry Dev or not, I still have to leave. Friedrich will only find someone else for him.”

“Don’t you let him.” Astrid closed the distance between them, took Felice by the elbows, and squeezed. For such a small woman, she had a lot of strength.

“I’m not stepping out of his life just so Friedrich can make another huge mistake,” Astrid said. “I’ve done my best to make the old man see reality. You finish the job.”

“You told him?”

“Of course, I told him I wouldn’t be marrying his son.” Astrid dropped her hands to her sides. “I didn’t tell Dev, though. His father can do that.”

Of course. Astrid wouldn’t have had the strength to face Dev, any more than Felice did. Both of them were cowards in that regard, it seemed, but at least Astrid had the backbone to stand up for what she wanted.

“I’m sorry,” Felice said. What weak, pointless words. “I never meant to hurt anyone.”

"Nor did I," Astrid said. "I wish we'd met under better circumstances."

Felice touched Astrid's hand. "Me, too."

A man in livery appeared at the palace entrance. "Your car is ready, My Lady."

"Thank you, Dieter." Astrid left, her chin high and her back straight. The man gathered up Astrid's luggage and followed.

Well, great. Other people could get out of this blessed palace easily enough. Why couldn't she? She'd give the staff two more minutes to appear with her cell phone, and then she'd go off herself to see what had happened to their car.

"What in bloody hell?"

Catastrophe. It was Dev's voice, as if she'd ever in her life forget the sound of it. He came bounding down the stairs, his shirt hanging open and half his face covered with shaving cream. Kicking aside suitcases, he charged to her and grabbed her shoulders.

"You'd leave me without so much as a word?" he shouted.

"Please, keep your voice down."

"I'll be as loud as I want," he said. "You owe me an explanation."

"Dev, I can't…" She stopped before her voice broke. Did he have to be so damned handsome with his broad shoulders, dark skin, and huge brown eyes? Did he have to stand there with his chest exposed, exactly as she'd watched him shave so many times now? Did he have to keep his hands on her shoulders as if he'd pull her into his embrace?

"I wouldn't have known if Kurt hadn't told me, and then you would have gone," he said. "For the love of God, Felice, would you really have left me?"

"I am leaving you, damn it," she shouted back as the tears started. "I can't stay. You know I can't."

"You're wrong. I worked it all out in my head last night when I couldn't sleep." He ran his fingers through his hair in much the same way he had when he'd pretended to be a dork. That gesture and the redness in his eyes said that he hadn't gotten much more rest the night before than she had. In fact, he looked a bit wild.

"This is the twenty-first century, and I don't have to marry someone because of her pedigree or because my father arranged it."

"Friedrich would never agree—"

"He has to, or I won't marry anyone, and Kurt or Ulrich will have to give him an heir." He paused, and his gaze bore into hers. "Better yet, I'll abdicate."

"Now you're being ridiculous."

"Not at all. Kurt would make a fine Prince Royal."

She put her hands on either side of his face, and one got a fistful of shaving cream for her trouble. "Think of what you're saying."

"I have thought about it. Marry me, Felice. We'll deal with Friedrich together."

"But what would you do? You've dedicated your life to assuming the throne."

"I don't know. I'd..." He stuttered to a stop. He hadn't figured everything out. This whole fine speech was built on impulse and nothing more.

"We'll move to Vogelsheim," he declared finally. "I'll make cheese."

"Cheese? For heaven's sake, listen to yourself." Hopeless. He was obviously drunk on lack of sleep and not dealing with a full deck.

"Frau Baumgarten told me to marry you."

"She didn't want me to make you into the village cheesemeister."

"Marry me, Felice." He wrapped his arms around her and pulled her against his chest. She was probably getting shaving cream in her hair now, but how could she care about that now that Dev was holding her?

"Don't leave me, Felice," he murmured. "I need you."

"Damn you, I'm trying to be noble." The tears started again, and this time, she wouldn't be able to stop them. She pounded her fist against his chest, but it came off as little more than a love tap.

"Don't be noble. Just love me."

Her voice would never have worked, so she nodded into his chest.

"Well, isn't this a fine state of affairs?" another voice boomed into the entryway, this time from the direction of Friedrich's study. Felice's stomach sank even further, although a moment ago she wouldn't have thought that possible. She pushed out of Dev's embrace and turned to find the Prince Royal glowering at them. The lethal stare in his eyes would have done a bird of prey proud.

"That Kurt gets around," she said. "Did he send for you, too?"

"He didn't have to," Friedrich said. "I could hear you two all over the palace."

"I'll deal with you later, old man," Dev said. "Can't you see Felice is upset?"

"Maybe if you stopped shouting at her, she'd calm down," Friedrich hollered.

"You're a fine one to talk," Dev hollered back.

"Enough of this nonsense. Wilson," Friedrich bellowed. "Wilson!"

The butler appeared, wearing a look of abject horror, which was quite an accomplishment for a man who hardly ever moved a facial muscle. "Your Majesty."

"Have Miss Larson's things taken back to her room," Friedrich ordered. "Tell Greta to unpack them."

"You can't." Felice's knees threatened to buckle. She'd gone through all this, had hardly slept five minutes and had almost made her escape, and now Friedrich would ruin all her resolve. Curse that cell phone. She wished it had never been invented.

While Wilson scrambled to obey his sovereign, the man himself pointed in the direction of the gold sitting room. "Come along. The three of us will settle this in privacy."

*

He'd almost lost her. Dev's bowels still felt like ice. He sat next to her on the same couch they'd occupied on her first day here, clutching her hand. He'd sit on her if she tried to get away again. A few more minutes and no warning from Kurt, and she'd be on her way to the airport and out of his life forever.

No, he wouldn't have allowed that, but he'd have had to chase her, and who knows how long it would have taken to convince her to come back? He couldn't spare the time…time they needed to spend starting their life together.

Before his father started browbeating them into his way of seeing things, he launched into what he'd planned to say.

"I was hoping to have this discussion with you in private, old man," he began. "But if you want an audience, Felice can hear it."

"Oh really?" Friedrich lowered himself into an armchair and crossed his legs. The posture might appear casual, but in reality, the man was coiled as tightly as a spring. Dev had done battle with him before but not about anything this important.

"Really." He stared at his father straight in the eyes. "I'm not going to marry Astrid."

"I know that," Friedrich answered.

"You do?"

"He does," Felice said.

"She told me so herself a few minutes before you two staged that Greek tragedy in the entryway," Friedrich said. "She said she wouldn't marry a man who didn't love her. Silliest collection of hogwash I'd ever heard, but I couldn't force her to do it."

The dark cloud of guilt that had floated around Dev's brain lifted. He had disappointed Astrid, but he wouldn't have to hurt her any further. She'd made the decision for them.

"Then there's no reason I can't marry Felice," he said.

"What, are you crazy?" she said. "There's every reason you can't marry me."

She tried to pull her hand away, but he held onto it. He'd deal with her so-called objections when he'd finished with his father's.

"I know you respect tradition, and I do, too," he said to Friedrich. "But I won't let you parade another young woman and another through here so I can disappoint them. I won't do it. I'm going to marry Felice, and if that means Kurt takes my place on the throne, so be it."

Friedrich hmphed. "So you've decided, have you?"

"I have." Dev stood so he'd dominate the older man. If Felice made a dash for the door, he could catch her. "I'll marry Felice or no one at all. This is not negotiable."

"All right, all right." Friedrich waved his hand as if a fly were bothering him. "Don't scream before you're hurt."

Felice's eyebrows shot up. "Where did you learn that expression?"

"You aren't the first American I've ever met, young lady," Friedrich said. "Now if my son will sit down again, we can discuss this rationally."

Dev resumed his seat, this time putting his arm around Felice's shoulders. He waited for a moment to see what his father would do, dredging up from memory all the arguments for marrying Felice he'd rehearsed through the night. They all boiled down to one thing—he loved her.

After a moment, his father reached into his pocket and pulled out a cell phone. Felice's. "I'm afraid you're going to have to be angry with me, my dear."

"My phone," she said. "You had it."

"I found it last night." Friedrich stood long enough to place the phone on the table next to her and then walked to the fireplace and rested his arm on the mantle. "I used it to invade your privacy."

She picked up the phone and rubbed her thumb over the face. At least, she'd stopped crying. Each sob had torn a little piece of his heart out.

"I used the speed dial to call your father," Friedrich said.

"Why?" she said.

"After speaking to him, I have to ask myself the same question." For the first time in Dev's life, his father managed to look ashamed of himself, although he did even that with a regal lift of one brow. "I told him you were very unhappy and asked him what he planned to do about it."

Felice groaned and crumpled against Dev. So he rubbed her back.

"The answer was not much, and though I didn't talk to your mother, I wouldn't have expected anything different from her," Friedrich said.

"How embarrassing," Felice said.

"You have nothing to be embarrassed about," Friedrich said, his umbrage restored. "They have a great deal they ought to be ashamed of, but they hardly seem to realize it."

"That's who they are." Felice said with a futile lift to her shoulders. "They never meant to have children."

"It isn't good enough." Friedrich drummed his fingers on the mantle. "So it seemed to me…because I've never had a daughter…you might as well become mine."

Lieber Gott. For a moment, Dev couldn't breathe. Had his father really said that? Had Friedrich put generations of tradition behind him to accept Felice as Dev's wife? All the obstacles, all the hurt fell away in an instant. He'd have the woman he loved, after all.

"Ohhh." Felice buried her face in her hands. "The two of you are insane."

"No, darling, we're not." Dev took her chin in his hand and lifted her head so he could place his lips over hers. Days had passed since he'd kissed her. How had he endured all those hours without her sweetness, the way she yielded and responded? Before they could get carried away, he pulled back and gazed into the deep green of her eyes. "Of all of us, only Astrid saw the truth, but we've come around finally. It's time for you to do the same."

"I can't be a princess. I don't have the faintest idea how," she said.

"But you do. You're wonderful with people. You have an emotional honesty that shines through everything you do," Dev said. "And you're generous with your praise and love."

"My son's right about that, my dear," Friedrich said. "You charmed the Bürgermeister. Marta and all the relatives loved you instantly."

"Think of the Baumgartens," Dev added, rubbing her lips with his thumb. "Everyone in Vogelsheim wants you to be my wife."

"Vogelsheim?" Friedrich said. "So that's where you go."

Dev felt his cheeks warm. His father had discovered where he went. No matter. If that helped convince Felice to marry him, he'd happily give up his secret.

"You're a natural," Dev said. "I can teach you everything else."

"Once you've learned German, you'll fit in like a native," Friedrich said.

Her eyes grew wet again, but this time, she smiled brightly enough to light up the room. And his heart. He'd kiss these tears away. He'd spend a lifetime keeping her as happy as she was right now.

"Your Majesty…Friedrich…I don't know what to call you," she said.

"Call him old man," Dev said.

"I will not." She pushed at his chest, but her hands still clung to his shirt. He'd never bothered to button it.

"You can call me father," Friedrich said. "As my sons do."

"Well then." Felice fanned her face, and for a minute, she became so pale she might have passed out. Eventually, she recovered her composure to give Dev another megawatt smile. "I guess I'll be a princess."

"Not just any princess," he corrected softly. "My princess."

Epilogue

The wedding took place in the national cathedral, with many of the crowned heads of Europe in attendance and a great deal of international media coverage. If Felice had had time for fear, she probably would have been terrified, but with all the rushing about, her bridesmaids made it to the ceremony barely in time for them to precede her and her father down the aisle. Crystal and Sandra—once her colleagues in grad school and the very people who'd put her up to seducing "virgin" Dev—had been her foundation during the last hectic days, and now they looked beautiful in their gowns.

As soon as she reached Dev, who looked as regal and handsome in his uniform as he'd ever had, the butterflies in her stomach settled down, and a sense of calm settled over her. He was her rock and her foundation, and although she might have to shoulder the responsibilities that came with being his princess, she was also marrying the man who could make her happier than she'd ever dared to dream.

Everything else went by in a blur as she gazed up into his face—Kurt standing beside him, the child with the rings, her parents seated in the front, next to Ben and Alex, the rest of her labmates from school.

She and Dev spoke their vows in German, as she'd rehearsed and rehearsed until her new father had given his blessing to her pronunciation. She would have learned Old Church Slavonic if it would have bound her to this beautiful and loving man. His eyes misted over a bit as she spoke the words without stumbling, and honestly, his image might have blurred a bit, too, when he repeated the vows.

When the archbishop had pronounced them man and wife, Dev gave her a kiss so full of promise, it stole her breath. He held her tightly as if he'd never let her go until Kurt cleared his throat to remind them they had a very large audience.

A cheer went up as they turned to face the crowd, and then they proceeded out of the cathedral and into an open carriage with Dev's father. Correction, her father. The three of them waved to the people who'd crowded around the cathedral.

Dev squeezed her free hand. "You were perfect through the ceremony."

"Of course, she was," Friedrich said. "I wouldn't let you marry a woman who wasn't."

"So this was all your idea, old man?" Dev said as he continued smiling to the crowd and waving.

"Not initially, I'll admit, but I do change my mind on occasion," Friedrich said, to which Dev snorted a laugh.

Friedrich leaned toward her. "Is this too much for you, my dear?"

"Not at all."

"A few hours, and it'll be over," Friedrich said.

"I wouldn't mind if it went on forever," she said. She spotted a woman holding up a child near the carriage's route. The little girl tossed a flower in her direction, and Felice reached out to catch it and then blew the child and her mother a kiss. Though it was nothing more exotic than a daisy, she'd press it in a book to remind her of this day.

"You see?" Friedrich said. "You were born to this."

They had to pass through another crush to get into the palace, and when they did, they found the reception already gaining steam. Waiters circulated with trays of champagne and hors d'oeuvres, and the orchestra struck up a waltz. She scarcely had time to hand the daisy to Wilson with instructions he pass it on to Greta before Dev took her directly to her parents. After all, they'd planned on following the American custom of the bride sharing the first dance with her father. After a hug and a kiss from her mother, who'd done a respectable job of crying through the service, her dad led her onto the dance floor. In his formal attire, he looked pretty darned handsome himself.

"Well, sweetie, who would have thought we'd end up with a princess in the family?" he said.

"I hope you're not too disappointed I didn't get my Ph.D."

"That wasn't what you wanted, was it?" he said.

"Nope. Just what I thought I wanted." Now that her life had settled into a perfect dream, there was no point telling him the idea of her Ph.D. had come from her parents.

He stopped dancing long enough to press his lips to her forehead. "Then, we're happy for you."

"You'll be going back to Peru soon?"

"Tomorrow. You have things under control here."

And so she did, in no small part because of the support of the man who now stood at her dad's elbow. Friedrich tapped her father on the shoulder, indicating he was cutting in. Her father nodded and blended back into the crowd.

"So," Friedrich said as he put his arm around her and led her in the waltz. "It seems I won't have to lecture him in parenting, after all."

"I'd be very grateful if you didn't."

"And while we're speaking of being a parent, when do you two plan to give me grandchildren?" Friedrich asked.

She tossed back her head and laughed. Partly because she had no answer to the question and partly because she had the option now of making a baby with her life mate.

Friedrich hmphed in that faux disapproval way he had. "I got the same answer from my son."

"Ask us again in a year or two," she said.

"Two years?" he said. "I have to wait two years?"

They both knew he'd waited longer before his wife had given birth to Dev, but if he wanted to pretend at being stern, he could feel free. He wasn't about to change at his age. And honestly, she didn't want to change him.

"Did you see the vase Astrid sent?" she asked. "It's lovely and very old. I can't imagine where she found it."

"You should think of donating it to the national museum," he said.

"I'd rather keep it with us," she said. "Do you think she'll ever be able to come to visit?"

"Probably," he said. "She's a lovely woman. I have excellent taste in those."

Felice bit her lip for a moment. Their relationship was young, and who knew for sure where the bounds lay? Still, she couldn't quite help herself. "Does that include Lady Marta?"

Friedrich stumbled to a stop, and he leaned away from her, obviously startled. "Marta? Why would you mention her?"

"She's especially beautiful today, don't you think?"

Friedrich lifted a finger and waved it at her. His mouth opened, but no words came out. She couldn't suppress a giggle.

"By God, you've rendered him speechless." Ulrich had appeared beside Friedrich. "However did you manage that?"

"I'll tell you later."

"My turn then." The youngest VonRamsberg led her off in the dance, and when that one ended, he claimed the next. After a bit, they passed by another familiar face, and a not entirely welcome one.

Vaclav tapped Ulrich's shoulder. "May I?"

"No," Ulrich answered and whirled her away. "He had to be invited, I'm afraid."

"Fine with me as long as I don't have to dance with him."

"And what if he tries to bother you at dinner?" Ulrich said.

"I'll call him a coprophage, and he can go look it up in the dictionary."

Ulrich lifted a brow. "I'd have to look it up, too."

"It's an animal that eats its own dung."

Ulrich stopped dancing and laughed so loudly he attracted attention, not the least of which came from her brand new husband.

"You've confounded first my father and now my brother," Dev said as he circled his arm around her. "You have quite a way with the men in my family."

"And I haven't even started on Kurt," she said. "When I'm through with him, there's always Grigori."

"Did I mention he complimented me on my selection of a princess?"

"Really?" She glimpsed toward the corner of the ballroom where his once-dour advisor gazed over the proceedings with what looked like a smile on his face.

"Really. His exact words," Dev said. "I do adore you."

"And I you."

"I have only one question." He bent his mouth to her ear. "When do I get to make love to my wife?"

"Not for several hours, I imagine."

"I'll never last that long."

They danced for a while, her hand resting on the shoulder of his uniform, his palm warm at the small of her back. From time to time, she stared still unbelieving at the wedding set on the third finger of her left hand. It had been his mother's and his grandmother's and so forth, back for many generations. She still wore the ring he'd given her on her right hand and would continue to do until their own son gave the family rings to his wife. Then she'd switch Dev's ring to the place where it had always belonged.

"I suppose you've heard my father's suggestion for a honeymoon," Dev said. "We can do whatever we want. London, Paris, you name it."

"Friedrich's right, as usual. A royal tour of Danislova," she said. "With a long layover in Vogelsheim."

"We already brought Vogelsheim here." Dev nodded toward where the Baumgartens stood in the crowd, both flushed with pride. Frau Baumgarten had cried as copiously as Felice's mother through the ceremony.

"Aren't they adorable?" she said. "And speaking of adorable…"

"Hm?"

"Over there."

Dev followed her gaze and spotted his father dancing with Lady Marta. The two were gazing deeply into each other's eyes as they moved in perfect synchrony.

"Well, I'll be damned," Dev said. "Did you accomplish that?"

"I might have given him a nudge."

"I wish you could nudge us toward our bedroom."

She laughed. "I'll see what I can do."

It was several hours before they could be alone. The party didn't wind down enough for them to steal away until after midnight. And though the day had exhausted them both, they still lay naked between silk sheets, Dev's body covering hers as he moved, their bodies joined, their hearts and minds united so profoundly they didn't need words. When she finally came apart in his arms, shouting his name, he released the proof of his love inside her. And though he was surely the finest man alive, he was still male and promptly fell asleep.

She didn't mind. She'd have thousands more nights and days with him. Now that the mattress had stopped moving, Sneakers jumped onto the bed and purred in Felice's ear. Luther, the iguana, was safely in his tank in their sitting room and wouldn't join them, thank you. Happy beyond her wildest imaginings, Felice lay with her husband's head on her shoulder, stroking his hair and feeling his breath against her skin, and she knew that her fairy tale had come true.

Alice Gaines has been published in erotic and romance since 1996 with publishers such as Red Sage, Changeling, Ellora's Cave, Harlequin Spice Briefs, and Avon Impulse. She loves to hear from readers at authoralicegaines@gmail.com. She'd be happy to add you to her mailing list if you drop her a line. Her blog/website is http://www.alicegaines.blogspot.com. Every Friday she posts an X-rated excerpt at http://www.alicesexcerpts.blogspot.com. You can find her at the usual social media as AliceGaines.

And now for a bit of Kurt's's story…

THE GLASS SLIPPER

CHAPTER ONE

Getting dumped ought to hurt more. Poets wrote about lost love, pining away as if the world would stop turning on its axis. Half the popular songs Kurt VonRamsberg knew were about the one who got away. People became obsessed with their ex's. Late night phone calls, orgies of liquor and tears. Restraining orders. They were the stuff of a lover cast aside. And he couldn't muster more than a sense of regret as he walked the few blocks from his apartment building to his office at the UN. What kind of future husband did that make him to care so little?

Kurt had built his life around three things – service to his country, his family, and the woman who'd give him his very own family to continue the traditions his father had taught him. He'd just lost number three, and he ought to be teetering like a stool missing a leg. He ought to be mourning the loss of Ilsa's kisses or planning some way to get her back. Maybe she'd had it right when she'd written that his passions didn't run very deep.

A car horn blared, pulling him back to reality. For the love of God, he'd almost stepped into First Avenue without looking.

"Mister, you'll get yourself killed," a man called.

Kurt didn't look back to find him. Embarrassing enough he'd almost stepped in front of that cab without having to face witnesses. He waited for the light to change and crossed the street more carefully.

He could have had his driver take him to the UN as he usually did, but walking helped him clear his mind. And this was one of those mornings when you couldn't imagine anything more wonderful than Manhattan in the spring. It would cheer him up if he were heartbroken. But damn it all, he couldn't figure out what he was. A failure, perhaps. He'd had the perfect woman for a prince of Danislova. Beautiful, cultured, royal in her own right. They got along. By all indications, they'd suit well in bed. And he'd failed to hold her interest.

"My dear Kurt," he recited the letter in his head. On stationery, through the international mail, not over the computer. Cultured. "I hate to hurt you, blah, blah, blah. You're a sweet man, and you deserve a woman who can love you blah, blah, blah."

What man wanted women to think of him as sweet? No one he knew. At least, Ilsa didn't seem familiar with the American kiss of death – I love you but I'm not in love with you – or she might have thrown that in, too.

As he continued, the sun warmed his shoulders, and the scents of spring seeped into his brain, turning his thoughts into oatmeal. Bland but nutritious for the most part, but occasionally he'd stumble across a raisin – something substantial to gnaw on. He ought to want Ilsa, or at the very least, he ought to think about dating someone who could fit the role of princess. But to be perfectly honest, the only thing bubbling up inside him was relief. Relief that he'd failed?

"As much as I adore your father," Ilsa's letter continued. Of course. All women adored his father. No woman would ever tell Friedrich VonRamsberg, the Prince Royal, she loved him but she wasn't in love with him. Kurt even looked like the old man, or he would when his hair turned white. But where Friedrich was commanding and alluring, even in his sixties, Kurt was solid and reliable.

Solid and reliable. Sweet. He stopped in his tracks in the lush garden in front of the vintage apartment building on 42nd Street. For a moment, his feet seemed nailed to the pavement. Before him stood the UN and his work. This morning's meeting with the Minister for Eastern European Rural Development. A dispute about goats no one else seemed able to settle except for good-old, dependable Kurt. Behind him waited his apartment. Luxurious but neat and ordered, just like the rest of his life. Going back there wouldn't solve anything, either. What the hell was he doing with his life? Did he even have a life? And was he going to stand in the middle of one of the most expensive parts of Manhattan and have a mid-life crisis? Would anyone notice?

He ended up so caught up in mental self-flagellation he didn't notice the woman approach until she had her hand on his arm.

Instinctively, he pulled back. "I beg your pardon."

"You're late," she said. "And you're going to get me in a lot of trouble."

"I? I don't even know you, madam." She was hardly a madam but more like a miss, and a young one at that. The top of her head scarcely came up to his nose, but her grip remained firm as she stared at him out of eyes almost as dark blue as sapphires. Barely restrained at the nape of her neck, sable curls spilled down her back, making a contrast with pale skin. Pale except for her cheeks, which were flushed with excitement or, more likely, irritation.

"You don't have to be in character," she said. "You just have to be inside."

"Character?"

She paid no attention to his objections as she tugged on his arm, leading into the apartment building. "I have one of the city's most expensive photographers and another model waiting for you. My ass is going to be grass if we don't get some good shots."

"Grass?" She *had* said that her ass, or arse as the case might be, would be grass, hadn't she? Well now, he couldn't very well let that happen. Especially because the arse in question looked like a nice one, based on the few quick glances he'd managed. And who was he to keep an expensive photographer and model waiting for him? Of course, none of this could possibly have anything to do with him. She must have mistaken him for someone else, but…sure. If he could help her out for a few minutes, the escapade could help fill the urges he'd been having lately to do something just for the hell of it.

She nearly dragged him toward the elevators, with the receptionists at the front desk looking on as if they witnessed this sort of scene every day.

"You're in the wrong costume, do you know that?" she said as she continued, pulling him along through the marble and brass reception area.

He flatly refused to repeat the word costume just because it didn't make any more sense than being in character or having one's ass turn into grass. When the elevator doors whished closed behind them, she crossed her arms over her chest and studied him. "We'll find something for you to wear."

"For my character," he said.

"Exactly."

"Dare I ask what that might be?" he said.

"Gumshoe."

Right. Gumshoe. That explained absolutely nothing, but who cared? This didn't have to make sense. He'd help her out, and he'd only be a few minutes late for his meeting. Somehow, assuming the character of a gumshoe to keep her ass from turning into grass held more promise than a meeting on a warm, spring morning like this.

"Here we are," she declared when the elevator doors opened.

"Right you are."

Still holding his arm, she paused. "You're not American, are you?"

"Sorry, no."

"Not English, either. You have a different accent."

"German," he lied. If he mentioned Danislova, she might recognize him. If he was to give a performance as a gumshoe, whatever that was, he'd best do it incognito.

"That's okay. No one has to listen to you." The elevator doors threatened to close, but she stuck her hand out to keep them open. "Hurry up."

Now committed to whatever she had in mind for him, he followed her down the hallway to a pair of double doors. She pulled a key from the pocket of her slacks and opened one. It let them into a living room with a view of the river. She only gave him a glimpse of plush carpets and modern furniture before she led him to another room full of exercise equipment.

At one end of the space, a sheet hung from some scaffolding. A man waited there with a camera slung around his neck. Nearby on one of the machines, a woman sat, dangling one leg over the other, her foot wagging with impatience. She wore several layers of makeup, and her clothes hugged her slender hips and artificially large breasts. What passed for beauty these days, at least in magazines.

"We have our hero," his young woman said. "We can get started."

The man with the camera checked his watch. "It's half past."

"You only paid me for an hour," the model said.

The young woman held her hands up as if to keep them where they were. “We’ll get it done. I promise. No more screw-ups.”

“What do you want me to do?” Kurt said.

“Get changed, of course,” the young woman answered. “You’re not supposed to be a CEO or international financier.”

“Right here? In front of everyone?” Not that he’d do that, of course. Escaping the Minister for Eastern European Rural Development was one thing, but his cooperation did have limits.

She pointed toward a corner of the room where a screen stood with female clothes draped over it. No doubt where the model had changed into her costume.

“I see,” he said.

The young woman sighed. “Why do the pretty ones have heads full of Styrofoam?”

He could have stood there contemplating the fact that she thought he was empty-headed or the even more interesting fact that she found him pretty, but all three of them were staring at him. Waiting for him to change his clothes, no doubt. So, he went behind the screen and glanced around for what he was supposed to wear. He only found feminine things, and he’d no more try fitting into that than he’d undress in front of the rest of them.

He hesitated for a moment before asking what he was supposed to change into. As pleasant as the pretty comment had been, he didn’t particularly relish having to listen to another one about his head being filled with plastic.

After a moment, a hand snaked around the screen, holding a pair of pants and a shirt. He grabbed her arm and pulled the young woman to him. Her eyes widened until she noticed he hadn’t undressed.

“More questions?” she asked.

“What’s your name?”

“Casey. What’s yours?”

“Kurt,” he answered.

“Nice. Now get dressed,” she ordered as she stepped back around the screen.

He obliged, folding his clothing as carefully as possible and setting it into a pile on the floor. He quickly put on his costume and had just sat on the floor to put his socks and shoes back on when an irritated huff came from the other side of the screen.

“We aren’t getting any younger out here,” Casey called.

“Just putting on my shoes.”

“We’re not going to be taking pictures of your feet,” she called back.

“Right.” He rose and walked barefoot around the screen. He almost collided with Casey on the other side.

She stepped back and let her gaze wander over him. “Not bad.”

“The pants are tight.”

She said nothing but gave him a look that had “Styrofoam” written all over it. Then she reached for the buttons of his shirt and began undoing them.

“Wait.” He covered her hands with his own. “What do you think you’re doing?”

“Exposing your chest, of course. How long have you been in this business?”

With no idea what business she was referring to, he had no way to answer that. But she probably hadn’t really expected a reply, so he dropped his hands and let her continue. With his shirt only. If she went for his pants, he’d let her know exactly who she was dealing with and end the whole charade.

She stopped just north of his belt and for a moment did nothing but stare at him, her head cocked to one side. The air thickened around them as her hand came up in slow motion and she pressed her palm to the place just over his heart. She had small fingers, although by now, he knew their strength. They felt warm against his skin. Some devil inside him made him lift his own hand and cover hers, squeezing gently. As natural as if he'd done this dozens of times before or planned to do it for a long, long time.

Finally, a throat cleared. The camera man snapped a few pictures and then pointedly stared at his watch. The model, on the other hand, seemed almost as intent on studying his chest as Casey was. Though he was certainly no stranger to what went on between men and women, all this female adoration was something new and slightly intoxicating, especially when it came so freely from the little dynamo standing so close he could detect the scent of shampoo in her hair.

"Can we take a picture now?" the camera man asked. "Please?"

Casey dropped her hand and gave him a sheepish smile. "You know what to do?"

Under the circumstances, honesty seemed like the best policy. "No."

"Don't worry. We'll make it up as we go along."

"Delightful," he said. "Now, if you'll explain what a gumshoe is…"

The camera man groaned.

Casey turned toward the man. "He's not American, okay?"

"I hope they take pictures wherever he comes from," the man said.

"He'll be fine. Just give me a second," Casey said.

"Well, I'm outta here in a couple," the model said. "You only paid for an hour."

"It's very simple." Casey put her hands on his shoulders and looked up at him. This close, she had to tip her head upward, and for a mini-second, she appeared to be asking for a kiss. Kurt had to mentally shake the idea out of his mind, but it wasn't easy. He hadn't notice before that freckles adorned her nose. Five of them exactly. And her blue eyes seemed to have golden highlights.

"You're a private detective," she said. "You spend your days chasing down the ugly underside of life. It's made you hard to the world."

"I see." He squinted in imitation of a Hollywood actor who played a tough guy.

"Uh, maybe not that hard," she said. "Just try for intensity."

"Could we try for a picture instead?" the camera man said.

"Sure, sure." Casey waved her hand in the general direction of the camera man. "This woman has hired you to do something especially seedy, but you're going to make her pay a special price first."

Across the room, the model stepped in front of the sheet. She struck a saucy pose, her hands on her hips. Her blouse open far enough to expose the black lace of her bra, she stood there, waiting for him to complete the scene.

"Okay, go get her, tiger." Casey clapped him on the shoulder and then nudged him in the direction of the model.

When Kurt joined the model in front of the camera, she immediately stepped into his embrace. To make things even more provocative, she tipped her head back in a pose that showcased the length of her neck and pulled her bosom away from his chest so the camera could catch some cleavage. Casey had told him to try for intensity, so he did his best to smolder, staring at a spot above her collarbone.

"Well, shit," the cameraman said. "That's about as sexy as my aunt's canasta parties."

"I know." Casey joined them and placed her hand on the back of Kurt's head to bend it toward the model. "Kiss her neck."

"He's a detective, not a vampire," the cameraman said.

"Try it," Casey said.

Kurt bent closer to the model. Now with his face only inches from her skin the scent of her make-up and hairspray was overpowering. He pulled back but not in time to keep him from sneezing. Twice.

"That does it." The model stepped away from him. "Your time's up. I'm tail lights."

"No, please." Casey reached for the woman's arm, but the model avoided her and went behind the screen. Pieces of clothing disappeared, one at a time, from where they'd been hanging, and after a moment, the model re-emerged with a large bag draped over her shoulder. Bits of fabric stuck out of the top as the woman walked out.

Casey turned toward the cameraman. "You have to stay. I need to finish this, or I could lose my job."

Damn. That explained the ass being grass remark. Whoever was supposed to serve as the male character had failed her completely by not showing up, and Kurt hadn't done a lot better with his miserable performance. At least he'd tried, even if he'd been a disaster.

"You want me to take solo pictures of him?" The cameraman gestured with his head toward Kurt.

"No," Casey said. "I need to get another female."

"I'm not sticking around for that," the cameraman said. "It took long enough to get him here."

"All right, we will all remain calm." She rubbed her forehead as if trying to ward off a headache. "I'm a female. I'll pose with him."

"You?" the camera man said. "You're not even made up."

"You can cut out my head and insert the model's, right?" Casey said.

"If you want to look like Frankenstein," the man said. "All stitched together."

"It's my only hope, and you have to do it. Raven Publishing paid you a lot of money," Casey said.

"Sure, why not?" The cameraman threw his hands into the air in frustration. "Knock yourself out."

She unbuttoned her blouse…not quite as far as the model had but enough to show the swell of small but firm breasts. Then she pulled the clip that held her hair in place, dropped it to the floor, and shook out her curls. A waterfall of sable fell around her face and graced the length of her throat. The warm brown contrasted with her pale skin, drawing his gaze downward.

Before he knew what was happening, she'd pressed herself against him from his pelvis to his chest. In contrast to the nothing-but-bones body of the model, Casey felt soft everywhere. Exactly the way a woman should melt against a man, and his man's anatomy responded in a very predictable, if embarrassing, manner.

He might be a prince and an ambassador to the UN, bound by courtesy and protocol, but he was also human. He hadn't become so fully erect so quickly since his youth, but within seconds he'd reached a state that would normally lead to lovemaking.

Casey's eyes widened as she gazed up at him. She'd noticed his hardness. She couldn't have missed it, snuggled up against him as she was. She didn't say anything, but her lips parted. The model had pretended an invitation. Casey meant it, and he couldn't help but bend toward her, seeking a taste of her mouth.

"That's hot," the cameraman said as he clicked away. "Give me more."

Kurt shook himself mentally. For a moment, he'd lost track of reality. He'd only just met this woman and knew nothing about her but her first name. Even if they hadn't had a witness, he couldn't kiss her less than an hour after meeting her. And they did have an audience. He shouldn't have reacted this way, and he shouldn't want nothing more than to strip her slowly and guide them both to the carpet so he could sink into her.

She gave him a hazy smile, full of sin and seduction. It set his heart to racing. The click of the camera grew constant so that he hardly noticed it any longer. He had a woman in his arms, soft in all the right places and as excited by the situation as he was.

"You two are dynamite together," the cameraman said. "Smoking hot."

"Let me try something else." Casey stretched backward as the model had before. This time, the pose made sense…a woman offering her neck to her lover in hopes of a caress. Her skin had a rosy hue to it, and her pulse beat visibly at the base of her throat. This time when he bent toward the woman in his arms, he encountered the pleasant scent of shampoo he'd noticed before.

"Hold it right there," the cameraman shouted. "Don't kiss her. Just anticipate. That's it…hold it…hold it…"

As soon as the man told Kurt not to kiss her, the need to do exactly that consumed him. He paused, his lips an inch away from her soft skin, her curls brushing his nose. One more movement, and he could taste her. Instead he had to hold himself away. So unnatural. He should place caress after caress along a path up to her ear, and he would…if only that man would disappear and take his clacking camera with him.

She made no secret that she felt the same way he did. She trembled in his embrace, and her breath grew unsteady. In a moment, he could have her moaning.

Soon after that, he could hear her gasps and finally the cry that signaled her satisfaction. If only he were free to do what his body demanded.

In the end, his willpower deserted him. He had to kiss her, or the lost opportunity would haunt his dreams. He closed the distance and pressed his lips to the place where her pulse raced. Now her perfume surrounded him, fogging his brain for anything but her. When she let out a soft gasp, he continued upward caressing her neck up to her ear.

Abruptly, she pulled back, holding his face between her hands. “Do you have what you need now?”

“Need?” Kurt repeated.

“I meant Joe,” she said. “The guy taking pictures.”

“Do I ever,” Joe said. “There should be at least eight or ten shots we can use.”

“Well then…” she said.

“Right.” Joe grinned. “I get the message.”

Whatever message the man had received, it helped him to gather up his lenses and pack them in a case quickly. A moment after that, Joe left. Kurt was alone with his arms around a woman who obviously had the power to make him more than a little crazy.

“You’re something else, Kurt,” she said.

She was right. Something else or someone else. He’d started out the day his normal, predictable self. Now he found himself locked in an embrace with a perfect stranger, and it felt like the most natural thing in the world.

Because that stranger was smiling and not stepping out of that embrace, he could show her just how perfect she was. He did that by kissing her again. Not a press of his lips against her neck, but a total possession of her mouth. The word “sweet” exploded at the back of his brain as he nibbled, and stroked, and sucked.

He'd had as much sexual experience as most men and rather more than some, but none of that prepared him for the power of his response to her. Even with her short stature, they fit together perfectly. Her softness welcomed him everywhere, especially where his stiff member pressed against her belly.

For her part, she seemed as caught up in the passion of the moment as he was. She clung to his neck as she parted her lips under his, and her tongue darted out to make explorations. When he touched it with his own, a shock traveled through him. Hot and strong, it sent a clear message—stop here or continue to the end.

No. He didn't know this woman. He didn't have any protection. Though his body craved the ultimate with a hunger that shook him to his bones, his mind had to win out. He gently took her shoulders and put her away from him. Not far. Just enough to say "no more."

"I'm sorry," he said. "I never lose control like that."

"Never?" She ran her tongue over her lips as if to taste him there. The gesture almost snapped his tenuous hold on sanity, so he closed his eyes for a moment and took even breaths.

He searched through his lust-addled brain for an honest answer to her question. Had a woman ever moved him so completely with no more than a kiss? "Never."

"I think I'm flattered."

"I'm relieved." He'd take flattered over angry at his forwardness. He really had pressed the kiss too far.

"You thought I'd be offended?" Her blue eyes held the twinkle of a woman who knows she has a man at a disadvantage. "They must do things differently in Germany."

The reference to Germany shook him for a second. But then, he'd told her he was German to explain his accent. "I assure you men don't take advantage of women in my country."

"I can slap your face, if you like, but it's really not that big a deal." She bit her lip, and the gleam in her eye turned positively wicked. "On the other hand, something was a big deal, wasn't it?"

"*Lieber Gott.*" His cheeks burned. He'd be blushing so brightly she'd have to notice.

"Hey, look, I didn't mean to embarrass you."

In the outer room—the living room they'd walked through—a door closed.

"Casey?" a man's voice called. "Casey, where are you?"

She flinched. "Shit, you have to get out of here."

He just stopped himself before he said "*Lieber Gott*" again, this time shouting. "That's your husband? We've been standing here, doing…*this*…when you have a husband?"

"My boss, and he can't catch you here." She went to the door, opened it, and stuck her head around the side. "I'm exercising, Phil. I'll be out in a bit."

"At this hour? You're supposed to be working on my blog tour," the man's voice called back.

"I had to get my heart rate up, get the old juices flowing," she said. "I'm really sweaty. Don't come in."

"All right. I'll be in the library. Ten minutes, Casey. I mean it," Phil said.

"Ten minutes. No problem." She waited for a while and then let out a breath. "He's gone. Out the back way. Hurry."

She once again grabbed him by the arm and started to lead him somewhere, but he hung back. "My clothes."

"Okay, but hurry up, will you?"

He'd barely gone behind the screen and grabbed his things before she reached for his arm again and pulled him out the door and into a short corridor. That ended in a huge, state-of-the-art kitchen. He hardly had time to admire many hundreds of dollars worth of copper pots and pans hanging over a butcher-block work table before she propelled him toward another door.

"Why do I have to hide from your boss?" he said.

"If you knew Phil, you wouldn't ask. He's going to want to bite the head off everyone involved in that cover shoot."

Kurt dug in his heels, jerking her to a stop. "That includes you."

"I get my head bitten off at least once I week."

"Then why do you work for him?" Kurt demanded.

"No time to explain." She released him and opened the door to reveal a hallway of the kind servants used so as not to disturb their employers. "You have to leave."

He stood his ground. "How will I see you again?"

"I don't know…um…"

"I can come back here when you finish work," he said.

"No. " She put up both hands as if to warn him off. "Not here."

"Then where?" If he could pursue a more rational relationship with her, he might rightfully enjoy more of those kisses and follow them to their logical conclusion. He might be old world and cautious in how he approached affairs of the heart—at least he had been in the past—but he wasn't foolish enough to throw away the promise of their embrace.

"I'll give you my phone number." He fumbled with the suit draped over his arm and found the pocket of his jacket. After pulling out his pen, he reached for a business card. He couldn't use that, though, without revealing his status as prince of Danislova and United Nations ambassador. "Do you have a piece of paper?"

"Reams of it," she said. "In the other room. With Phil."

He handed her his pen and continued fumbling.

"Give me your hand," she said.

"My hand?"

"Just do it."

He did as she ordered and she pressed the pen to his palm. After a moment, she'd written her phone number on his skin. "There you go. Now, you really have to leave."

With that, she pushed him out the door and closed it behind him. Prince Kurt Wilhelm Richard VonRamsberg, third in line to the throne of Danislova, found himself standing in a servants' corridor wearing too-tight pants and a shirt open to his waist, his own clothes tangled in his arms and a young woman's phone number scrawled on his palm.

For the love of God, what had just happened to him?

*

Casey took the ninth and tenth minutes her boss had given her to snatch the sheet off the machines and stuff it and the screen into the closet of the exercise room. Then she took a few seconds Phil hadn't given her to check around and make sure she'd hidden all evidence of the crime. Everything appeared in order, including the towels hanging where Phil liked them and his precise setting on the elliptical machine.

"Casey!" he yelled from the other room.

She straightened her clothes and did her best to get her hair out of her face without the clip, which she must have dropped somewhere. That done, she plastered a smile on her face and went into the living room.

All six feet of spoiled, self-absorbed male author stood by the window, his back to a spectacular view of the East River. "What took you so long?"

"I had to freshen up before I changed clothes."

"Well, you're here now. Let's get to work."

If anyone were to send down to central casting for a surfer dude, they might well end up with Philip Comstock. Sandy-haired, tall, handsome, and oh-so male, he hardly seemed the type to have started out writing historical romance novels under the pseudonym Lisa Parnell. Lisa Parnell had penned stories so compelling and so sexy, they still graced Casey's keeper shelf. Naturally, Casey had jumped at the chance to work for that writer—even knowing Lisa was a man. Instead she'd ended up an assistant to Philip Comstock, author of hard-boiled detective mysteries.

"Publicity at Raven set me up with a blog tour," Phil said. "The first is due in a week, and we don't have a topic yet."

She went to one of the couches and sat down. He could stand in the middle of the room, if he wanted. She'd already run herself ragged, and it wasn't even noon.

"Character interviews usually work well as blogs," she said.

"I already interviewed Joe Stark on Gun for Hire dot Com," he said.

"How about the mystery female? If the interview asked more questions than it answered, that could pique readers' interest."

"I suppose we could do that." he said.

Of course, the "we" in this deal meant she'd end up writing the piece. Just as she'd written the blog for Phil's gumshoe hero, Joe Stark. She shouldn't complain. That's what she got paid to do, after all.

"Put in a bunch of sexual innuendo, too," he added. "You know that's a hallmark of a Joe Stark mystery."

"How high on the Crude-O-Meter?"

"The blog's PG," he answered.

"Got it."

He crossed his arms over his muscular chest. "Shouldn't you be taking notes?"

"My pad's in the library."

Phil didn't move except for the slight arch to his eyebrow that told her she'd given him the wrong answer.

"Be right back." She got up and walked across the thick carpet and then up two stairs to the door to the library. Once inside, she had to flip through magazines and press releases at her small work station to find her steno pad. Amazing that anyone still made these things as no one in the world gave dictation or took shorthand any longer. But Phil insisted on them, probably because they made her look properly secretarial. She'd just found a pen when her cell phone rang. She pulled it from the pocket of her skirt and glanced at the number…the modeling agency.

"Casey Vaughn here," she said.

"This is the Midtown Agency. We apologize for our male model this morning."

"No need. He was late, but we got the pictures we needed." And she'd gotten a whole lot more than pictures. She had to hope he wasn't the type for sweaty palms or her phone number would smear. But then, if that happened she could probably track him through Midtown.

A silence of several seconds came through the ether to her ear. Finally, the woman cleared her throat. "There must be some mistake."

"You sent over a German guy named Kurt, right?"

"Uh, no. Our model was Steve from the Bronx. He called a while ago to say he'd overslept and missed the appointment completely."

"You mean…" Casey rummaged through her memories of the morning and everything Kurt had said and done. He'd never represented himself as a model. In fact, he'd appeared quite surprised when she'd found him on the street and dragged him inside. So, if the agency hadn't sent him over, why had he gone along with posing for the shoot?

He'd seemed reluctant at first. In fact, he'd acted pretty clueless about the whole process. She'd…oh, God…she'd grabbed at his shirt and unbuttoned it. Then she'd posed with him, forcing herself on him. Bad enough that she'd done that with a guy who'd been paid to pose, but she'd thrown herself at a stranger. You could probably consider that assault except for the very obvious and very enticing fact that he'd enjoyed the encounter.

"We're very sorry to have disappointed you," the agency woman said.

"Oh, he didn't disappoint, not one little bit."

"I beg your pardon?" the woman said.

"Excuse me. Figure of speech."

"Needless to say, we'll be returning your check."

"Great. Thanks." Casey's mind drifted off to interesting territory as she broke the connection.

One…she'd grabbed a stranger off the street and made him pose for a suggestive book cover. Given his incredible good looks—his wavy brown hair, glowing, tanned skin, and sensually curved lips—she'd naturally mistaken him for a model. Two…she'd ended up in clinch with him that had nothing to do with fiction. There were some things guys couldn't fake, and he hadn't had a gun in his pocket when he'd entered the building lobby. He'd had a rapid and forceful reaction to their embrace.

Which left one more problem. If she didn't know who the hell he was and if he didn't call her, how could she find him? She had to for at least one reason—she owed him money for his work.

She smiled as a warm feeling suffused her chest. Yes, indeed. One way or another she had to give him everything he deserved.

Made in the USA
Middletown, DE
04 June 2015